Also by David Markson

The Ballad of Dingus Magee
Going Down
Springer's Progress

Malcolm Lowry's Volcano: Myth, Symbol, Meaning

Wittgenstein's Mistress

David Markson

The Dalkey Archive Press

ISBN: 0-916583-50-3
LC: 87-73068

First Edition, May 1988
  second printing, July 1988
First paperback edition, February 1990
  second printing, May 1990
  third printing, September 1990

Partially funded by grants from The National Endowment for the Arts and
The Illinois Arts Council.

Dalkey Archive Press
1817 North 79th Avenue
Elmwood Park, IL 60635 USA

*Printed on permanent/durable acid-free paper and bound in the United
States of America.*

= 71 - fata morgana (an illusion of a depeopled
    world - or a voice that
    creates a depeopled world
    that the voice can inhabit)

78

For Joan Semmel

Tractatus

r.1 — 2.161

[katz]
her invention of her
adventures as the sole
living creature on earth
means our invention.
one imagines her life
and past as solitary, that which
art tells us of that which
never happened except one
in our mind, as our reality,
invent reality

"What an extraordinary change takes place . . . when for the first time the fact that everything depends upon how a thing is thought first enters the consciousness, when, in consequence, thought in its absoluteness replaces an apparent reality."

—Kierkegaard

"When I was still doubtful as to his ability, I asked G. E. Moore for his opinion. Moore replied, 'I think very well of him indeed.' When I enquired the reason for his opinion, he said that it was because Wittgenstein was the only man who looked puzzled at his lectures."

—Bertrand Russell

"I can well understand why children love sand."

—Wittgenstein

IN THE BEGINNING, sometimes I left messages in the street.

Somebody is living in the Louvre, certain of the messages would say. Or in the National Gallery.

Naturally they could only say that when I was in Paris or in London. Somebody is living in the Metropolitan Museum, being what they would say when I was still in New York.

Nobody came, of course. Eventually I stopped leaving the messages.

To tell the truth, perhaps I left only three or four messages altogether.

I have no idea how long ago it was when I was doing that. If I were forced to guess, I believe I would guess ten years.

Possibly it was several years longer ago than that, however.

And of course I was quite out of my mind for a certain period too, back then.

I do not know for how long a period, but for a certain period.

Time out of mind. Which is a phrase I suspect I may have never properly understood, now that I happen to use it.

 ⊛

Time out of mind meaning mad, or time out of mind meaning simply forgotten?

But in either case there was little question about that madness. As when I drove that time to that obscure corner of Turkey, for instance, to visit at the site of ancient Troy.

And for some reason wished especially to look at the river there, that I had read about as well, flowing past the citadel to the sea.

I have forgotten the name of the river, which was actually a muddy stream.

And at any rate I do not mean to the sea, but to the Dardanelles, which used to be called the Hellespont.

The name of Troy had been changed too, naturally. Hisarlik, being what it was changed to.

In many ways my visit was a disappointment, the site being astonishingly small. Like little more than your ordinary city block and a few stories in height, practically.

Still, from the ruins one could see Mount Ida, all of that distance away.

Even in late spring, there was snow on the mountain.

Somebody went there to die, I believe, in one of the old stories. Paris, perhaps.

I mean the Paris who had been Helen's lover, naturally. And who was wounded quite near the end of that war.

As a matter of fact it was Helen I mostly thought about, when I was at Troy.

I was about to add that I even dreamed, for a while, that the Greek ships were beached there still.

Well, it would have been a harmless enough thing to dream.

From Hisarlik, the water is perhaps an hour's walk away. What I had planned to do next was to take an ordinary rowboat across, and then drive on into Europe through Yugoslavia.

Possibly I mean Yugoslavia. In any case on that side of the channel there are monuments to the soldiers who died there in the first World War.

On the side where Troy is, one can find a monument where Achilles was buried, so much longer ago.

Well, they say it is where Achilles was buried.

Still, I find it extraordinary that young men died there in a war that long ago, and then died in the same place three thousand years after that.

But be that as it may, I changed my mind about crossing the Hellespont. By which I mean the Dardanelles. What I did was pick out a motor launch and go by way of the Greek islands and Athens, instead.

Even with only a page torn out of an atlas, instead of maritime charts, it took me only two unhurried days to get to Greece. A good deal about that ancient war was doubtless greatly exaggerated.

Still, certain things can touch a chord.

Such as for instance a day or two after that, seeing the Parthenon by the late afternoon sun.

It was that winter during which I lived in the Louvre, I believe. Burning artifacts and picture frames for warmth, in a poorly ventilated room.

But then with the first signs of thaw, switching vehicles whenever I ran low on gas, started back across central Russia to make my way home again.

All of this being indisputably true, if as I say long ago. And if as I also say, I may well have been mad.

Then again I am not at all certain I was mad when I drove to Mexico, before that.

Possibly before that. To visit at the grave of a child I had lost, even longer ago than all of this, named Adam.

Why have I written that his name was Adam?

Simon is what my little boy was named.

Time out of mind. Meaning that one can even momentarily forget the name of one's only child, who would be thirty by now?

I doubt thirty. Say twenty-six, or twenty-seven.

Am I fifty, then?

There is only one mirror, here in this house on this beach. Perhaps the mirror says fifty.

My hands say that. It has come to show on the backs of my hands.

Conversely I am still menstruating. Irregularly, so that often it will go on for weeks, but then will not occur again until I have almost forgotten about it.

Perhaps I am no more than forty-seven or forty-eight. I am certain that I once attempted to keep a makeshift accounting, possibly of the months but surely at least of the seasons. But I do not even remember any longer when it was that I understood I had already long since lost track.

Still, I believe I was soon going to be forty, back when all of this began.

How I left those messages was with white paint. In huge block letters, at intersections, where anybody coming or going would see.

I burned artifacts and certain other objects when I was at the Metropolitan Museum too, naturally.

Well, I had a fire there perpetually, winters.

That fire was different from the fire I had at the Louvre. Where I built the fire in the Metropolitan was in that great hall, just where one goes in and out.

As a matter of fact I manufactured a high tin chimney above it, too. So that the smoke could drift to the skylights high above that.

What I had to do was shoot holes in the skylight, once I had constructed the chimney.

I did that with a pistol, quite carefully, at an angle from one of the balconies, so that the smoke would go out but the rain would not come in.

Rain came in. Not much rain, but some.

Well, eventually it came in through other windows as well, when those broke of themselves. Or of the weather.

Windows break still. Several are broken here, in this house.

It is summer at present, however. Nor do I mind the rain.

Upstairs, one can see the ocean. Down here there are dunes, which obstruct one's view.

Actually this is my second house on this same beach. The

first, I burned to the ground. I am still not certain how that happened, though perhaps I had been cooking. For a moment I walked to the dunes to urinate, and when I looked back everything was ablaze.

These beach houses are all wood, of course. All I could do was sit at the dunes and watch it burn. It burned all night.

I still notice the burned house, mornings, when I walk along the beach.

Well, obviously I do not notice the house. What I notice is what remains of the house.

One is still prone to think of a house as a house, however, even if there is not remarkably much left of it.

This one has weathered fairly well, come to think about it. The next snows will be my third here, I believe.

Probably I should compose a list of where else I have been, if only for my own edification. I mean beginning with my old loft in SoHo, before the Metropolitan. And then my trips.

Although doubtless I have lost track of a good deal of that by now, as well.

I do remember sitting one morning in an automobile with a right-hand drive and watching Stratford-on-Avon fill up with snow, which must surely be rare.

Well, and once that same winter being almost hit by a car with nobody driving it, which came rolling down a hill near Hampstead Heath.

There was an explanation for the car coming down the hill with nobody driving it.

The explanation having been the hill, obviously.

That car, too, had a right-hand drive. Although perhaps that is not especially relevant to anything.

And in either case I may have made an error, earlier, when I said I left a message in the street saying that somebody was living in the National Gallery.

Where I lived in London was the Tate Gallery, where so many of the paintings by Joseph Mallord William Turner are.

I am quite certain that I lived at the Tate.

There is an explanation for this, too. The explanation being that one can see the river, from there.

Living alone, one is apt to prefer a view of water.

I have always admired Turner as well, however. In fact his own paintings of water may well have been a part of what led to my decision.

Once, Turner had himself lashed to the mast of a ship for several hours, during a furious storm, so that he could later paint the storm.

Obviously, it was not the storm itself that Turner intended to paint. What he intended to paint was a representation of the storm.

One's language is frequently imprecise in that manner, I have discovered.

 Actually, the story of Turner being lashed to the mast reminds me of something, even though I cannot remember what it reminds me of.

I also seem not to remember what sort of a fire I had at the Tate.

At the Rijksmuseum, in Amsterdam, I removed *The Night Watch* by Rembrandt from its frame when I was keeping warm there too, incidentally.

I am quite certain I intended to get to Madrid around that time also, since there is one painting at the Prado by Rogier van der Weyden, *The Descent from the Cross,* that I had wished to see again. But for some reason, at Bordeaux, I switched to a car that was facing back in the other direction.

Then again perhaps I had actually crossed the Spanish border as far as to Pamplona.

Well, often I did unpremeditated things in those days, as I have said. Once, from the top of the Spanish Steps in Rome, for no reason except that I had come upon a Volkswagen van full of them, I let hundreds and hundreds of tennis balls bounce one after the other to the bottom, every which way possible.

Watching how they struck tiny irregularities or worn spots in the stone, and changed direction, or guessing how far across the piazza down below each one of them would go.

Several of them bounced catty-corner and struck the house where John Keats died, in fact.

There is a plaque on the house, stating that John Keats died there.

The plaque is in Italian, naturally. Giovanni Keats, it calls him.

The name of the river at Hisarlik is the Scamander, I now remember.

In the *Iliad,* by Homer, it is referred to as a mighty river.

Well, perhaps it was, at one time. Many things can change, in three thousand years.

Even so, sitting above it one evening on the excavated walls, and gazing toward the channel, I was almost positive one could still see the Greek watchfires, being lighted along the shore.

Well, as I have said, perhaps I did not really let myself think that.

Still, certain things are harmless enough to think.

The next morning, when dawn appeared, I was quite content to consider it a rosy-fingered dawn, for instance. Even though the sky was murky.

Meanwhile I have just taken time to move my bowels. I do not go to the dunes for that, but down to the ocean itself, where the tide will wash in.

Going, I stopped first in the woods beside the house for some leaves.

And afterward went for water from my spring, which is perhaps a hundred paces along the path in the opposite direction from the beach.

I have a stream, too. Even if it is hardly the Thames.

At the Tate I did bring in my water from the river, however. One has been able to do that sort of thing for a long while, now.

Well, one could drink from the Arno, in Florence, as long ago as when I lived at the Uffizi. Or from the Seine, when I would carry a pitcher down the quay from the Louvre.

⁒ In the beginning I drank only bottled water, naturally.

In the beginning I had accouterments, as well. Such as generators, for use with electrical heating devices.

Water and warmth were the essentials, of course.

I do not remember which came first, becoming adept at maintaining fires, and so shedding devices of that sort, or discovering that one could drink any water one wished again.

Perhaps becoming adept at fires came first. Even if I have burned two houses to the ground, over the years.

The more recent, as I have noted, was accidental.

Why I burned the first one I would rather not go too deeply into. I did that quite deliberately, however.

That was in Mexico, on the morning after I had visited poor Simon's grave.

Well, it was the house we had all lived in. I honestly believed I had planned to stay on, for a time.

What I did was spill gasoline all over Simon's old room.

Much of the morning I could still see the smoke rise and rise, in my rearview mirror.

Now I have two enormous fireplaces. Here in this house by the sea, I am talking about. And in the kitchen an antiquated potbellied stove.

I have grown quite fond of the stove.

Simon had been seven, by the way.

A variety of berries grow nearby. And less than minutes past my stream there are various vegetables, in fields that were once cultivated but are of course now wildly overgrown.

Beyond the window at which I am sitting the breeze is frisking with ten thousand leaves. Sunlight breaks through the woods in mottled bright patches.

Flowers grow too, in great profusion.

It is a day for some music, actually, although I have no means of providing myself with any.

For years, wherever I was, I generally did contrive to play some. But when I began to get rid of devices I had to give up the music as well.

Baggage, basically, is what I got rid of. Well, things.

Now and again one happens to hear certain music in one's head, however.

Well, a fragment of something or other, in any case. Antonio Vivaldi, say. Or Joan Baez, singing.

Not too long ago I even heard a passage from *Les Troyens,* by Berlioz.

When I say heard, I am saying so only in a manner of speaking, of course.

Still, perhaps there is baggage after all, for all that I believed I had left baggage behind.

Of a sort. The baggage that remains in one's head, meaning remnants of whatever one ever knew.

Such as the birthdays of people like Pablo Picasso or Jackson Pollock, for instance, which I am convinced I might still recite if I wished.

Or telephone numbers, from all of those years ago.

There is a telephone right here, actually, no more than three or four steps behind where I am sitting.

Naturally I was speaking about numbers for telephones which function, however.

In fact there is a second telephone upstairs, near the cushioned window seat from which I watch the sun go down, most evenings.

The cushions, like so much else here at the beach, are musty. Even on the hottest days, one senses the dampness.

Books become ruined by it.

Books being more of the baggage I got rid of, incidentally. Even if there are still many in this house, that were here when I arrived.

I should perhaps indicate that there are eight rooms in the house, although I make use of only two or three.

Actually I did read, at times, over the years. Especially when I was mad, I read a good deal.

One winter, I read almost all of the ancient Greek plays. As a matter of fact I read them out loud. And throughout, finishing the reverse side of each page would tear it from the book and drop it into my fire.

Aeschylus and Sophocles and Euripides, I turned into smoke.

In a manner of speaking, one might think of it that way.

In a different manner of speaking, one might declare it was Helen and Clytemnestra and Electra, whom I did that with.

For the life of me I have no idea why I did that.

If I had understood why I was doing that, doubtless I would not have been mad.

Had I not been mad, doubtless I would not have done it at all.

I am less than positive that those last two sentences make any particular sense.

In either case neither do I remember where it was, exactly, that I read the plays and burned the pages.

Possibly it was after I had gone to ancient Troy, which may have been what put me in mind of the plays to begin with.

Or would reading the plays have been what put me in mind of going to ancient Troy?

It did run on, that madness.

I was not necessarily mad when I went to Mexico, however. Surely one does not have to be mad to decide to visit the grave of one's dead little boy.

But certainly I was mad when I drove the breadth of Alaska, to Nome, and then pointed a boat across the Bering Strait.

Even if I did seek out charts, that time.

Well, and had once known boats, as well. But still.

Yet after that paradoxically made my way westward across all of Russia with scarcely any maps at all. Driving out of the sun each morning and then waiting for it to appear ahead of me as the day progressed, simply following the sun.

✓Brooding upon Fyodor Dostoievski as I went.

Actually, I was keeping a weather eye out for Rodion Romanovitch Raskolnikov.

Did I stop at the Hermitage? Why do I not remember if I stopped in Moscow at all?

Well, quite possibly I drove right past Moscow without knowing it, not speaking one word of Russian.

When I say not speaking one word, I mean not reading one either, obviously.

✓ And why did I write that pretentious line about Dostoievski, when I do not have any notion now if I allotted a moment's thought to the man?

More baggage, then. At least here and now while I am typing, if not at that earlier time.

As a matter of fact when I docked the launch after the last island and went hunting for an automobile again I was possibly even surprised that they had Russian printing on their license plates. Having half imagined that I ought to be in China.

Though it strikes me at only this instant that one possesses certain Chinese baggage too, of course.

Some. There seems no point in illustrating the fact.

Even if I happen to be drinking souchong tea as I say that.

And in either case the Hermitage may be in Leningrad.

Then again there is no question that I was, decidedly, looking for Raskolnikov.

Using Raskolnikov as a symbol, one can decidedly say that I was looking for Raskolnikov.

Though one could also say that I was looking for Anna Karenina, just as readily. Or for Dmitri Shostakovitch.

I was looking when I went to Mexico too, naturally.

Hardly for Simon, since I knew all too well that Simon was in that grave. Looking for Emiliano Zapata then, perhaps.

Again symbolically, looking for Zapata. Or for Benito Juárez. Or for David Alfaro Siqueiros.

Looking for anybody, anywhere at all.

Well, even mad was looking, or for what earthly reason else, would I have gone wandering off to all of those other places?

And had been looking on every streetcorner in New York before that, naturally. Even before I moved out of SoHo, had been looking everywhere in New York.

And so was still looking that winter when I lived in Madrid, as well.

I am not certain whether I have mentioned my period in Madrid.

In Madrid I did not live at the Prado, as it turned out. Perhaps I have suggested that I had thought to do so, but it was too badly lighted.

It is natural light that I am speaking about in this case, already having begun to shed most of my devices by then.

Only when the sun is especially fierce can one begin to see that Rogier van der Weyden the way it wants to be seen.

I can attest to this categorically, having even washed the windows nearest it.

Where I lived in Madrid was in a hotel. Choosing the one they had named after Velázquez.

Looking, there, for Don Quixote. Or for El Greco. Or for Francisco de Goya.

How poetic most Spanish names generally sound. One can say them over and over.

Sor Juana Inés de la Cruz. Marco Antonio Montes de Oca.

Though in fact both of those may be names from Mexico again.

Looking. Dear heaven, how anxiously I looked.

I do not remember when it was that I stopped looking.

In the Adriatic, when I was on my way from Troy to Greece, a ketch swooped toward me swiftly, its tall spinnaker taking noisy wind.

Just imagine how that startled me, and how I felt.

One moment I was sailing, as alone as ever, and a moment after that there was the ketch.

But it had only been adrift. Through all of that time, presumably.

Would it have been as long as four or five years, by then? I am almost certain that I remained in New York for at least two winters, before I went looking elsewhere.

Near Lesbos, I saw that ketch. Or perhaps Scyros.

Is Scyros one of the Greek islands?

One forgets. There is a loss of baggage unwittingly, too.

As a matter of fact I now suspect I ought to have said the Aegean when I said the Adriatic, a few paragraphs ago. Surely it is the Aegean, between Troy and Greece.

This tea is baggage of a sort also, I suppose. Though in this case I did seek it out again, after that other beach house burned. Little as I burden myself with, did wish for tea.

And some cigarettes as well, although I smoke very little, these days.

Well, and other staples too, naturally.

The cigarettes are the sort that come in tins. Those in paper had begun to taste stale some while ago.

Most things did, which were packaged that way. Not to spoil, necessarily, but to turn dry.

As a matter of fact my cigarettes happen to be Russian. That is just coincidence, however.

Hereabouts, everything stays damp.

I have said that.

Still, when I remove it from a drawer, often my clothing feels clammy.

Generally, summers as now, I wear nothing at all.

I do have underpants and shorts, and several denim skirts that wrap around, and some few cotton jerseys. I wash everything at the stream, and then spread it across bushes to dry.

Well, I have more clothing than that. Winter makes demands.

Except for gathering firewood beforehand, however, I have taken to worrying about winter when winter appears.

When it is here, it will be here.

When the leaves fall, generally the woods remain barren for a time before the snows, and I can see all the way to the spring, or even to the continuation of my path to the highway beyond.

It requires perhaps forty minutes to walk along the highway to the town.

There are stores, some few, and there is a gas station.

Kerosene is still to be found at the latter.

I rarely make use of my lamps, however. Even when what seems the last glimmer of sunset is gone, traces still reach the room I climb upstairs to sleep in.

Through another window at its opposite side the rosy-fingered dawn awakens me.

Certain mornings the phrase does happen to fit, as a matter of fact.

The houses along this beach would appear to continue endlessly, by the way. In any case infinitely farther than I have chosen to walk in either direction and still be able to return by nightfall.

Somewhere I have a flashlight. In the glove compartment of the pickup truck, possibly.

The pickup truck is at the highway. I suspect that I may have neglected to run the battery for some time, now.

Doubtless there are still unused batteries at the gas station.

Sister Juana Inés de la Cruz. I no longer have any idea who she may have been, to tell the truth.

To tell the truth I would be equally hard pressed to identify Marco Antonio Montes de Oca.

In the National Portrait Gallery, in London, which is not one of the museums I chose to live in, I was not able to recognize eight out of ten of the faces in the portraits. Or even almost that many of the names, identifying the portraits.

I do not mean in the cases of people like Winston Churchill or the Brontë sisters or the Queen or Dylan Thomas, obviously.

Still, this saddened me.

And why does it come into mind that I would like to inform Dylan Thomas that one can now kneel and drink from the Loire, or the Po, or the Mississippi?

Or would Dylan Thomas have already been dead <u>before it</u> became impossible to do such <u>things</u>, meaning that he would look at me as if I were mad all over again?

Certainly Achilles would. Or Shakespeare. Or Emiliano Zapata.

I do not remember Dylan Thomas's dates. And anyway, doubtless there was no specific date for pollution.

One one eight six, the last four digits of somebody's phone number may have been.

Actually, I have never been to the Mississippi either. Going and coming from Mexico I did drink from the Rio Grande, however.

Why do I say such things? Obviously I would have had to cross the Mississippi as well, both ways, on the same trip.

Still, it appears I have no recollection of that. Or was I mad then also?

The queer selection of books that I read in that period, good heavens. Virtually every solitary one of them about that identical war.

But frequently making up new versions of the stories on my own part, too, one's fanciful private improvisations.

Such as Helen, slipping down from the battlements and meeting Achilles beside the Scamander on the sly.

Or Penelope, making love to one after another of all of those suitors, while Odysseus was away.

Wouldn't she have? Surely, with so many of them hanging about? And if it was truly ten years for the war and still another ten before that husband of hers materialized?

For some reason a part I always liked was Achilles dressing like a girl and hiding, so that they would not make him go to fight.

There is a painting of Penelope weaving in the National

Gallery, actually, by somebody named Pintoricchio.

I have said that quite badly, I suspect.

One scarcely meaning that where Penelope is doing her weaving is in the National Gallery. Where she is doing that is on the island of Ithaca, naturally.

Ithaca being in neither the Adriatic nor the Aegean Sea, incidentally, but in the Ionian.

The things that do remain in one's head after all.

I should also perhaps point out that the National Gallery and the National Portrait Gallery are not the same museum, even though they are both in London.

As a matter of fact they are not the same museum even though they are both in the same building.

Conversely I know next to nothing about Pintoricchio, though I once knew a great deal about many painters.

Well, I knew a great deal about many painters for the same reason that Achilles must surely have known a great deal about Hector, say.

All I can remember about the painting of Penelope is that there is a cat in it, however, playing with a ball of yarn.

Doubtless the inclusion of the cat was scarcely innovative on Pintoricchio's part. Still, it is perhaps agreeable to think about Penelope with a pet, especially if I have been wrong about her and the suitors.

I should have also perhaps said long before this that I harbor sincere doubts that that war did last those ten years.

Or that Helen was the cause of it.

A single Spartan girl, as somebody once called her. After all.

But what I am basically thinking about here is how disappointingly small the ruins of Troy turn out to be.

Like little more than your ordinary city block and only a few stories in height, practically.

Well, though with people having lived outside of the citadel too, on the plains.

But still.

In the *Odyssey,* when she is older, Helen has a splendid radiant dignity. I read those pages two or three times, where Odysseus's son Telemachus comes to visit.

Which means I could not have been tearing them out and dropping them into the fire, as I did when I read the plays.

Meanwhile I have just been to the dunes again. For some reason while I was peeing I thought about Lawrence of Arabia.

Well, I can hardly be said to have thought about him, since I know little more about Lawrence of Arabia than I do about Pintoricchio. Still, Lawrence of Arabia did come into mind.

I can think of no connection between making a pee and Lawrence of Arabia.

There is still that frisky breeze. It is early August, possibly.

For a moment, strolling back, I may have been hearing some Brahms. I would say *The Alto Rhapsody,* though I doubt that I remember *The Alto Rhapsody.*

Doubtless there was a portrait of Lawrence of Arabia at the National Portrait Gallery.

And now I have the name T. E. Shaw in my head. But it is one more of those flitting identities that I cannot at all catch hold of.

None of that troubles me, by the way.

Very little does, as I may or may not have made evident.

Well, how ridiculous under the circumstances, should I let anything do so.

I do fret now and again, if fret is the word, over an arthritic shoulder. The left, which at times leaves me moderately incapacitated.

Sunshine is a help, however.

My teeth, on the other hand, do not speak of fifty years at all. Knock on wood, about my teeth.

I cannot remember anything about my mother's teeth, trying to think back. Or my father's.

At any rate perhaps I am no more than forty-seven.

I cannot envision Helen of Troy with dental problems. Or Clytemnestra with arthritis.

There was Cézanne, of course.

Although it was not Cézanne but was Renoir.

I have no idea, any longer, where any of my own painting materials may have gotten to, by the way.

Once during these years I did stretch one canvas, actually. A monstrosity of a canvas, in fact, at least nine feet by five. In fact I also sized it with no less than four coats of gesso.

And thereafter gazed at it.

Months, I suspect, I gazed at that canvas. Possibly I even foolishly squeezed out some pigments onto my pallet.

As a matter of fact I believe it was when I went back to Mexico, that I did that. In the house where I had once lived with Simon, and with Adam.

I am basically positive that my husband was named Adam.

And then after months of gazing set fire to the canvas with gasoline one morning and drove away.

Across the wide Mississippi.

Once in a great while I could almost see things in that canvas, however.

Almost. Achilles, for instance, in his grief after the death of his friend, when he covered himself with ashes. Or Clytemnestra, after Agamemnon had sacrificed their daughter to raise wind for the Greek ships.

I have no idea why Achilles dressing like a girl is a part that I always liked.

For that matter it was a woman who wrote the *Odyssey,* somebody once said.

When I was back in Mexico, all through that winter I could not rid myself of the old habit of turning my shoes upside down each morning, so that any scorpions inside might fall out.

Any number of habits died hard, that way. For some years I continued to find myself locking doors, similarly.

Well, and in London. Frequently taking the trouble to drive

Samuel Butler

on the British side of the road.

After his grief, Achilles got even by slaying Hector, although Hector ran and ran.

I was about to add that this was the sort of thing men used to do. But after her own grief Clytemnestra killed Agamemnon.

Needing some assistance. But nonetheless.

Something tells me, obliquely, that that may have been one of the notions I had, for my canvas. Agamemnon at his bath, ensnared in that net and being stabbed through it.

Heaven only knows why anybody could have wished for such a bloody subject, however.

As a matter of fact whom I really may have thought to paint was Helen. At one of the burned-out boats along the strand, when the siege was finally ended, being kept prisoner.

But with that splendid dignity, even so.

To tell the truth it was actually just below the central staircase in the Metropolitan, where I set that canvas up. Under those high skylights where my bullet holes were.

Where I had situated my bed was on one of the balconies, overlooking that area.

The bed itself I had taken from one of the reconstructed period rooms, I believe, possibly American Colonial.

What I had done about that chimney I had constructed was to wire it to the same balconies, so that it would not list.

Though I was still making use of all sorts of devices, in those days. And so had electric heaters also.

Well, and innumerable lights, particularly where the canvas was.

A nine-foot brilliantly illuminated Electra, I might have painted, had I thought about it.

I did not think about it until this immediate instant.

Poor Electra. To wish to murder one's own mother.

Well, all of those people. Wrist deep in it, the lot of them, when one comes down to that.

Irene Papas would have been an effective Electra, however.

In fact she was an effective Helen, in *The Trojan Women,* by Euripides.

Perhaps I have not indicated that I watched a certain few films while I still possessed devices, also.

Irene Papas and Katherine Hepburn in *The Trojan Women* was one. Maria Callas in *Medea* was another.

My mother did have false teeth, I now remember.

Well, and in that glass beside her bed, those final weeks in the hospital.

Oh, dear.

Though I have a vague recollection that the projector I brought into the museum stopped functioning after I had used it no more than three or four times, and that I did not trouble to replace it.

When I was still at my loft, in the beginning, I brought in at least thirty portable radios, and tuned each one to a different number on the dial.

Actually those worked by batteries, not electricity.

Obviously that was how they worked, since I doubt that I would have solved how a generator operated, that early on.

My aunt Esther died of cancer, as well. Though Esther was my father's sister, actually.

Here, at least, there is always a sound of the sea.

And right at this moment a strand of tape at a broken window in the room next to this one is making scratching sounds, from my breeze.

Mornings, when the leaves are dewy, some of them are like jewels where the earliest sunlight glistens.

A cat scratching, that loose strip of tape could be.

Where would it have been, that I read all of those bloody stories out loud?

I am fairly certain that I had not yet gone to Europe when I wore my last wristwatches, if that is at all relevant.

I doubt that wearing thirteen or fourteen wristwatches, along the length of one's forearm, is especially relevant.

Well, and for a period several gold pocket watches also, on a cord around my neck.

Actually somebody wore an alarm clock that very way in a novel I once read.

I would say it was in *The Recognitions,* by William Gaddis, except that I do not believe I have ever read *The Recognitions* by William Gaddis.

In any case I am more likely thinking of Taddeo Gaddi, even though Taddeo Gaddi was a painter and not a writer.

What did I do with those watches, I wonder?

Wore them.

Well. But each of them with an alarm of its own, as well.

What I normally did was set the alarms so that each one of the watches would ring at a different hour.

I did that for some time. All day long, every hour, a different watch would ring.

In the evening I would set all fourteen of them all over again. Except that in that case I would set them to ring simultaneously.

This was before I had learned to depend upon the dawn, doubtless.

They rarely did that anyway. Ring simultaneously, I mean.

Even when that appeared to be the case, one learned to wait for those which had not started ringing yet.

When I say they rang, I mean that they buzzed, more truthfully.

In a town called Corinth, in Mississippi, which is not near the Mississippi River, parking a car on a small bridge I divested myself of the watches.

I believe Corinth. I would need an atlas, to reassure myself.

Actually, there is an atlas in this house. Somewhere. Perhaps in one of the rooms I have stopped going into.

For an entire day I sat in the car and waited for each watch to ring in its turn.

And then dropped each as it did so into the water. Whatever body of water that may have been.

One or two did not ring. What I did was reset them and sleep in the car and then get rid of those when they rang for morning.

Still ringing like all of the rest when I discarded them.

To tell the truth, I did that in a town somewhere in Pennsylvania. The name of the town was Lititz, Pennsylvania.

All of this was some time before I rolled the tennis balls down the Spanish Steps in Rome, by the way.

I make the connection between getting rid of the watches and rolling the tennis balls down the Spanish Steps because I am positive that getting rid of the watches also occurred before I saw the cat, which was likewise in Rome.

When I say that I saw a cat I mean that I believed I saw one, naturally.

And the reason I am positive that this happened in Rome is because it happened at the Colosseum, which is indisputably in that city.

Where I believed I saw the cat was at one of the archways in the Colosseum, quite far up.

How I felt. In the midst of all that looking.

And so went scurrying to a supermarket for canned cat food.

As quickly as I realized I could not locate the cat again, that would have been.

And then every morning for a week, opened cans by the carton and went about setting them out on the stone seats.

As many cans as there must have been Romans watching the Christians, practically.

But next speculated that the cat might possibly reappear only at night, being frightened, and so rigged up yet another generator and floodlights, even.

Though of course I had no way of telling if the cat had nibbled at any of the food behind my back, since most of the cans had not seemed quite full to begin with.

Still, I felt that to be unquestionably worth checking on, several times each day.

What I named the cat was Nero.

Here, Nero, I would call.

Well, I suspect I may have tried Julius Caesar and Herodotus and Pontius Pilate at various moments, also.

Herodotus may have been a waste of time with a cat in Rome, now that I think about it.

Doubtless the cans are still there in either case, lined up across all of those seats.

Rains would have emptied them completely by now, assuredly.

Doubtless there was no cat at the Colosseum.

Though I also called the cat Calpurnia, after a time, when it struck me that I should cover all bases.

Doubtless there was no seagull either.

It is the seagull which brought me to this beach, that I am speaking about now.

High, high, against the clouds, little more than a speck, but then swooping in the direction of the sea.

I will be truthful. In Rome, when I thought I saw the cat, I was undeniably mad. And so I thought I saw the cat.

Here, when I thought I saw the seagull, I was not mad. So I knew I had not seen the seagull.

Now and again, things burn. I do not mean only when I have set fire to them myself, but out of natural happenstance. And so bits and pieces of residue will sometimes be wafted great distances, or to astonishing heights.

I had finally gotten accustomed to those.

Still, I would have vastly preferred to believe I had seen the seagull.

As a matter of fact it was much more probably the thought of sunsets, which brought me to this beach.

Well, or of the sound of the sea.

After I had finally determined that I may as well stop looking, this is.

Have I mentioned looking in Damascus, Syria, or in Bethlehem, or in Troy, New York?

Once, near Lake Como, at a stone stairway that reminded me somewhat of the Spanish Steps, I put several loose coins that had been lying in my Jeep into a public telephone, intending to ask for Giovanni Keats.

I had no idea if Keats had ever visited Lake Como, actually.

For some weeks in Mexico I drove a Jeep also. And so was able to maneuver directly up the hillside, instead of taking the road, each time I went to the cemetery.

How many different vehicles have I made use of, I suddenly wonder, since all of this started?

Well, more than one could have kept track of just down to Cuernavaca or back, surely. What with having to switch at so many obstacles, even disregarding when one ran out of gas.

By obstacles I most generally mean other cars, naturally. In whatever nuisance locations they had come to a stop.

And on top of which I always foolishly troubled to transfer all of my baggage as well, in those days.

Excepting when I was forced to walk too considerable a distance between one vehicle and the next, of course.

But even then, would repeatedly burden myself with more of the same in no time.

Here, I have three denim skirts that wrap around, and some cotton jerseys.

Most of which at the moment are lying across bushes, drying in the sun.

I drive only rarely now, as well.

As a matter of fact the clothing out at the spring has been dry for some days.

In autumn, after the leaves have fallen, I would be able to see it from exactly where I am sitting at this moment, possibly.

The cat at the Colosseum was russet colored, incidentally.

The gull was your ordinary gull.

Actually it was ash, carried astonishingly high and rocked by breezes.

Every last one of those skirts and jerseys has gotten faded, because I almost always forget about them out there like this.

I am wearing underpants, but only because the seat of this chair has no cushion.

I have also just brought blueberries in from the kitchen.

Was it really some other person I was so anxious to discover, when I did all of that looking, or was it only my own solitude that I could not abide?

Wandering through this endless nothingness. Once in a while, when I was not mad, I would turn poetic instead. I honestly did let myself think about things in such ways.

The eternal silence of these infinite spaces frightens me. For instance I thought about them like that, also.

In a manner of speaking, I thought about them like that.

Actually I underlined that sentence in a book, named the *Pensées,* when I was in college.

Doubtless I underlined the sentence about wandering through an endless nothingness in somebody else's book, as well.

The cat that Pintoricchio put into the painting of Penelope weaving may have been gray, I have a feeling.

Once, I had a dream of fame.

Generally, even then, I was lonely.

Later today I will possibly masturbate.

I do not mean today, since it is already tomorrow.

Well, it is already tomorrow insofar as that I have watched a sunset and had a night's sleep since I began typing these pages. Which I began yesterday.

Perhaps I ought to have noted that.

When the woods started to fill up with shadows, and this corner darkened, I went into the kitchen and ate more of the blueberries, and then I went upstairs.

Yesterday's sunset was an abstract expressionist sunset. It is about a week since the last time I had a Turner.

I do not masturbate often. Though at times I do so almost without being aware of it, actually.

At the dunes, perhaps. Just sitting, being lulled by the surf.

There is an ebb, is all.

I suspect I have done it while driving too, however.

I am quite certain that I masturbated on a road in La Mancha once, near a castle that I kept on seeing and seeing, but that I never appeared to get any closer to.

There was an explanation for not getting any closer to the castle.

The explanation being that the castle was built on a hill, and that the road went in a flat circle around the bottom of the hill that the castle was built on.

Very likely one could have driven around that castle eternally, never actually arriving at it.

Before I ever saw one, I would have supposed that castles in Spain was just a phrase.

There are castles.

Near someplace called Savona, which is not in Spain but in Italy, I went off the road, once.

Part of the embankment had fallen away. This is on the seacoast, that I am talking about, so that if one goes off an embankment one has gone into water.

Instead of watching a castle I had been watching the water, doubtless.

As a matter of fact the car turned over.

Only my shoulder hurt, some moments afterward.

Well, the very shoulder that is now arthritic, come to think about it. I had never made that connection before.

Perhaps there is no connection.

In either case the car also began to fill up with water.

Interestingly, I did not feel frightened in the least. Or perhaps it was the realization that I had not badly injured myself, which reassured me.

Still, I understood that opening my door and getting out would be a sensible notion under the circumstances.

I was not able to open my door.

During all of this time I was on the roof of the car, by the way.

I mean on the inside of the roof, obviously. And with the rubber mat from the floor having fallen on top of me.

I do not remember what kind of a car I was driving at the time.

Well, one was scarcely driving it any longer in either case.

What I was doing was trying to crawl across to the opposite door.

The water came up only to the tops of my sandal straps.

Still, the entire experience terrified me.

I am aware that I have just said it had not frightened me in the least.

As a matter of fact what happened was that it did not frighten me until it was over.

Once I had climbed back onto the embankment, and could see the car upside down in the water, it frightened me rather impressively.

I cannot say with any certainty that I had been masturbating when I failed to notice the collapsed embankment.

Or whether I had been driving toward Savona, or had already passed Savona.

What is fairly certain is that I was driving into Italy, and not out, since in driving into Italy along that coast one would have the sea at one's right hand, which is the side I went into it from.

Even if I have no recollection whatsoever of ever having driven into Italy from the direction I am talking about.

Doubtless it is partly age, which blurs such distinctions.

When one comes down to it, I could actually be well past fifty.

Again, the mirror is of no real help. One would need some kind of yardstick, or a field of comparison.

There was a tiny, pocket sort of mirror on that same table beside my mother's bed, those final weeks.

You will never know how much it has meant to me that you are an artist, Kate, she said, one evening.

There are no painting materials in this house.

[handwritten top margin] eg. ekphrasis — a representation of one visual/graphic work inside a literary work.

Actually there was one canvas on a wall, when I came. Directly above and to the side of where this typewriter is, in fact.

A painting of this very house, although it took me some days to recognize that.

Not because it was not a satisfactory representation, but because I had not happened to look at the house from that perspective, as yet.

I had already removed the painting into another room by the time I did so.

Still, I believed it was a painting of this house.

After I had concluded that it was, or that it appeared to be, I did not go back into the other room to verify my conclusion.

I go into those rooms infrequently, and have closed those doors.

There was nothing extraordinary in the fact of my closing them. Possibly I closed them only because I did not feel like sweeping.

Leaves blow in, and fluffy cottonwood seeds.

This room is quite large. There is a deck outside, constructed on two sides of the house so that it faces both the forest and the dunes.

Two of the five closed doors are upstairs.

None of this is counting the bathroom, where the mirror is.

In fact there could well be additional paintings in those other rooms. I could look.

There are no paintings in the closed rooms. Or at least not in the three closed rooms that are downstairs.

Though I have just replaced the painting of the house.

It is agreeable to have some art about.

In my mother's living room, in Bayonne, New Jersey, there were several of my own paintings. Two of those were portraits, of her and my father.

Never was I able to find the courage to ask her if she wished me to remove that mirror.

One afternoon the mirror was no longer there, however.

To tell the truth, I rarely did portraits.

Those of my mother and father are now at the Metropolitan Museum, in one of the main painting galleries on the second floor.

Well, all of my paintings are now in those galleries in the Metropolitan Museum.

What I did was stand them between various canvases in the permanent collection, wherever there was sufficient wall space.

Some few overlapped those others, but only at their lower corners, generally.

Very likely a certain amount of warp has occurred in mine since, however.

From having been leaning for so many years rather than being hung, that would be.

Well, and a number of them had never been framed, either.

Then again, when I say all of my paintings I am speaking only about the paintings I had not sold, naturally.

Though in fact some few were in group shows, or out on loan, also.

One of those I saw by sheer chance when I was in Rome, as a matter of fact.

Actually I had almost forgotten about it. And then in the window of a municipal gallery on a street near the Via Vittorio Veneto, there was my name on a poster.

To tell the truth, it was Louise Nevelson's name that caught my eye first. But still.

Sitting in an automobile with English license plates and a right-hand drive, only a day after that, I watched the Piazza Navona fill up with snow, which must surely be rare.

Early in the Renaissance, although also in Rome, Brunelleschi and Donatello went about measuring ruins with such industry that people believed they were mad.

But after that Brunelleschi returned home to Florence and put up the largest dome since antiquity.

Well, this being one of the reasons they named it the Renaissance, obviously.

It was Giotto who built the beautiful campanile next door to that same cathedral.

Once, being asked to submit a sample of his work, what Giotto submitted was a circle.

Well, the point being that it was a perfect circle.

And that Giotto had painted it freehand.

When my father died, less than a year after my mother, I came upon that same tiny mirror in a drawer full of old snapshots.

An authentic snow falls in Rome no more than once every seventy years or so, as a matter of fact.

Which is approximately how often the Arno overflows its banks too, at Florence. Though perhaps there is no connection there.

Yet it is not impossible that people like Leonardo da Vinci or Andrea del Sarto or Taddeo Gaddi went through their entire lives without ever watching boys throw snowballs.

Had they been born somewhat later they could have seen Bruegel's paintings of youngsters doing that, at least.

I happen to believe the story about Giotto and the circle, by the way. Certain stories being gratifying to believe.

I also believe I met William Gaddis once. He did not look Italian.

Conversely I do not believe one word of what I wrote, a few lines ago, about Leonardo da Vinci and Andrea del Sarto and Taddeo Gaddi never seeing snow, which was ridiculous.

Nor can I remember, any longer, if I happened onto the poster with my name on it before or after I saw the cat at the Colosseum.

The cat at the Colosseum was orange, if I have not indicated, and had lost an eye.

In fact it was hardly your most appealing cat, for all that I was so anxious to see it again.

Simon had a cat, once. Which we could never seem to decide on a name for.

Cat, being all we ever called it.

Here, when the snows come, the trees write a strange calligraphy against the whiteness. The sky itself is often white, and the dunes are hidden, and the beach is white down to the water's edge, as well.

In a manner of speaking almost everything I am able to see, then, is like that nine-foot canvas of mine, with its opaque four white coats of gesso.

Now and again I build fires along the beach, however.

Well, autumns, or in early spring, I am most apt to do that.

Once, after doing that, I tore the pages out of a book and lighted those too, tossing each page into the breeze to see if the breeze might make it fly.

Most of the pages fell right next to me.

The book was a life of Brahms, which had been standing askew on one of the shelves here and which the dampness had left permanently misshapen. Although it had been printed on extraordinarily cheap paper to begin with.

When I say that I sometimes hear music in my head, incidentally, I often even know whose voice I am hearing, if the music is vocal music.

I do not remember who it was yesterday for *The Alto Rhapsody,* however.

I had not read the life of Brahms. But I do believe there is one book in this house which I did read, since I came.

As a matter of fact one could say two books, since it was a two-volume edition of the ancient Greek plays.

Although where I actually read that book was in the other house, farther down the beach, which I burned to the ground. The only book I have looked into in this house is an atlas, wishing to remind myself where Savona is.

As a matter of fact I did that not ten minutes ago, when I decided to bring the painting of the house back out here.

Which I now cannot be positive is a painting of this house, or of a house that is simply very much like this house.

The atlas was on a shelf directly behind where the painting had been leaning.

And directly beside a life of Brahms, printed on extraordinarily cheap paper and standing askew in such a way that it has become permanently misshapen.

Presumably it was another book altogether, from which I tore the pages and set fire to them, in wishing to simulate a seagull.

Unless of course there were two lives of Brahms in this house, both printed on cheap paper and both ruined by dampness.

Kathleen Ferrier is who was singing *The Alto Rhapsody*.

I assume I do not have to explain that any version of any music that comes into my head would be the version I was once most familiar with.

In SoHo, my recording of *The Alto Rhapsody* was an old Kathleen Ferrier recording.

And now that strand of tape is scratching at the window in the next room again, again sounding like a cat.

One does not name a seagull.

Once, when I was listening to myself read the Greek plays out loud, certain of the lines sounded as if they had been written under the influence of William Shakespeare.

One had to be quite perplexed as to how Aeschylus or Euripides might have read Shakespeare.

I did remember an anecdote, about some other Greek author, who had remarked that if he could be positive of a life after death he would happily hang himself to see Euripides. Basically this did not seem relevant, however.

Finally it occurred to me that the translator had no doubt read Shakespeare.

Normally I would not consider that a memorable insight, except for the fact that I was otherwise undeniably mad at the time when I read the plays.

As a matter of fact I only now realize that I may not have been cooking after all, when I burned that other house to the ground, but may well have burned it in the process of dropping the pages of *The Trojan Women* into the fire after I had finished reading their reverse sides.

Conversely I have no idea why I would have stated that it was a life of Brahms I had set fire to, out on the beach, when it was not ten minutes earlier that I had noticed the life of Brahms next to the atlas behind where the painting was.

Certain questions would appear unanswerable.

Such as, in addition, what my father may have thought about, looking through old snapshots and then looking into the mirror that had been beside my mother's bed.

Or whether one would have ever arrived at the castle or not, had one continued to follow that same road.

Well, in that case doubtless there was ultimately a cutoff.

To the castle, a sign must have said.

In a Jeep, one could have maneuvered directly up the hillside, instead of following the road.

Meanwhile one does not spend any time viewing castles in La Mancha without being reminded of Don Quixote also, of course.

Any more than one can spend time in Toledo without being reminded of El Greco, even if it happens that El Greco was not Spanish.

All too often one hears of him spoken of as if he were, however.

The famous Spanish artists such as Velázquez or Zurbarán or El Greco, being the sort of thing that one hears.

One hardly ever hears of him being spoken of as a Greek, on the other hand.

The famous Greek artists such as Phidias or Theophanes the Greek or El Greco, being the sort of thing that one almost never hears.

Yet it is not beyond imagining that El Greco was even

(NB) painting passages

directly descended from some of those other Greeks, when one stops to think about it.

Surely it would have been easy to lose track, in so many years. But who is to say that it might not go back even farther than that, to somebody like Achilles, why not?

I am almost certain that Helen had at least one child, at any rate.

Now the painting does appear to be of this house.

As a matter of fact there also appears to be somebody at the very window, upstairs, from which I watch the sunset.

I had not noticed her at all, before this.

If it is a she. The brushwork is fairly abstract, at that point, so that there is little more than a hint of anybody, really.

 Still, it is interesting to speculate suddenly about just who might be lurking at my bedroom window while I am typing down here right below.

 Well, and on the wall just above and to the side of me, at the same time.

All of this being merely in a manner of speaking, of course.

 Although I have also just closed my eyes, and so could additionally say that for the moment the person was not only both upstairs and on the wall, but in my head as well.

Were I to walk outside to where I can see the window, and do the same thing all over again, the arrangement could become much more complicated than that.

For that matter I have only now noticed something else in the painting.

The door that I generally use, coming and going from the front deck, is open.

Not two minutes ago, I happen to have closed that same door.

Obviously no action of my own, such as that, changes anything in the painting.

Nonetheless I have again just closed my eyes, trying to see if I could imagine the painting with the door to the deck closed.

I was not able to close the door to the deck in the version of the painting in my head.

Had I any pigments, I could paint it closed in the painting itself, should this begin to trouble me seriously.

There are no painting materials in this house.

Unquestionably there would have had to be all sorts of such materials here at one time, however.

Well, with the exception of those that she carried to the dunes, where else would the painter have deposited them?

Now I have made the painter a she, also. Doubtless because of my continued sense of it being a she at the window.

But in either case one may still assume that there must be additional painting materials inside of the house in the painting, even if one cannot see any of them in the painting itself.

As a matter of fact it is no less possible that there are additional people inside of the house as well, above and beyond the woman at my window.

Then again, very likely the others could be at the beach, since it is late on a summer afternoon in the canvas, although no later than four o'clock.

So that next one is forced to wonder why the woman at the window did not go to the beach herself, for that matter.

Although on second thought I have decided that the woman may well be a child.

So that perhaps she had been made to remain at home as a punishment, after having misbehaved.

Or perhaps she was even ill.

Possibly there is nobody at the window in the canvas.

At four o'clock I will try to estimate exactly where at the dunes the painter took her perspective, and then see how the shadows fall, up there.

Even if I will be forced to guess at when it is four o'clock, there being no clocks or watches in this house, either.

All one will have to do is to match the real shadows on the house with the painted shadows in the painting, however.

Although perhaps the real shadows at the window when I go out will not solve a thing in regard to the painting.

Perhaps I will not go out.

Once, I believed I saw somebody at a real window, while I am on the subject.

In Athens, this was, and while I was still looking, which made it something of an occurrence.

Well. And even more so than the cat at the Colosseum, rather.

As a matter of fact one could also see the Acropolis, from beside the very window in question.

Which was in a street full of taverns.

Still, when the sun had gotten to the angle from which Phidias had taken his perspective, the Parthenon almost seemed to glow.

Actually, the best time to see that is generally also at four o'clock.

Doubtless the taverns from which one could see that did better business than the taverns from which one could not, in fact, even though they were all in the same street.

Unless of course the latter were patronized by people who had lived in Athens long enough to have gotten tired of seeing it.

Such things can happen. As in the case of Guy de Maupassant, who ate his lunch every day at the Eiffel Tower.

Well, the point being that this was the only place in Paris from which he did not have to look at it.

For the life of me I have no idea how I know that. Any more than I have any idea how I also happen to know that Guy de Maupassant liked to row.

When I said that Guy de Maupassant ate his lunch every day at the Eiffel Tower, so that he did not have to look at it, I meant that it was the Eiffel Tower he did not wish to look at, naturally, and not his lunch.

One's language being frequently imprecise in such ways, I have discovered.

Although I have a rowboat of my own, as it happens.

Now and again, I row out a good distance.

Beyond the breakers, the currents will do most of the work.

The row back can be difficult, however, if one allows one's self to be carried too far.

Actually, the rowboat is my second rowboat.

The first rowboat disappeared.

Doubtless I had not beached it securely enough. One morning, or possibly one afternoon, it was simply gone.

Some days afterward I walked along the beach farther than I had ever walked before, but it had not come ashore.

It would scarcely be the only boat adrift, of course, if it is still adrift.

Well, like that ketch in the Aegean, for starters.

Sometimes I like to believe it has been carried all of the way across the ocean by now, however. As far as to the Canary Islands, say, or to Cádiz, on the coast of Spain.

Well, or who is to argue that it might not have gotten to Scyros itself, even?

I do not remember the name of the street with all of those taverns in it.

Possibly I never knew the names of any of the streets in Athens in either case, not speaking one word of Greek.

When I say not speaking one word, I mean not reading one either, obviously.

One would certainly wish to conceive of the Greeks as having been imaginative in that regard, however.

Penelope Avenue being an agreeable possibility, for instance. Or Cassandra Street.

At least there must have been an Aristotle Boulevard, surely. Or a Herodotus Square.

Why did I imply that it was Phidias who built the Parthenon when it was somebody named Ictinus?

In spite of frequently underlining sentences in books that had not been assigned, I did well in college, actually.

So that one could even generally identify the floor plans of such structures, on final exams.

But so what poem am I now thinking about, then, about singing birds sweet, being sold in the shops for the people to eat?

Being sold in the shops, does it go, on Stupidity Street?

I do not believe I have ever mentioned Cassandra in any of these pages before, come to think about it. Let me name the street with the taverns in it Cassandra Street.

Cassandra certainly being an appropriate name for a street in which I believed I saw somebody at a window in either case.

Well, and especially lurking at it.

Or is it simply the notion of somebody lurking at my window in the painting that has made me make this connection?

Still, lurking at such a window is exactly where one is apt to visualize Cassandra after Agamemnon had brought her back as one of his spoils from Troy, as a matter of fact.

Even while Clytemnestra is saying hello to Agamemnon and suggesting a nice hot bath, one is apt to visualize her that way.

Well, but with Cassandra also always able to see things, of course. So that even without a window to lurk at, she would have soon known about those swords near the tub.

Not that anybody ever learned to pay any attention to a word Cassandra ever said, however.

Well, those mad trances of hers.

Nor would there have been a street in Athens named for her after all, obviously. Any more than there would have been one named for Hector, or for Paris.

Then again it is not impossible that people's sentiments might change, after so many years.

At the intersection of Cassandra Street and El Greco Road, at four o'clock in the afternoon, I saw somebody at a window, lurking.

There was nobody at the window, which was a window in a shop selling artists' supplies.

It was a small stretched canvas, coated with gesso, that had highlighted my own reflection as I passed.

Still, how I nearly felt. In the midst of all that looking.

Though as a matter of fact where I saw my own reflection may well have been in a bookstore window.

At any rate the two stores were adjacent. The one with the books was the one that I chose to let myself into.

All of the books in the store were in Greek, naturally.

Possibly some few of them were actually books that I had even read, in English, although naturally I would have had no way of knowing which ones.

Possibly one of them was even a Greek edition of William Shakespeare's plays. By a translator who had been under the influence of Euripides.

Gesso has such a silly look, for a word, when one types it.

It would have helped to prevent my canvases from warping if I had not shot holes into those skylights, obviously.

Had the smoke backed up, winters there at the Metropolitan would have been difficult, however.

Actually one can be saddened, letting one's self into a store full of books and not being able to recognize a single one.

The bookstore on the street below the Acropolis saddened me.

Although I have now made a categorical decision that the painting is not a painting of this house.

Assuredly, it is a painting of the other house, farther down the beach, which burned.

To tell the truth I cannot call that other house to mind at all, any longer.

Although perhaps that house and this house were identical. Or quite similar, at any rate.

Houses along a beach are often that way, being constructed by people with basically similar tastes.

Though as a matter of fact I cannot be absolutely certain that the painting is on the wall beside me any longer itself, since I am no longer looking at it.

Quite possibly I put it back into the room with the atlas and the life of Brahms. I have a distinct suspicion that it had entered my mind to do that.

The painting is on the wall.

And at least we have verified that it was not the life of Brahms that I set fire to the pages from also, out on the beach.

Unless as I have suggested somebody in this house had owned two lives of Brahms, both printed on cheap paper and both ruined by dampness.

Or two people had owned them, which is perhaps more likely.

Perhaps two people who were not particularly friendly with each other, in fact. Though both of whom were interested in Brahms.

Perhaps one of those was the painter. Well, and the other the person in the window, why not?

Perhaps the painter, being a landscape painter, did not wish to paint the other person at all, actually. But perhaps the other person insisted upon looking out of the window while the painter was at work.

Very possibly this could have been what made them angry with each other to begin with.

If the painter had closed her eyes, or had simply refused to look, would the other person have still been at the window?

One might as well ask if the house itself would have been there.

And why have I troubled to close my own eyes again?

I am still feeling the typewriter, naturally. And hearing the keys.

Also I can feel the seat of this chair, through my underpants.

Doing this out at the dunes, the painter would have felt the breeze. And a sense of the sunshine.

Well, and she would have heard the surf.

Yesterday, when I was hearing Kirsten Flagstad singing *The Alto Rhapsody,* what exactly was I hearing?

Winters, when the snow covers everything, leaving only that

strange calligraphy of the spines of the trees, it is a little like closing one's eyes.

Certainly reality is altered.

One morning you awaken, and all color has ceased to exist.

Everything that one is able to see, then, is like that nine-foot canvas of mine, with its opaque four white coats of plaster and glue.

I have said that.

Still, it is almost as if one might paint the entire world, and in any manner one wished.

Letting one's brushing become abstract at a window, or not.

Though perhaps it was Cassandra whom I had intended to portray to begin with, on those forty-five square feet, rather than Electra.

Even if a part I have always liked is when Orestes finally comes back, after so many years, and Electra does not recognize her own brother.

What do you want, strange man? I believe this is what Electra says to him.

Well, it is the opera that I am thinking about now, I suspect.

At the intersection of Richard Strauss Avenue and Johannes Brahms Road, at four o'clock in the afternoon, somebody called my name.

You? Can that be you?

Imagine! And here, of all places!

It was only the Parthenon, I am quite certain, so beautiful in the afternoon sun, that had touched a chord.

In Greece, no less, from where all arts and all stories came.

Still, for a time I almost wished to weep.

Perhaps I did weep, that one afternoon.

Though perhaps it was weariness too, behind the veil of madness that had protected me, and which, that afternoon, had slipped away.

One afternoon you see the Parthenon, and with that one glance your madness has momentarily slipped away.

Weeping, you walk the streets whose names you do not know, and somebody calls out after you.

I ran into an alley, which was actually a cul-de-sac.

Surely that is you!

I also had a weapon. My pistol, from the skylights.

Well, when I was looking, I almost always carried that.

Looking in desperation, as I have said.

But still, never knowing just whom one might find, as well.

Not until dusk did I emerge from the cul-de-sac.

And saw my own reflection behind the window of an artists' supplies shop, highlighted there against a small stretched canvas.

To tell the truth, one book in the shop next door to that one did happen to be in English.

This was a guide to the birds of Southern Connecticut and Long Island Sound.

I slept in the car that I was making use of at the time. Which was a Volkswagen van, filled with musical instruments.

Kathleen Ferrier had very possibly died even before I had purchased that old recording, I now believe.

I have forgotten whatever point I might have intended to make by mentioning that, however.

Veil of madness was a terribly pretentious phrase for me to have written, too.

The next morning I drove counterclockwise, among mountains, toward Sparta, which I wished to visit before departing Greece.

Not thinking to look into the book on birds for what it might have told me about seagulls.

Halfway to Sparta, I got my period.

Throughout my life, my period has always managed to surprise me.

Even in spite of my generally having been out of sorts for some days beforehand, this is, which I will almost invariably have attributed to other causes.

So doubtless it was not the Parthenon which had made me weep after all.

Or even necessarily my madness temporarily slipping away.

Already, obviously, the other had been coming on.

And so somebody called my name.

I still do menstruate today, incidentally, if irregularly.

Or else I will stain. For weeks on end.

But then may not do so again for months.

There is naturally nothing in the *Iliad,* or in any of the plays, about anybody menstruating.

Or in the *Odyssey.* So doubtless a woman did not write that after all.

Before I was married, my mother discovered that Terry and I were sleeping together.

Was there anybody else before Terry? This was one of the first questions my mother then asked me.

I told her that there had been.

Does Terry know?

I said yes to that, also.

Oh you young fool, my mother said.

As the years passed I often felt a great sadness, over much of the life that my mother had lived.

What do any of us ever truly know, however?

I can think of no reason why this should remind me of the time when having my period caused me to fall down the central staircase in the Metropolitan and break my ankle.

Actually it may not have been broken but only sprained.

The next morning it was swollen to twice its normal size nonetheless.

One moment I had been halfway up the stairs, and a moment after that I was making believe I was Icarus.

What I had been doing was carrying that monstrosity of a canvas, which was extraordinarily unwieldy.

How one carries such a monstrosity is by gripping the cross-bars between the stretchers, at its back, meaning that one has no way whatsoever of seeing where one is going.

Still, I had believed I was managing. Until such time as the entire contraption floated away from me.

Possibly it was a wind, which caused that, since there were many more broken windows in the museum than those I had broken on purpose, by that time.

Presumably it was a wind from below, in fact, since what the canvas seemed to do was to rise up in front of me. And then to rise up some more.

Remarkably soon after that it was underneath me, however.

The pain was excruciating.

I am gushing, being what I thought at first, however. And I do not even have underpants on, under this wraparound skirt.

To tell the truth, when I had actually thought that had been perhaps two seconds earlier.

And so had shifted the way in which I was standing, naturally, to close my thighs.

Forgetting for the same instant that I was carrying forty-five square feet of canvas, on stretchers, up a stone stairway.

In retrospect it does not even become unlikely that there had been no wind after all.

And naturally all of this had occurred with what seemed no warning whatsoever, either.

Although doubtless I had been feeling out of sorts for some days, which I would have invariably laid to other causes.

The museum of course possessed crutches, and even wheelchairs, for just such emergencies.

Well, perhaps not for exactly just such.

All of these were on the main floor, in any event, along with other first aid items.

It would have been inordinately easier for me to crawl to the top of the stairs, rather than to the bottom.

Most of my accouterments were down there too, however. I believe I have mentioned having still possessed accouterments, in those days.

As it turned out, I became astonishingly adept at maneuvering my wheelchair in next to no time.

Skittering from one end of the main floor to the other, in fact, when the mood took me.

From the Greek and Roman antiquities to the Egyptian, or whoosh! and here we go round the Temple of Dendur.

Often even with music by Berlioz, or Igor Stravinsky, to accompany myself.

Now and again, the same ankle still pains me.

This is generally only in regard to the weather, actually.

For the life of me I cannot remember what I had been trying to get that canvas up the stairway for, on the other hand.

To paint on it, would be a natural supposition.

Then again, after not having painted on it for months, perhaps I had wished to put it someplace where I would not have to be continually reminded that I had not done so.

A canvas nine feet tall and five feet wide being hardly your most easily ignored reminder.

Doubtless I had had something in mind, at any rate.

There is a tape deck in the pickup truck here, now that I think about it.

There would appear to be no tapes, however.

Once, changing vehicles beside some tennis courts at Bayonne, in France, I turned an ignition key and found myself hearing the *Four Serious Songs,* by Brahms.

Though I am possibly thinking about the *Four Last Songs,* by Richard Strauss.

In either event it was not Kathleen Ferrier singing.

Actually, a fairly high percentage of the vehicles that one comes upon will have tape decks, many still set to the on position.

Rarely would it occur to me to give this any attention, however.

Obviously, one's chief interest at such moments would concern whether the battery on hand still functioned.

Assuming one had already determined that there was a key in the vehicle, and gasoline.

Kirsten Flagstad was singing, at Bayonne. Which was in fact Bordeaux.

To tell the truth, one was generally pleased enough that a car was moving so as to have driven some distance before noticing whether a tape deck was playing or not.

Or at least to have gotten clear of whatever obstacles had made it necessary to switch vehicles to begin with.

Often, bridges caused such switching. One solitary nuisance car can render your average bridge impassable.

For some years I normally troubled to transfer my baggage from one vehicle to the next, as well. On certain trips I even thought to carry along a hand truck.

When I was living at the Metropolitan I towed clear a number of my access routes, finally.

Well, or sometimes made use of a Land Rover, and came or went directly across the lawns in Central Park.

There is no longer any problem in regard to my husband's name, by the way. Even if I never saw him again, once we separated after Simon died.

As a matter of fact there is a hand truck in the basement of this house.

It is not one of my own, since I rarely make use of such contrivances any longer. Rather it was there when I came.

There are eight or nine cartons of books in the basement also, in addition to the many books in the various rooms up here.

The hand truck is badly rusted, as are the several bicycles.

The basement is even more damp than the remainder of the house. I leave that door closed.

The entrance to the basement is at the rear of the house, and below a sandy embankment, so that one does not see that in the painting.

The perspective in the painting having been taken from out in front, if I have not indicated that.

There are several baseballs in the basement also, on a ledge.

There is also a lawnmower, although there is only one exceedingly small patch of grass, at one side of the house, that I can imagine ever having been mowed.

That patch, on the other hand, does appear to be discernible in the painting.

I can see now that it had, in fact, been mowed at the time when the painter painted it.

The things one tardily becomes aware of.

Which reminds me that I am now convinced that the sentence that came into my head yesterday, or the day before yesterday, about wandering through an endless nothingness, was written by Friedrich Nietzsche.

Even if I am equally convinced that I have never read a single word written by Friedrich Nietzsche.

I do believe that I once read *Wuthering Heights,* however, which I mention because all that I seem able to remember about it is that people are continually looking in or out of windows.

The book called the *Pensées* was written by Pascal, by the way.

I also believe I have not indicated that this is another day of typing, which is why I expressed hesitation as to whether quoting Friedrich Nietzsche had occurred yesterday or the day before yesterday.

I did not make any sort of note about where I stopped, simply leaving that sheet in the machine.

Possibly I stopped at the point where I came to the baseballs in the basement, since the topic of baseball has always bored me.

Afterward I went for a walk along the beach, as far as the other house, which burned.

Yesterday's sunset was a Vincent Van Gogh sunset, with a certain amount of anxiety in it.

Perhaps I am only thinking about streaks.

I have more than once wondered why the books in the basement are not upstairs with the others, actually.

[54]

There is space. Many of the shelves up here are half empty.

Although doubtless when I say they are half empty I should really be saying they are half filled, since presumably they were totally empty before somebody half filled them.

Then again it is not impossible that they were once filled completely, becoming half empty only when somebody removed half of the books to the basement.

I find this second possibility less likely than the first, although it is not utterly beyond consideration.

In either event the present state of the shelves is an explanation for why so many of the books in the house are tilted, or standing askew. And thus have become permanently misshapen.

Baseball When the Grass Was Real is actually the name of one of those, I believe.

In that case one is at least made halfway curious about the meaning of the title, I must admit.

Less than inordinately curious, baseball remaining baseball, but at least halfway curious.

As a matter of fact perhaps I will mow my own grass, which is undeniably real, even if it is inordinately overgrown.

I cannot mow the grass. Not with the lawnmower being as badly rusted as the hand truck and the bicycles.

I have other bicycles, actually.

One is doubtless beside the pickup truck. Another may be at the gas station, in the town.

There was a bicycle in the cul-de-sac beneath the Acropolis, come to think about it.

Perhaps the books in the basement are duplicate books.

Like the two lives of Brahms, that would be. Even if both of those would appear to have been upstairs.

There is nobody at the window in the painting of the house, by the way.

I have now concluded that what I believed to be a person is a shadow.

If it is not a shadow, it is perhaps a curtain.

As a matter of fact it could actually be nothing more than an attempt to imply depths, within the room.

Although in a manner of speaking all that is really in the window is burnt sienna pigment. And some yellow ochre.

In fact there is no window either, in that same manner of speaking, but only shape.

So that any few speculations I may have made about the person at the window would therefore now appear to be rendered meaningless, obviously.

Unless of course I subsequently become convinced that there is somebody at the window all over again.

I have put that badly.

What I intended to say was that I may possibly become newly convinced that there is somebody at the window, hardly that somebody who had been at the window has gone away but might come back.

In either case it remains a fact that no altered perception of my own, such as this one, changes anything in the painting.

So that perhaps my earlier speculations remain valid after all.

I have very little idea what I mean by that.

✓ One can scarcely speculate about a person when there is no person to speculate about.

✓ Yet there is no way of denying that one did make such speculations.

Two days ago, when I was hearing Kathleen Ferrier, what exactly was I hearing?

✓ Yesterday, when I was speculating about a person at the window in the painting, what exactly was I speculating about?

I have just put the painting back into the room with the atlas and the life of Brahms.

As a matter of fact I have now also had another night's sleep.

I mention that, this time, only because in a manner of speaking one could now say that it has this quickly become the day after tomorrow.

Certain questions would still continue to appear unanswerable, however.

Such as, for instance, if I have concluded that there is nothing in the painting except shapes, am I also concluding that there is nothing on these pages except letters of the alphabet?

If one understood only the Greek alphabet, what would be on these pages?

Doubtless, in Russia, I drove right past St. Petersburg without knowing it was St. Petersburg.

As a matter of fact Anna Karenina could have driven right past without knowing it was St. Petersburg either.

Seeing a sign indicating Stalingrad, how would Anna Karenina have been able to tell?

Especially since the sign would have more likely indicated Leningrad?

I have obviously now lost my train of thought altogether.

Once, Robert Rauschenberg erased most of a drawing by Willem de Kooning, and then named it *Erased de Kooning Drawing*.

I am in no way certain what this is connected to either, but I suspect it is connected to more than I once believed it to be connected to.

Robert Rauschenberg came to my loft in SoHo one afternoon, actually. I do not remember that he erased anything.

The reason for one of my bicycles being at the gas station is that I sometimes decide to walk home, after having ridden somewhere.

Although what I really decided that day was to bring back kerosene, which was difficult to ride with.

I say was difficult, instead of is difficult, since I no longer carry kerosene, no longer making use of those lamps.

When I stopped making use of them was after I knocked over the one that set fire to the other house, although doubtless I have mentioned this.

One moment I was adjusting the wick, and a moment after

that the entire bedroom was ablaze.

These beach houses are all wood, of course. All I could do was sit at the dunes and watch it burn.

For most of the night the entire sky was Homeric.

It was on that same night that my rowboat disappeared, as it happened, although that is perhaps beside the point.

One hardly pays attention to a missing rowboat when one's house is burning to the ground.

Still, there it was, no longer on the beach.

Sometimes I like to believe that it has been carried all of the way across the ocean by now, to tell the truth.

As far as to the island of Lesbos, say. Or to Ithaca, even.

Frequently, certain objects wash up onto the shore here that could well have been carried just as far in the opposite direction, as a matter of fact.

Such as my stick, for instance, which I sometimes take with me when I walk.

Doubtless the stick served some other purpose than simply being taken along on walks, at one time. One can no longer guess at what other purpose, however, because of the way it has been worn smooth by waves.

Now and again I have also made use of the stick to write in the sand with, actually.

In fact I have even written in Greek.

Well, or in what looked like Greek, although I was actually only inventing that.

What I would write were messages, to tell the truth, like the ones I sometimes used to write in the street.

Somebody is living on this beach, the messages would say.

Obviously it did not matter by then that the messages were only in an invented writing that nobody could read.

Actually, nothing that I wrote was ever still there when I went back in any case, always being washed away.

Still, if I have concluded that there is nothing in the painting except shapes, am I also concluding that there was not even

⌈invented writing in the sand, but only grooves from my stick?

Doubtless the stick was originally nothing more interesting than the handle of a carpet sweeper.

Once, when I had set it aside to drag a piece of driftwood along the beach, I worried that I might have lost it.

When I looked back it was standing upright, however, where I had had the foresight to place it without really paying attention.

Then again it is quite possible that the question of loss had not entered my mind until I was already in the process of looking back, which is to say that the stick was already not lost before I had worried that it might be.

I am not particularly happy over this new habit of saying things that I have very little idea what I mean by saying, to tell the truth.

It was somebody named Ralph Hodgson, who wrote the poem about the birds being sold in the shops for people to eat.

I do not remember that I ever read any other poem by Ralph Hodgson.

I do remember that Leonardo da Vinci used to buy such birds, however, in Florence, and then let them out of their cages.

And that Helen of Troy did have at least one daughter, named Hermione.

And that Leonardo also thought up a method to prevent the Arno from overflowing its banks, to which nobody obviously paid any attention.

For that matter Leonardo at least once put snow into one of his paintings too, even if I cannot remember whether Andrea del Sarto or Taddeo Gaddi ever did.

In addition to which, Rembrandt's pupils used to paint gold coins on the floor of his studio and make them look so real that Rembrandt would stoop to pick them up, although I am uncertain as to why this reminds me of Robert Rauschenberg again.

I have always harbored sincere doubts that Helen was the cause of that war, by the way.

A single Spartan girl, after all.

As a matter of fact the whole thing was undeniably a mercantile proposition. All ten years of it, just to see who would pay tariff to whom, so as to be able to make use of a channel of water.

A different poet, named Rupert Brooke, died in the Dardanelles during the first World War, even if I do not believe that I remembered this when I visited the Dardanelles, by which I mean the Hellespont.

Still, I find it extraordinary that young men died there in a war that long ago, and then died in the same place three thousand years after that.

And on second thought the gold coins that Rembrandt's pupils painted on the floor of his studio are exactly what I was talking about when I was talking about Robert Rauschenberg.

Or rather what I was talking about when I was talking about the person who is not at the window in the painting of this house.

The coins having only been coins until Rembrandt bent over.

Which did not deter me from rigging up a generator and floodlights in the Colosseum, however.

Or from being shrewd enough to call the cat Calpurnia, after having gotten no response with Nero and Caligula.

Still, if Rembrandt had had a cat, it would have strolled right past the coins without so much as a glance.

Which does not imply that Rembrandt's cat was more intelligent than Rembrandt.

Even if it so happens that Rembrandt kept on doing that, incidentally, no matter how many times they tricked him.

The world being full of stories about pupils playing tricks on their teachers, of course.

Leonardo once played a trick on Verrocchio by filling in part of a canvas so beautifully that Verrocchio decided to go into another line of work.

One finds it difficult to think of Aristotle playing tricks on Plato, on the other hand.

Or even to think of Aristotle doing lessons.

One can easily manage to visualize Helen doing them, however. One can even see her chewing on a pencil.

Assuming the Greeks had had pencils, that would be.

As a matter of fact even Archimedes sometimes did his geometry by writing in the sand. With a stick.

I accept the fact that it is doubtless not the same stick.

Even if it could well have drifted for years. Over and back any number of times, in fact.

Helen left Hermione at home when she deserted Menelaus and ran off with Paris, which is the one thing Helen did that one wishes she hadn't.

Though it is not impossible that the ancient writers are not to be fully trusted in regard to such topics, having been mostly men.

What one really wishes is that Sappho had written some plays.

Though in fact there are other versions anyhow.

Such as in the painting by Tiepolo, for instance, where Helen is shown being carried off by force.

The Rape of Helen, in fact, being what Tiepolo called the painting.

Medea is a little harder to visualize chewing on a pencil.

Perhaps at seven or eight. After that she would have been Germaine Greer.

For the life of me I cannot remember when the last time I thought about Germaine Greer was. Possibly there are some books by her in this house, however.

Though I still cannot imagine what that other title might mean, about grass no longer being real.

Perhaps my stick was once a baseball bat.

Perhaps Rembrandt's pupils once played baseball.

Cassandra was raped too, of course, after Troy fell.

Doubtless there is no way of verifying that El Greco was descended from Hermione, however, after practically three thousand years.

Near the end of his life, Titian manipulated his pigments as much with his fingers as with a brush, which was surely not the way Giovanni Bellini taught him.

Naturally I had no way of knowing if the cat at the Colosseum had nibbled at anything behind my back, since most of the cans had seemed less than full to begin with.

Doubtless Brahms was once a pupil, also.

Even if, when he was only twelve, he was already playing the piano in a dance hall, which was more likely a house of prostitution.

In fact Brahms went to prostitutes for the rest of his life.

Nonetheless it is still not impossible to visualize Brahms doing scales.

Well, and perhaps the prostitutes when he was still only twelve were dancing girls after all.

Such as Jane Avril, for instance.

I have no idea if Brahms ever visited in Paris while Jane Avril was dancing there.

Still, for some reason it strikes me as agreeable to think of Brahms as having had an affair with Jane Avril.

Or at least with Cléopatre or Gazelle or Mlle. Églantine, who were some of the other dancers in Paris at that time.

How one remembers certain things is beyond me.

Perhaps Guy de Maupassant was rowing, when Brahms visited in Paris.

Once, Bertrand Russell took his pupil Ludwig Wittgenstein to watch Alfred North Whitehead row, at Cambridge. Wittgenstein became very angry with Bertrand Russell for having wasted his day.

In addition to remembering things that one does not know how one remembers, one would also appear to remember things that one has no idea how one knew to begin with.

to remember other people's memories as well as one's own — [or one's own ins]

Although perhaps Toulouse-Lautrec once handled my stick, even if Archimedes did not, having walked with a cane.

Then again, one of the popes made people burn most of what Sappho did write.

Doubtless my ankle was only sprained. Though it was swollen to twice its normal size.

Could that person T. E. Shaw have been a baseball player, perhaps?

And what have I been saying that has now made me think about Achilles again?

Now is perhaps not the correct word in any case.

By which I mean that I was undeniably thinking about Achilles at the moment when I started to type that sentence, but was no longer thinking about him by the time I had finished it.

One allows one's self to finish such sentences, of course. Even if by the time one has managed to indicate that one is thinking about one thing, one has actually begun thinking about another.

What happened after I started to write about Achilles was that halfway through the sentence I began to think about a cat, instead.

The cat I began to think about instead was the cat outside of the broken window in the room next to this one, at which the tape frequently scratches when there is a breeze.

Which is to say that I was not actually thinking about a cat either, there being no cat except insofar as the sound of the scratching reminds me of one.

As there were no coins on the floor of Rembrandt's studio, except insofar as the configuration of the pigment reminded Rembrandt of them.

As there was, or is, no person at the window in the painting of this house.

As for that matter there is not even a house in the painting of this house, should one wish to carry the matter that far.

Certain matters would appear to get carried certain distances whether one wishes them to or not, unfortunately.

Although perhaps this is the very subject of that other book, come to think about it. Quite possibly what I have taken to be a book about baseball is actually some sort of scholarly speculation about there having been no grass where people played baseball except insofar as the people playing baseball believed that there was.

At first glance one would scarcely have expected *Wuthering Heights* to be a book about windows, either.

Though it remains a fact that there was once some very real grass that had been mowed at the side of this house.

As can be readily verified by a glance at that same painting.

Though I am very likely now contradicting myself.

In either case the tape has now stopped scratching.

Nor am I thinking about a cat any longer.

Then again I certainly would have had to be thinking about one while I was typing that sentence, even though the sentence says just the opposite.

Surely one cannot type a sentence saying that one is not thinking about something without thinking about the very thing that one says one is not thinking about.

I believe I have only now noted this. Or something very much like this.

Possibly I should drop the subject.

Actually, all I had been thinking about in regard to Achilles was his heel.

Although I do not have any sort of limp, if I have possibly given that impression.

And meanwhile I am also now curious about the tape itself, since for the life of me I cannot remember having put it up.

Unquestionably I did put it up, however, since I can remember very distinctly when the window broke.

Oh, dear, the wind has just broken one of the windows in one of the rooms downstairs, I can even remember thinking.

This would have been right after I had heard the glass, naturally.

And on a windy night.

Yet for the life of me I cannot remember repairing that window.

In fact I am next to positive that I have never had any tape in this house.

The last time I can remember having seen any tape, anywhere, was on the afternoon when I drove the Volkswagen van full of first aid items into the Mediterranean.

As it happened there was a tape deck in the van also, although this is of course in no way connected to the sort of tape I am talking about.

The tape deck in the van was playing *The Seasons,* by Vivaldi.

Even after I had climbed back up the embankment, the tape deck continued to play. In my upside down car that was filling up with the sea.

As a matter of fact what it was playing was *Les Troyens,* by Berlioz.

This held a particular interest for me, in fact, what with my having been in Hisarlik not long before. For some time I sat on the embankment and listened to it.

Though to tell the truth I had much more recently been in Rome. And in Rimini and Perugia and Venice.

So that perhaps the tape deck was playing something else entirely.

For the life of me I cannot remember what I had been trying to get that monstrosity of a canvas up that stairway for.

Even if the question was soon enough rendered irrelevant, considering the manner in which I did not get it up.

And what have I been saying that has now made me think about Brahms's mother?

In this instance I can make an educated guess, since the poor woman had a crippled leg.

For the life of me I would not have believed that the life of Brahms was the book I had read in this house.

Evidently not every question falls into the category of questions that would appear to remain unanswerable, however.

Though what must now surprise me is that I would have troubled to read a book so badly damaged, or printed on such cheap paper.

Any number of books in this house are in considerably better condition, even if all of them show evidence of dampness.

Such as the atlas, for instance. Although the atlas has had the advantage of lying flat, generally, rather than standing askew.

In fact I returned it to that same position not two days ago, after having wished to remind myself where Lititz, Pennsylvania, and Ithaca, New York, might be.

The book about baseball has a green cover, incidentally, which is possibly appropriate.

Conversely there does not appear to be a single book about art in this house.

My reason for remarking on this is not personal. Rather I find it unusual simply because of another painter once seeming to have lived here.

Then again the other painter may have only been a guest. In which case the painting of the house may well have been done as a sort of gift, in return for her visit.

Though in suggesting that, I am of course forgetting the several other paintings in certain of the rooms here that I do not go into, and to which the doors are closed.

Possibly those other paintings are paintings by the same painter, as well.

In fact I am certain that they are, in spite of my not having looked at any of them since closing the doors, which I did some time ago.

The only one of the closed doors which I any longer open is the one to the room where the atlas and the life of Brahms are, and that has been happening only lately.

It is scarcely a demanding proposition to determine that all three paintings on the walls of the same house have been painted by the same painter, however.

More especially when all three are paintings of houses at, or near, a beach, as I have now remembered that the other two are also.

Though I naturally possess more practiced equipment for making such a determination, should that become necessary.

In either event, what now occurs to me is that the painter was doubtless not a guest in this house either, but more likely was somebody who lived nearby. Which would more readily explain why there are three paintings by her in a house in which there are an inordinate number of books but not one of those books is about art.

Being so closely familiar with the painter's subject matter, the people who did live in this house would have presumably been delighted to display such paintings.

No question of aesthetic understanding would have had to enter into the arrangement at all.

For that matter perhaps all of the houses along this beach, or many of them, contain other examples of the same painter's work.

Perhaps even the very house which I burned to the ground contained such examples, even though it would obviously not contain them any longer, no longer being a house.

Well, it is still a house.

Even if there is not remarkably much left of it, I am still prone to think of it as a house when I pass it in taking my walks.

There is the house that I burned to the ground, I might think. Or, soon I will be coming to the house that I burned to the ground.

None of the three paintings in this house is signed, incidentally.

Actually, I do not remember looking, but I am positive that looking is something I would have done.

Even in museums, it is something I often do.

I have even done it with paintings that I have been familiar with for years.

I hardly do it because I believe that there might be any error in the attribution of a painting.

In fact I have no idea why I do it.

Frequently, Modigliani would sign the work of other painters. This was so they would be able to sell paintings that they otherwise might not have sold.

Doubtless I should not have said frequently. Doubtless Modigliani did this only a handful of times.

Still, it was kind of Modigliani, since a certain number of his friends were not eating very well.

In fact Modigliani himself often did not eat well, although basically this would have been because he was drinking, instead.

Once, in the Borghese Gallery, in Rome, I signed a mirror.

I did that in one of the women's rooms, with a lipstick.

What I was signing was an image of myself, naturally.

Should anybody else have looked, where my signature would have been was under the other person's image, however.

Doubtless I would not have signed it, had there been anybody else to look.

Though in fact the name I put down was Giotto.

There is only one mirror in this house, incidentally.

What that mirror reflects is also an image of myself, of course.

Though in fact what it has also reflected now and again is an image of my mother.

What will happen is that I will glance into the mirror and for an instant I will see my mother looking back at me.

Naturally I will see myself during that same instant, as well.

In other words all that I am really seeing is my mother's image in my own.

I am assuming that such an illusion is quite ordinary, and comes with age.

Which is to say that it is not even an illusion, heredity being heredity.

Still, it is the sort of thing that can give one pause.

Even if it has also entered my mind to realize that I may be almost as old, by now, as my mother was then.

My mother was only fifty-eight.

Though she was exactly fifty, when I painted her portrait.

Well, it was that birthday for which I painted it.

Though I rarely did portraits.

There were times when I regretted that I had never done a portrait of Simon, however.

Other times I did not believe I would have wished to possess such a reminder.

And perhaps it was their anniversary that I painted my mother and father's portraits for.

In fact it was their thirtieth anniversary.

I painted both of the portraits from slides, meaning the gift to be a surprise.

What this made it necessary to do was to hang dropcloths in my studio, so as to contrive a dark corner in which I could make use of the projector.

Generally I seemed to spend more time walking in and out of the darkness, than actually painting.

To tell the truth, what I generally spent the greatest amount of time doing was sitting, whenever I painted.

At times one can sit endlessly, before getting up to add a single brushstroke to a canvas.

Leonardo was known to walk halfway across Milan to do that, with *The Last Supper,* even when anybody else would have believed it was finished.

Which did not keep *The Last Supper* from beginning to deteriorate in Leonardo's own lifetime, however, because of a foolish experiment he had tried, with oil tempera on the plaster.

In a manner of speaking, one could even say that *The Last Supper* was already deteriorating while it was still being painted.

For some reason the thought of this has always saddened me.

Often, too, I was surprised that so many people did not seem to know that *The Last Supper* was a painting of a Passover meal.

I did not stop in Milan, in any case, on my way from Venice to Savona.

For that matter I had hardly intended to stop at Savona.

An embankment gave way. I have no idea how long the embankment had been deteriorating before I got there.

Leonardo wrote in his notebooks backwards, from right to left, so that they had to be held up to a mirror to be read.

In a manner of speaking, the image of Leonardo's notebooks would be more real than the notebooks themselves.

Leonardo was also left-handed. And a vegetarian. And illegitimate.

The slides that I took of my mother and father still exist, presumably.

Presumably old slides of Simon still exist, too.

I suspect there is something ironical in my knowing so many things about Leonardo and yet not knowing if the slides that I took of my mother and father, or any of my little boy, still exist.

Or, if they exist, where.

Time out of mind.

I have snapshots of Simon, of course. For some time one of them was in a frame on the table beside my bed.

But quite suddenly I do not feel like typing any more of this, for now.

I have not been typing, for perhaps three hours.

All I had anticipated doing, actually, was going to the spring for water. But after I had filled the pitcher I decided to take a walk into the town.

The pitcher is actually a jar. On the way home I forgot about having left it, and so will have to go back out.

This is hardly a chore. And there is a frisky breeze.

In the town, I looked at the boats in the boat basin.

While I was there I also realized that there is an explanation for so many people forgetting that *The Last Supper* is a painting of a Passover meal, doubtless.

The explanation being that what they really forget is that everybody in the painting is Jewish.

For a long period, in the Borghese Gallery, I stood in front of a pediment carving of Cassandra being raped. Her hair is magnificently wild, for anonymous stone.

Cassandra and Helen, both, had told the Trojans there were Greeks in the wooden horse. Nobody paid attention to either of them, naturally.

Quite possibly I have not mentioned the boat basin before. There are several, nearby.

Very few of the boats would appear to be seaworthy any longer.

Though I rarely have any impulses in that regard any longer, either.

Once, I sailed to Byzantium, however. By which I mean Istanbul.

Though how I actually went, after the Bering Strait, was by various cars across Siberia. Next following the Volga River south, until I turned toward Troy.

Constantinople thus becoming very little out of my way.

Now and again I have regretted that I did not continue on across to Moscow and Leningrad, on the other hand. Especially having never been to the Hermitage.

And to tell the truth I have never done any sailing at all, when one comes down to it.

Every boat I have made use of has had an engine.

This is scarcely including my rowboats, naturally.

Which in either case I have rarely done more in than drift.

Though I did give serious thought to the notion of rowing out beyond the breakers on the night on which my house was burning to the ground, actually, once it had struck me to wonder from how far out the flames might be seen.

Doubtless I would not have rowed nearly far enough, even if

I had gone, since one would have surely had to row all the way beyond the horizon itself.

For that matter one might have actually been able to row as far as to where one was out of sight of the flames altogether, and yet still have been seeing the glow against the clouds.

Which is to say that one would have then been seeing the fire upside down, so to speak.

And not even the fire, but only an image of the fire.

Possibly there were no clouds, however.

And in either case I no longer had a rowboat.

Now, each time I go to the beach, I take a look to make certain that the new rowboat is in its place.

In fact I took such a look only moments ago, when I came back from the town.

Perhaps I have not mentioned that I came back from the town by way of the beach, instead of the way I had gone, which was by way of the road.

Which would explain why I did not remember to bring in my pitcher, which I had left at the spring.

Frequently I tend to think of my jar as a pitcher. Doubtless this is only because a pitcher has more of the sound of what one would wish to carry to a spring.

Though perhaps another reason why I did not remember it is that I am feeling somewhat tired.

Actually, I am not feeling tired. How I am feeling is not quite myself.

Well, perhaps what I am more truthfully feeling is a kind of depression. The whole thing is fairly abstract, at this point.

In any case, doubtless I was already feeling this way when I stopped typing. Doubtless my decision to stop typing had much to do with my feeling this way.

I have already forgotten what I had been typing when I began to feel this way.

Obviously, I could look back. Surely that part cannot be very many lines behind the line I am typing at this moment.

On second thought I will not look back. If there was something I was typing that had contributed to my feeling this way, doubtless it would contribute to it all over again.

I do not feel this way often, as a matter of fact.

Generally I feel quite well, considering.

Still, this other can happen.

It will pass. In the meantime there is little that one can do about it.

Anxiety being the fundamental mood of existence, as somebody once said, or unquestionably should have said.

Though to tell the truth I would have believed I had shed most of such feelings, as long ago as when I shed most of my other sort of baggage.

When winter is here, it will be here.

Even if one would appear never to be shed of the baggage in one's head, on the other hand.

Such as the birthdays of people like Pablo Picasso or Dylan Thomas, for instance, which I am convinced that I might still recite if I wished.

Or the name Sor Juana Inés de la Cruz, even if one still has no idea who she may have been.

I do not know who Marina Tsvetayeva may have been either, although in this case the name at least did not come into my mind until an hour ago, when I was at the boat basin.

Obviously, I was thinking about the other sort of marina.

Actually it was Helen Frankenthaler's name that caught my eye on that poster not far from the Via Vittorio Veneto. I do not remember ever having been in a show with Georgia O'Keeffe.

Though in fact perhaps it was Kierkegaard who said that, about anxiety being the fundamental mood of existence.

If it was not Kierkegaard it was Martin Heidegger.

In either case I suspect there is something ironical in my being able to guess that something was said by Kierkegaard, or by Martin Heidegger, when I am convinced that I have never read a single word written by Kierkegaard or Martin Heidegger.

A good deal of one's baggage would appear to be not even one's own, as I have perhaps elsewhere suggested.

Anna Akhmatova is somebody else whom I have never read, although doubtless she is in some way connected to Marina Tsvetayeva.

Then again it is not impossible that there are books by all of these people in this house.

I have noticed guides to several of the National Parks. As well as one to the birds of the southern Aegean and the Cyclades Islands.

There is an explanation for the atlas generally lying flat, incidentally, instead of standing askew.

The explanation being simply that the atlas is too tall for the shelves.

And in either event I have just now categorically determined where it was that I read the life of Brahms.

Where I read the life of Brahms was in London, in a bookstore near Hampstead Heath, on the morning when I was almost hit by the car.

I believe I have mentioned being almost hit by the car, which came rolling down a hill.

Perhaps I was not almost hit by the car. Still, one moment I was reading the life of Brahms, and a moment after that, whoosh! there went the frightening thing right past me.

Just imagine how this startled me, and how I felt.

Only a day before, I had sat in a vehicle with a right-hand drive and watched a street called Maiden Lane, near Covent Garden, fill up with snow, which must surely be rare.

Naturally the car that came down the hill had a right-hand drive also, this still being London.

My reason for emphasizing this is simply because that same side of the car was the side that was nearest me, and naturally my first reaction was to look for who in heaven's name could be driving.

Naturally nobody was driving.

Still, my condition of being startled continued for quite some time.

Unquestionably it was still continuing while I was realizing that what the car was going to do next was to crash into the car I had been driving myself, and which I had double parked a certain distance farther down the hill.

Instead it crashed into something else altogether.

As a matter of fact it did not crash into anything at all, that I saw, but kept right on down the hill and out of sight.

All I am assuming when I say it crashed into something else is that surely there would have had to be other obstacles in its path sooner or later.

Certainly it would have had to hit a street sign, or possibly even an English house, if it did not hit another car.

When one comes right down to it, on the other hand, I did not hear the sound of the crash either.

Then again it is quite possible that I was not really listening, what with the overall duration of that condition of being startled.

All that I was truthfully doing was continuing to stand in front of the bookstore, which was next door to a Mexican restaurant.

The restaurant had reproductions of paintings by David Alfaro Siqueiros in its window.

The car in question had been a London taxi cab, by the way.

To this day I have no idea what may have caused it to roll down that hill on a morning when I happened to be visiting in the same neighborhood.

Something had finally deteriorated, doubtless, that it had been wedged against.

Doubtless any number of other vehicles have been rolling down any number of other hills, in fact, through all of these years.

Quite possibly a certain number of them are doing exactly that at this very moment, even.

One has no idea what number, but a certain number, surely.

Then again the tires on many cars have become flat, which would indisputably have become a factor.

But be that as it may, eventually I walked some distance past my own car to see which of the various possible obstacles the taxi had crashed into.

I did not see the taxi anywhere.

The hill made a turn, as it happened.

Still, surely I would have eventually come upon it, if I had wished to pursue the matter.

And assuming of course that I did not mistake a different wrecked taxi for the taxi I was looking for.

What I appeared to be more interested in at the moment, however, was the Mexican restaurant, which I had not noticed earlier.

Although actually what I let myself into the restaurant for was a bottle of tequila.

Well, all of this having occurred during the period when I was still looking, if I have not indicated that. So that surely a drink was permitted.

Moreover I was doubtless also remembering having been identically startled by that ketch, in sight of Mount Ida.

Actually, what surprises me about the ketch in retrospect is that that spinnaker had not been shredded years before.

Although possibly the ketch had been sheltered somewhere, and had not begun to drift until lately.

As the taxi had not begun to roll until the same morning on which I stopped at the bookstore and read the life of Brahms.

I had not gone into the bookstore with anything approximating a life of Brahms in mind, incidentally. All I did was pick up the first book I happened to see, which was lying on a counter.

And which in fact was not a life of Brahms at all, but a history of music. For children.

But which had been open to a chapter on Brahms.

The book was printed in extraordinarily large type. Additionally, the chapter on Brahms could not have been more than six pages long.

Unquestionably there would have been nothing about dancing girls in it either.

Still, if I had not decided to read the chapter, certainly I would have been somewhere else by the time the taxi rolled down the hill.

Instead, there I was, forced to think, good heavens! here comes a car, and a moment after that, oh, well, of course it is not a car.

In thinking the latter I meant only that it was not a car with anybody driving it, obviously.

Naturally you can never find a taxi when you want one.

But again, all of this in the midst of all that looking, nonetheless.

Not to speak of all that anxiety.

Although as a matter of fact I noticed a taxi just today, at the boat basin.

That particular taxi has been in the identical spot since I came to this beach, however.

Nor will it leave, what with all four of the tires being flat in this case.

In fact its wheels are in deep sand, also.

The tires on the pickup truck are fine. Though naturally I check those.

There is an air pump under the seat, in any event.

Then again I suspect that I may have neglected to run the battery for some time, now.

I have just walked out to the pickup truck.

Actually where I walked was to the spring, which the truck is next to. I went for the pitcher, which is how I think of the jar.

Before bringing it back I emptied it out and filled it again, since the water had already turned warm from standing in the sun.

The water at the spring itself is always cool, however.

I have brought in lilacs, also.

It is Joan Baez, I believe, whom I would like to inform that one can now kneel and drink from the Loire, or the Po, or the Mississippi.

Winters, when the snows come and the trees write their strange calligraphy against the whiteness, sometimes the only other demarcation is that of my path to the spring.

Lowry

Well, and in the opposite direction too, of the path that I follow through the dunes to the beach.

Although I am completely forgetting the third path, just in back of the dunes, which is still another that can be seen at such times.

That third path is the path to the house that I have been dismantling.

Perhaps I have not mentioned that I am dismantling a house.

I am dismantling a house.

It is tedious work, but necessary.

I do not make a major project out of it, on the other hand. Basically I treat it in much the same way as I treat the question of my driftwood.

Perhaps I have not mentioned how I treat the question of my driftwood.

All that will happen, basically, is that now and again I will be walking past the house, and a board will catch my eye, and so I will dismantle the board and carry it home.

Assuming I am not already carrying driftwood, obviously.

Actually there was adequate firewood here already, for my first winter.

Well, there was almost adequate firewood here. Later along I burned certain items of furniture.

All of those were from the rooms that I no longer make use of, as it happens, and to which the doors are closed.

Now that I think about it, very possibly that is even why I have taken to closing those doors, although I cannot imagine why I would not have made this connection before.

In any case the house that I am dismantling contains almost no furniture at all. In fact it is quite indifferently built.

The only tool I have needed for any of the work is a crowbar, which I took from beneath the same seat in the pickup truck.

Well, there is also the saw, which I came upon in the house itself.

Then again I do not really think of the saw as a tool for dismantling. Rather I think of that as a tool for turning dismantled lumber into firewood.

After it has been dismantled.

Although perhaps this distinction is no more than one of semantics.

At any rate I have no idea why the house should have been constructed so indifferently.

One can only guess that it had been built to be rented, perhaps, rather than to be lived in, which is sometimes the case with houses along a beach.

The world is everything that is the case.

I have no idea what I mean by the sentence I have just typed, by the way.

For some reason I seem to have had it in my head all day, however, although without the vaguest notion about where it might have come from.

Such things can happen. One morning not too long ago all I could think about was the word *bricolage,* which I presume is French, even though I do not speak one word of French.

Well, perhaps I did not think about it at all, in the usual sense of thinking.

Still, when I went for my walk along the beach, or was picking up shells as I sometimes do, I must have said the word *bricolage* to myself a hundred times.

Eventually I stopped saying it. So today what I have been saying is that the world is everything that is the case, instead.

Oh, well.

In the meantime I have also been wondering if one's reading

of six pages in a history of music that was written for children, and had been printed in extraordinarily large type, can truly be considered as the reading of a life of Brahms?

Or did I also read certain additional pages in the more genuine life of Brahms, such as certain pages about dancing girls, when I was setting fire to those pages in trying to simulate a seagull?

Not knowing that there was a second copy of the identical book, with all of the pages still in it, still here in the house?

Doubtless these are inconsequential perplexities. Still, inconsequential perplexities have now and again been known to become the fundamental mood of existence, one suspects.

The world is everything that is the case.

Hm.

But I have just made one more connection that I had never thought about before either.

Will the house that I am dismantling become the second house on this beach that I have burned to the ground?

Granting that I am burning that house board by board, and that it will be quite some time before I have dismantled it fully enough to be able to consider it as having been burned to the ground, nonetheless the fact that I am doing exactly that would appear to be indisputable.

One day that house, too, will look as if Robert Rauschenberg had gotten to it.

There is the house that I dismantled board by board and erased to the ground, I will think in walking past.

Doubtless by then I will also be erasing another house.

Naturally I have been leaving out such things as stone chimneys when I have spoken about houses as still being houses even when they are no longer houses, by the way.

Well, and plumbing.

As a matter of fact one can still see a toilet fastened to pipes on the second floor of the house in which I knocked over the kerosene lamp.

Even if there is no longer a second floor.

There is the toilet on the second floor of the house that I burned to the ground, is what I will more truly think, in walking past. Or, soon I will be coming to the toilet on the second floor of the house that I burned to the ground.

In SoHo, back at the beginning, I now remember that I used to empty bottled water into the tank, so as to still be able to flush.

Any number of habits died hard, that way. For some period I continued carrying my driver's license and other identification, similarly.

Naturally I will have stopped taking the path to the beach once it has become genuinely snowy here, on the other hand.

Which is to say that I sometimes still do make use of a bathroom after all, even if in this case it is by having taken up a board from the bathroom floor.

Perhaps I have not mentioned having taken up a board from the bathroom floor.

I have taken up a board from the bathroom floor.

In a manner of speaking, doubtless it might be said that I am dismantling this house, too.

Although I have scarcely burned that particular board, which is in fact normally back in the identical place from which I have taken it.

As often as it has appeared necessary, I have shoveled away part of the embankment just outside.

Doubtless I had established some sort of similar hygienic arrangement in the house that I burned to the ground on the night that my rowboat disappeared, as well.

In fact my rowboat did not disappear on the night that I burned that house to the ground.

It was on that night that I happened to become aware of the rowboat's disappearance, which is something else altogether.

Very possibly the rowboat had already been gone for days, since I had scarcely yet taken to looking out for it as I do now.

I will not trouble to point out again how one's language is frequently imprecise in such ways.

One morning I was similarly convinced that all seventeen of my watches had disappeared too, now that I think about it.

What happened was that I woke up in a car beside the Pont Neuf, in Paris, and understood that I had not heard the alarms.

Why have I been awakened by the sun coming in through my windshield, I wondered, instead of by my seventeen simultaneous buzzings?

It was some moments before I remembered that I had divested myself of the watches on a different bridge altogether, some while before, I believe in Bethlehem, Pennsylvania.

Although I find it interesting that I can almost always make a distinction between periods when I was mad and periods when I was not, when one comes down to it.

Such as when I read certain books out loud, as I did with Aeschylus and Euripides when I was living in the Louvre, which was always a conclusive sign.

The Louvre is practically right beside the Pont Neuf, by the way.

The reverse of that statement being equally true, obviously.

In either case doubtless I was not yet living in the Louvre on the morning when I woke up in the car practically right beside it.

Surely I would have had no reason to sleep in a car if I had already taken to burning artifacts and picture frames in the museum itself, which I unquestionably eventually did.

Well, such as the frame from *La Gioconda* by Leonardo, for instance, from which the old varnish gave the smoke an astringent odor.

Although the sun actually woke me in cars far more times than that once, to tell the truth.

Frequently I watched the sun setting from cars, as well.

The latter was especially true in Russia, of course, where I kept on driving into the west for day after day after day.

Almost every one of the books I read about ancient Troy was

a book that I read out loud, come to think about it.

For some reason, a part I always liked was Odysseus pretending he was mad himself, so that they would not make him go to fight.

How he pretended this was by sowing salt into the ground, while he was plowing.

Somebody very shrewdly put Odysseus's little boy into one of the furrows, however, and naturally he did not plow his little boy.

Tiepolo painted this also, I believe. *The Madness of Ulysses,* being what he called it.

In fact I am quite certain that the painting is in the same museum with *The Rape of Helen,* even if I cannot remember which museum that is.

Possibly I should point out that Odysseus and Ulysses were the same person. For some reason the Romans changed his name.

Well, doubtless they did this for the identical reason that the Spaniards changed El Greco's name. Even if Odysseus seems hardly as difficult to pronounce as Domenikos Theotocopoulos.

La Gioconda is another name for the *Mona Lisa,* of course.

In the *Odyssey,* while he is waiting for Ulysses to come home, the same little boy goes to visit Helen and Menelaus, in Sparta, and Helen has a splendid radiant dignity.

Then again the little boy is hardly so little by then, it having been ten years for the war and still another ten with Odysseus being a tourist.

This is the same twenty years during which Penelope is said to have spent her time weaving, naturally, if one wishes to believe that.

I doubt that I believe one word of it, myself.

Penelope and Helen were cousins, incidentally.

The things one knows.

Well, this making her Clytemnestra's cousin too, of course, Helen and Clytemnestra having been sisters.

Although what I am now thinking about is the scene in which Odysseus has himself lashed to the mast of his ship, so that he can listen to the Sirens singing but will stay put.

For some reason this story reminds me of something, even though I cannot remember what it reminds me of.

Telemachus is the little boy's name, by the way. Although I believe I mentioned this a good many pages ago.

The name of the friend for whom Achilles weeps is Patroclus, which on the other hand I am quite certain I did leave out.

My last lover was named Lucien. I find it interesting that I have not included the name of a single one of my lovers in any of these pages, either.

Possibly those paintings by Tiepolo are in the Hermitage, at which I spent several days before leaving for home across Russia in the opposite direction.

As a matter of fact they are in Milan, where I saw them on the very day when I was so saddened by *The Last Supper.*

Where I watched the sunsets on that return trip, naturally, was more often than not in my rearview mirror.

Which would have made them images of sunsets rather than sunsets, come to think about it. And with the left side being the right, or vice versa, although one was doubtless less conscious of this with sunsets than one would have been with Michelangelo's notebooks.

Doubtless I was much more interested in keeping a weather eye out for Anna Karenina in either case, since I was naturally still looking, at the time.

Have I mentioned looking in Amsterdam, New York, or in Syracuse, or in Toledo, Ohio?

Meanwhile I have no idea why rearview mirrors should remind me that I was feeling a certain depression, yesterday.

In fact I have perhaps omitted to indicate that that was yesterday.

Last evening's sunset had a certain stillness about it, as if Piero della Francesca had done the color.

What I woke up to this morning were the lilacs, breathing them all over the house.

Later, I washed myself with some of the water I had brought in from the spring.

I am still wearing the underpants I wore yesterday, however.

This is because even though I went to the spring twice, on both trips I walked right past my laundry, which is spread across bushes.

To tell the truth, I am still feeling a touch of that same depression, as well.

Possibly what I had been thinking about yesterday was the tiny, pocket sort of mirror that had been beside my mother's bed, although I do not remember having thought about that yesterday.

There is a distinction to be made between this sort of depression and the depression I generally felt while I was still doing all of that looking, by the way, the latter having been much more decidedly a kind of anxiety.

Although I believe I have noted that.

One day I appeared to have finally stopped looking, in any event.

At the intersection of Anna Akhmatova Street and Rodion Romanovitch Raskolnikov Mews, perhaps this was.

Doubtless it would have been around that same time that I stopped reading out loud, also. Or in any case surely tearing out pages after having finished their reverse sides, so as to be able to drop them into the fire.

What I did later, with the pages from the life of Brahms, was to toss those into the breeze in the hope that the ash might take flight.

In Cádiz, where he was once writing his poems while living for a certain period near water, Marco Antonio Montes de Oca had a seagull which came to his window each morning, to be fed.

It was Lucien, in fact, who told me that. Lucien was once acquainted with William Gaddis also, I believe.

Though perhaps it was William Gaddis who lived for a certain period near water in Cádiz, and had a pet seagull.

The cat in the Colosseum was black, I am next to positive, and held up one paw as if it had hurt itself.

Nothing that I am writing in these moments should cause me to continue to feel depressed, I do not believe.

Although I am perhaps just enough disturbed by these underpants to have let that become a sort of nuisance factor.

I have just gone out for fresh underpants.

What I more exactly did was change while I was out there. There is always something pleasurable about changing into garments that are still warm from the sun.

Which will perhaps explain why I again left everything else on the bushes, in fact.

Then again, some of it may well remain there indefinitely, since I generally wear nothing at all, summers.

Once, I actually left out certain items which became frozen, when an early frost surprised me.

By the time I remembered to go for them, I was able to stand several of my wraparound denim skirts upright on the ground.

Skirt sculptures, one might have considered them.

And there can be no doubt at all that I had gotten rid of my anxiety by then, since I was even able to be amused by the concept.

Apparently, one day I had been looking and then one day I was not, as I have said.

Although very likely it was hardly that simple either.

Doubtless I had not even realized that anything had changed, for some time.

For some time I have been watching the sun go down every evening without anxiety, is perhaps what I finally one evening remembered to think.

Or, the eternal silence of these infinite spaces no longer makes me feel like Pascal.

I doubt very seriously that I thought that.

Sculpture is the art of taking away superfluous material, Leonardo once said, if that is at all relevant?

Although it was not Leonardo who said it but was Michelangelo.

And on third thought I believe that Leonardo did not put snow into one of his paintings after all. Certain whitish rocks in mist, were what I had had in mind.

Quite possibly Tiepolo did not paint either of those two paintings either, now that I think about it, although in this instance all I mean is that Tiepolo had a great many assistants in his workshop, and so may have done no more than the preliminary sketches.

Though as a matter of fact he also did, or did not, do a painting of Agamemnon sacrificing poor Iphigenia to raise winds for the Greek ships.

Painting is not my trade, is another thing that Michelangelo once said. When he said this was when a pope told him that the Sistine Chapel might look more agreeable with some pictures up on top.

Perhaps this was the same pope who once offered Michelangelo his chair, out of respect. This was a very significant moment in the history of art, since nothing of the sort had ever happened with an artist before.

I serve him who pays me, is something that Leonardo did say instead of Michelangelo, on the other hand. Doubtless there is a way in which this moment had its significance in the history of art, as well.

Actually, Tintoretto once threatened to shoot a critic with a gun, which many artists would have perhaps felt was a more significant moment than both of those put together.

And possibly it was only one of the Medici, who let Michelangelo sit down. Still, one would be pleased if the pope was not the same pope who made people burn Sappho's poems.

When I state that any of these things were done or said, incidentally, what I more truthfully mean is that they were alleged to have been done or said, of course.

As it was similarly alleged that Giotto once painted a perfect circle freehand.

Although I happen to believe it categorically about the circle, most of such tales being harmless enough to believe in any event.

Well, and I also see no reason not to believe that Piero di Cosimo would hide under a table when there was lightning. Or that Hugo van der Goes was not able to paint religious paintings in a church unless friars sang psalms to keep him from sobbing all day.

Piero di Cosimo is not to be confused with yesterday's sunset, by the way, which was a Piero della Francesca, nor is Hugo van der Goes to be confused with Rogier van der Weyden, whose *Descent from the Cross* is so badly lighted at the Prado.

Well, nor with Vincent Van Gogh, whose sunset was some days before Piero's.

Which symphony is it, by Shostakovitch, in which one can practically hear the tanks coming off the assembly line?

In any event all that any of these stories would appear to add up to, one suspects, is that many more people in this world than one's self were never able to shed certain baggage.

Surely walking halfway across Naples to add one brush-stroke to a wall is a form of baggage itself.

Doubtless cutting off one's ear is one too, if paradoxically.

Well, as is eating one's lunch every day at the Eiffel Tower. Or even lurking at windows.

Nonetheless, what would appear to remain the case on my own part is that one day I had baggage and then one day I did not.

Although very likely it was hardly that simple either.

Accouterments, I did get rid of. Things.

Conversely I can even now still call to mind the last four digits of Lucien's telephone number from all of those years ago.

Or recite the several rumors about Achilles and Patroclus

having been more than just dear friends.

In fact I have just even quoted Friedrich Nietzsche.

Actually, it was almost an hour ago when I quoted Friedrich Nietzsche, who was really Pascal.

Where I have been was at the spring again. This time I decided I may as well bring in everything.

Nor am I any longer depressed, incidentally, which I now understand that I had not been to begin with, having only been out of sorts.

Which is to say that I had changed into those fresh underpants perhaps fifteen minutes earlier than I ought to have, having now had to change again, having just gotten my period.

I have no intention of looking back to see what I wrote about inconsequential perplexities now and again becoming the fundamental mood of existence. Or about certain unanswerable questions becoming answerable.

Oh, well.

At any rate everything that had been washed is now in my upstairs bedroom.

For a moment or two, before I came back down, I looked out of the rear window.

I do not often look out of that one, which is not the one from which I watch the sun go down.

What I was looking at was the other house, which is deep in the woods some distance from here.

I do not believe I have ever mentioned the other house.

What I may have mentioned are houses in general, along the beach, but such a generalization would not have included this house, this house being nowhere near the water.

All one can see of it from that upper rear window is a corner of its roof.

In fact I was not aware of the other house at all, when I first came to this one.

Once I did become aware of it, I understood that there would also have to be a road leading to it from somewhere, of course.

Yet for the life of me I was not able to locate the road, and for the longest time.

Looking for it, what I did first was drive the pickup truck along the road one takes to the town, turning off at every other road I came to.

Every one of those roads led to a house which was on the beach, however, and as I have said, this house is not on the beach.

I should perhaps add that when I say I followed the road one takes to the town, there is a manner of speaking in which I was not doing that at all.

The road one takes to the town being naturally also the road one takes away from the town, and it is in that opposite direction that the house can be seen from my upper rear window.

Possibly I did not really need to make that distinction.

In any case my failure to locate the road eventually began to become a wholly new sort of perplexity in my existence.

Unquestionably there has got to be a road leading to that house, I more than once said to myself.

Still, no matter how many times I drove back and forth, I was not able to locate it.

One morning I finally determined to make a major project out of doing so, for all that I was convinced I had put an end to such things as major projects.

Today I am going to locate the road leading to that house no matter what, was what I finally determined.

How I had been looking before this was in the pickup truck, as I have said. How I decided to do so that morning was by walking directly through the woods to the house.

And naturally by this identical procedure I will have also walked directly to the road, being what I obviously now had in mind.

Indeed, I had been just enough distracted by the entire proposition so that the logic in this notion delighted me.

In fact what I additionally told myself was, as quickly as I get to the house I will next follow the road to wherever it comes out, and thus will have eliminated any trace of the mystery altogether.

The road came out at the road one takes in the direction away from the town.

Well, when I say came, obviously I mean comes, since to this day the road naturally remains exactly where it had been all the while.

The fallen tree naturally remains exactly where it had been all the while, as well.

Good heavens. And how long had I permitted myself to fret over not locating that road?

Surely I had driven past that fallen tree no less than six or eight times.

And meanwhile no sooner had I solved the problem than I understood that I no longer had any interest in the road whatsoever, of course.

Nor do I have very much interest in the house either, to tell the truth.

Except as perhaps something to gaze at the corner of the roof of, on certain occasions, as I just now did.

It is likely that I will now bleed for weeks, incidentally. Or at least stain for that long.

This is a matter of hormones, doubtless, and of change of life.

My hands would appear to indicate that it is time for this. Being a painter, one learns to read such things as the backs of hands.

Even if I rarely did portraits.

That other house is quite ordinary, by the way.

Well, except for being the only house in the vicinity which was constructed for people who preferred a view of the woods to a view of the water, obviously.

I imagine I can understand such a preference. It is hardly my own preference, but I imagine I can understand it.

Then again one would get little more than an inference of the sunset at best, over there, even from the upper windows.

Well, I have looked. Which is a thing one might do.

Although what I was more truthfully looking for was to see if one could see my own house from there.

This is a thing one might do, as well.

One cannot see this house from that one.

Obviously, this is a result of nothing more than where windows happen to be situated. Still, one could easily let it become a perplexity of a sort too, should one be so inclined.

After all, why on earth should one be able to see one house from another, but not vice versa? Surely there is no difference in the distance between this house and that, and that house and this?

Once, in the Rijksmuseum, I brought in new speakers for my phonograph. What the directions told me to do was to make certain that the two speakers were equidistant from each other.

One certainly had to wonder what the person who wrote the instructions could have believed he meant by that.

Well, or the person who had translated the instructions from the Japanese.

No matter where one situated them, how could there be any way in which any two objects could be any distance from each other except equidistant?

Even if there were some miraculous manner in which I were able to move this house, for instance, surely it would still end up being exactly the same distance from the other house that the other house would be from this.

Although in that case this one might at least land where it could finally be seen from the other after all.

As a matter of fact I actually once did see this house from that one anyway, now that I think about it.

What happened was that there was a fire in my potbellied stove, on an afternoon when I decided to take a walk through the woods.

Looking back, I could see the smoke above the trees.

There is my house, being what I thought when I looked.

I have noted the persistence of this sort of thinking before, I believe.

Doubtless I would have expressed an identical thought on the night when my earlier house was turning into little more than an upside down glow on the clouds, in fact, had I had a rowboat to express it in at the time.

Perhaps all such thoughts might very well fall into the same category as the thought that there is somebody at a window in a painting when there is nobody at the window in the painting, since I would appear to have verified that paintings are never basically what one thinks of them as being either.

Then again it is perhaps questionable that I have verified any such thing.

Continuing to think in such terms one might as well ask if I had ever truly walked to the other house to begin with.

Undeniably I walked to the other house, since I can distinctly remember the poster, which is taped to the living room wall.

The poster shows Jane Avril and three other Paris dancers. In fact it also lists all of the dancers' names, including hers.

The other names that the poster lists are Cléopatre and Gazelle and Mlle. Églantine.

Well, I have a vague recollection that I may have spoken about this before, even.

On the other hand there is no way of telling if the poster had been painted before or after Toulouse-Lautrec may have handled my stick, of course.

There is nothing in Jane Avril's expression which gives any hint about her affair with Brahms either, as it happens.

Still, one remembers other paintings of her in which she appears more than sensitive enough to have attracted him.

Unfortunately there is no life of Brahms in the other house in which I might have looked up more about this.

The life of Beethoven would have been of no help, one presumed.

The title of the life of Beethoven in the other house is

Beethoven, by the way.

The title of the life of Brahms that I did once look into, insofar as I can remember, was *A Life of Brahms.*

Well, doubtless I could readily verify this, there being a second copy of the life of Brahms still accessible right where I am.

Then again, what one is now perhaps forced to wonder is if the title of the life of Brahms would remain *A Life of Brahms* if there did not happen to be that second copy still at hand.

If there were no more copies accessible anywhere of *Anna Karenina,* in other words, would its title still be *Anna Karenina?*

I am perhaps less than certain what I mean by that question.

Still, it would undeniably appear that I have more than once thought about a life of Brahms when I was not seeing a life of Brahms.

For that matter I have more than once thought about *The Recognitions,* by William Gaddis, when I have not seen a copy of *The Recognitions* by William Gaddis in twelve or fifteen years.

I have even thought about William Gaddis himself, when I have not seen William Gaddis for twelve or fifteen years either.

In fact I may never have seen William Gaddis.

Moreover I have also thought about T. E. Shaw and I do not even know who T. E. Shaw was.

Although having finally remembered that Marco Antonio Montes de Oca wrote poetry, perhaps I can at least safely assume that Sor Juana Inés de la Cruz did also.

But what I am actually now thinking about, for some reason, is the scene in *The Trojan Women* where the Greek soldiers throw Hector's poor baby boy over the city's walls, so that he will not grow up to take revenge for his father or for Troy.

God, the things men used to do.

Irene Papas was an effective Helen in the film of *The Trojan Women,* however.

Katherine Hepburn was an effective Hecuba, as well.

Hecuba was Hector's mother. Well, which is to say she was the baby boy's grandmother also, of course.

Just imagine how Katherine Hepburn must have felt.

Very likely one might have driven right past that fallen tree eternally, I suppose, without ever having noticed the road. Especially since the road turned sharply at once, too.

Although I now remember that I watched a certain few other films as well, before the projector I had brought into my loft stopped functioning.

Peter O'Toole playing the part of Lawrence of Arabia may have been one.

Marlon Brando as Zapata was possibly another.

Meanwhile I have just eaten a dish of sardines.

Most items in cans would still appear to be edible, by the way. It is only foods packaged in paper that I have stopped trusting.

Although two fresh sunnyside eggs are what I would give almost anything for.

What I would more seriously give almost anything for, in all truth, would be to understand how my head sometimes manages to jump about the way it does.

For instance I am now thinking about that castle in La Mancha again.

And for what earthly reason am I also remembering that it was Odysseus who found out where Achilles was, when Achilles was hiding among the women so that they would not make him go to fight?

Granting, that what Odysseus doubtless felt was that if he himself had to go, everybody else should have to go, too.

But still.

In fact I was about to add that this was still another episode that Tiepolo did, or did not, paint, but it was Van Dyck who painted this.

Even if Van Dyck rarely did anything except portraits.

In either event, one aspect of things that Odysseus was

presumably not aware of was that Achilles had gotten one of the women pregnant.

One wonders if Patroclus was ever aware of this, either.

To the castle, a sign must have said.

And something else I believe I watched, just by accident, was an interesting Russian film about Andrei Roublev and Theophanes the Greek.

Who were two Russian painters.

Even if Theophanes was not really Russian, obviously.

None of which has anything to do with the fact that there is no life of Brahms in the other house, I imagine, whatever its title would have been if there were one.

In addition to the life of Beethoven, which is called *Beethoven*, there is also a book called *Baseball When the Grass Was Real*.

As I have indicated, there is a copy of the identical book in this house.

I have decided that this is not a scholarly speculation in the manner of Kierkegaard or Martin Heidegger after all, by the way.

Although quite possibly it may have something to do with meteorology. What I am thinking about, in that regard, is the question of the time of year in which baseball was presumably played.

In which case the book would appear to have been astonishingly ill edited, however, *Baseball When the Grass Is Real* having surely been the title that was intended.

In fact *Baseball When the Grass Is Growing* would have been more appropriate yet.

What one can doubtless be certain of, on the other hand, is that the author would have been a friend of people who lived in both of these houses. Or perhaps even lived nearby himself.

Surely two different people in two such close houses would not have each actually spent money for an identical book about baseball.

Then again, had there been a copy of *Wuthering Heights* in

each house, it is perhaps doubtful that I would have speculated that somebody from each had known Emily Brontë.

Or that Emily Brontë had once lived on this beach.

Incidentally, there is an explanation for my generally speaking of Kierkegaard as Kierkegaard, but of Martin Heidegger as Martin Heidegger.

The explanation being that Kierkegaard's first name was Søren, and in typing that I would repeatedly have to go back to put in the stroke.

There would appear to be no way of avoiding the two dots over Brontë, however.

In any event, none of the few other books I have noticed over there interests me remarkably either.

Although I am perhaps forgetting the one-volume selection from among the Greek plays, which is an edition I had never seen before.

Conversely, I have no more intention of even opening something called *The Origin of Table Manners* than I do of reading the book about grass.

One other is actually called *The Eiffel Tower*, of all nonsense subjects.

There is naturally nothing in any of the plays about anybody menstruating, incidentally.

Although when one comes right down to it, one can often make an educated guess about that sort of thing despite the silence.

One has a fairly acute inkling as to when Cassandra may be having her period, for instance.

Cassandra is feeling out of sorts again, one can even imagine Troilus or certain of the other Trojans now and again saying.

Then again, Helen could be having hers even when she still possesses that radiant dignity, being Helen.

My own generally makes my face turn puffy.

One is next to positive that Sappho would have never beaten around the bush about any of this, on the other hand.

Which could well explain why certain of her poems were used as the stuffing for mummies, even before the friars got their hands on those that were left.

On my honor, pieces of Sappho's lost work were found cut into strips inside dead Egyptians.

Have I mentioned that Sappho's father was named Scamandros, for the river near Hisarlik that I once went to see, by the way?

I am by no means implying that there is anything significant about this, which merely strikes me as an agreeable fact to include.

Once, in the National Portrait Gallery, in London, looking at Branwell Brontë's group portrait of his three sisters, I decided that Emily Brontë looked exactly like what Sappho must have looked like.

Even though the pair of them could have scarcely been more different, of course, what with the considerable likelihood that Emily Brontë never even once had a lover.

Which is presumably an explanation for why so many people in *Wuthering Heights* are continually looking in and out of windows, in fact.

Or climbing in and out of them, even.

Still, the thought of this sort of life has always saddened me.

What do any of us ever truly know, however?

The name of Hector's little boy was Astyanax, incidentally.

As a matter of fact that was only a nickname. What he was really named was Scamandrius.

I have no wish to imply anything in regard to this coincidence, either.

A certain number of such connections do appear to keep on coming up, however. A few days ago, for instance, when I remarked that Aristotle had once been Plato's pupil, I also remembered that Alexander the Great was later Aristotle's.

What that reminded me of was that Helen's lover Paris was really named Alexandros. And for that matter that Cassandra was often called Alexandra.

There seemed no point whatsoever in mentioning any of this. Even if it happens that Alexander the Great always kept a copy of the *Iliad* right next to his bed, and actually believed that he was directly descended from Achilles.

Or that Achilles once almost drowned in the Scamander.

Although I have also now remembered that Jane Avril kept a certain book right next to her bed too, even if I have forgotten what book.

And now I further remember that it was Odysseus, again, who convinced the other Greeks that they should not leave any male survivors at Troy.

God, the things men used to do.

I have just said that, I know.

Still, what especially distresses me, in this instance, is how quickly Odysseus had forgotten that plow, and his own little boy.

At least one can be gratified that Sappho had a child of her own, too. Well, a daughter, like Helen.

Which is to say that any number of later Greeks could have been directly descended from Sappho as well, even if one would have surely lost track, after a certain period of years.

But who is to argue that it might not have come all the way down to somebody like Irene Papas, even?

Plato's own teacher was of course Socrates, if I have not said.

Meanwhile the title of that life of Brahms, I suddenly suspect, may well have been *The Life of Brahms,* and not *A Life of Brahms* after all.

Undeniably *The Life of Brahms* would have been more appropriate, the man having had only one life.

Which is perhaps failing to consider the possibility of its having been called simply *Brahms,* however.

Or that there also happens to be a life of Shostakovitch in the other house, the title of which is *Shostakovitch, A Biography.*

There is no poster showing Jane Avril and three other Paris dancers taped to the living room wall in the other house, incidentally.

The poster is on the floor of the living room in the other house.

After so much discussion, when I went out for my walk yesterday I decided to walk through the woods rather than along the beach.

Which is also to say that it is again tomorrow. And which I imagine needs no further explanation, by this juncture.

Except to perhaps note that everything is still all lilac.

What I do wish to mention, however, is that the poster had indisputably fallen some time ago, since it was covered with leaves. And with fluffy cottonwood seeds.

The reason I wish to mention this is that through all of that time, in my head, the poster was still on the wall.

In fact the very way I was able to verify that I had ever even been to the other house, some few pages ago, was by saying that I could distinctly remember the poster.

On the wall.

 Where was the poster when it was on the wall in my head but was not on the wall in the other house?

Where was my house, when all I was seeing was smoke but was thinking, there is my house?

A certain amount of this is almost beginning to worry me, to tell the truth.

I have no idea what amount, but a certain amount.

Actually, I did well in college, in spite of frequently under-lining sentences in books that had not been assigned.

One is now forced to wonder if underlining sentences in Kierkegaard or Martin Heidegger might have shown more foresight, however.

Or if some of these very questions may have even been answered as long ago as when Alexander the Great happened to raise his hand in class.

Perhaps they were the identical questions that Ludwig Witt-genstein would have preferred to think about on the afternoon when Bertrand Russell made him waste his time by watching

Guy de Maupassant row, in fact.

Although come to think about it I once read somewhere that Ludwig Wittgenstein himself had never read one word of Aristotle.

In fact I have more than once taken comfort in knowing this, there being so many people one has never read one word of one's self.

Such as Ludwig Wittgenstein.

Even if one was always told that Wittgenstein was too hard to read in any case.

And to tell the truth I did once read one sentence by him after all, which I did not find difficult in the least.

In fact I became very fond of what it said.

You do not need a lot of money to buy a nice present, but you do need a lot of time, was the sentence.

On my honor, Wittgenstein once said that.

Still, yesterday, if he had been hearing the tanks coming off the assembly line in Tchaikovsky's sixth symphony, what exactly would Wittgenstein have been hearing?

When people first heard Brahms's first symphony, all that most of them could say was that it sounded a lot like Beethoven's ninth symphony.

Any donkey can see that, being what Brahms said in turn.

I believe I would have liked Brahms.

Well, and I certainly would have found it agreeable to tell Ludwig Wittgenstein how fond I am of his sentence.

Then again I harbor sincere doubts that I would have liked John Ruskin, even if I have no idea what I have been saying that has now made me think about John Ruskin.

Well, Ruskin being still another of the assignments I skipped, was doubtless what.

And what I more truthfully happen to feel in regard to John Ruskin is sorry for him.

This is because of the silly man having spent so many years looking at so many ancient statues that he almost went into shock on his wedding night, what with nobody ever having told him that living women had pubic hair.

Normally, the person one might more probably feel sorry for under such circumstances would be Mrs. Ruskin. Except that she was sensible enough to soon go running off with John Everett Millais.

When I comment that she was sensible, incidentally, I do not mean only because she ran off, but because it was with Millais, who had been a child prodigy. Which is to say that he had been painting from models with no clothes on since he was eleven.

Sappho is said to have taught music, by the way.

Well, and Achilles also played an instrument.

I enjoy knowing both of those things.

Although I additionally know that Achilles had a mistress at Troy, named Briseis. Some of that does begin to get a little confusing, finally.

Actually, it is too bad that John Ruskin was not friendly with Robert Rauschenberg, who presumably could have thought up some way of rectifying things.

Ludwig has such a silly look, for a name, when one types it.

Doubtless I would have settled for calling a biography I had written myself simply *Beethoven,* too.

Although now what I tardily might wish I had done, while I was at the other house, was to see if any of the versions in that one-volume selection from the plays were by the translator who made Euripides sound as if he had been under the influence of William Shakespeare.

In spite of that, one has a fairly acute inkling as to when Medea is having her period also, incidentally.

And if it is true that Odysseus was away from Ithaca for twenty years, Penelope would have had hers approximately two hundred and fifty times.

I hardly mean to go on about this, even if one does now and again become preoccupied.

Especially while sitting here with a puffy face.

But all that I actually have in mind is all of that giveaway silence again, which would surely appear to verify that Samuel Butler was wrong about a woman having written the *Odyssey*.

How curious. Even when I had already begun typing that sentence, I would have sworn I still had no idea who it was who had made that suggestion.

So now I also remember that the translator who read Shakespeare too many times was named Gilbert Murray.

Other than that I have no notion of who Samuel Butler was, however, unless perhaps he was the same Samuel Butler who wrote *The Way of All Flesh*.

Although all I know about *The Way of All Flesh*, in turn, is that I would be pleased to hear that Ludwig Wittgenstein had not read one word of it.

Gilbert Murray, I believe one can meanwhile assume, was somebody who translated Greek plays.

When he was not reading Shakespeare.

Rubens painted a version of Achilles hiding among the women also, by the way.

Too, there is a drawing by him of Achilles slaying Hector, with a spear through the throat.

One of the things people generally admired about Rubens, even if they were not always aware of it, was the way everybody in his paintings is always touching everybody else.

Well, hardly including the way Achilles is touching Hector, obviously.

Meantime I may have made an error, earlier, in saying that where Rupert Brooke died during the first World War was at the Hellespont, by which I mean the Dardanelles.

Where I believe he actually died was on the island of Scyros, even though the latter is only a little bit south in the Aegean.

I bring this up only because Scyros was the same island on which Achilles did all that hiding.

Again, however, I am by no means implying that there is any significance in such connections.

Even if the child born to the woman on Scyros who Achilles made pregnant grew up to become the very soldier who threw Hector's little boy over the walls.

And after that became the husband of Helen's daughter Hermione.

Which in either case still leaves me in the dark as to how I know about Samuel Butler.

Although doubtless I read about him in a footnote, in one of the books about the Greeks I did pay attention to.

At any rate I unquestionably paid enough attention to be certain that Achilles's son would have been far too young to be at Troy when he was supposed to. And that Hermione would have been practically old enough to be his mother.

Then again I almost never read footnotes.

Though once I did read a lovely poem by Rupert Brooke, about Helen growing older.

Actually, the poem made her a nag.

Besides Briseis, the name of another mistress I remember is Jeanne Hébuterne, who had a child by Modigliani. Although that particular story is one of the saddest I know.

What happened was that Jeanne Hébuterne threw herself out of a window, on the morning after Modigliani died.

While again being pregnant.

The things women used to do, too, one is almost tempted to add.

What do any of us ever truly know, however?

And at least the word mistress had finally gone out of style.

Meanwhile, Samuel Butler, the author of *The Way of All Flesh,* has suggested that the *Odyssey* was written by a woman, I am assuming the footnote said.

Although doubtless there was rather more to it than that, it being a fairly safe guess that one does not change Homer from a man to a woman after three thousand years without including some sort of interesting explanation.

I have no idea what that explanation may have been, however.

Even though any number of people often insisted that there had never been any Homer to begin with, but were only various bards.

There having been no pencils then either, being a reason for that insistence.

Then again perhaps the footnote was in some book that had nothing to do with the Greeks at all.

Many books frequently containing things that are connected to other things that one would have never expected them to be connected to.

Even in these very pages that I am writing myself, for instance, one would have scarcely expected that T. E. Shaw would be connected to anything, even though I have only at this instant remembered that an additional book in the other house is a translation which was done by somebody with that identical name.

What it is a translation of is the *Odyssey,* in fact.

Then again, indicating that I now know approximately as much about T. E. Shaw as I know about Gilbert Murray may be less than the most impressive manner in which to make my point.

In either case, doubtless the footnote was in no way connected to the opera about Medea, even if that also now happens to be in my head.

Once, in Florence, sitting in a Land Rover with a right-hand drive and watching the piazza below Brunelleschi's dome fill up with snow, which must surely be rare, I listened to Maria Callas singing that.

I had only a few moments earlier switched vehicles, after carrying several suitcases across one of the bridges over the Arno, and so had not even noticed immediately that the new tape deck was set to the on position.

Medea was written by Luigi Cherubini, I might mention.

Basically, I do that because of Luigi Cherubini being somebody I often mix up with Vincenzo Bellini, who wrote *Norma,* which is another opera that Maria Callas frequently sang.

Although now and again I have mixed up Vincenzo Bellini with Giovanni Bellini in turn, even if Giovanni Bellini is one of the painters I have always most deeply admired.

Well, even Albrecht Dürer, whom I admire to almost the same degree, once said that Bellini was still the best painter alive.

I say still, since Dürer happened to be visiting in Venice at a time when Bellini was quite old.

On the other hand this would have been before Dürer himself became practically as mad as Piero di Cosimo, presumably. Or as Hugo van der Goes.

Well, or as Friedrich Nietzsche, for all that I was once extremely fond of one of Friedrich Nietzsche's sentences too.

As a matter of fact still another person I was once fond of a sentence by, meaning Pascal, could doubtless be added to this same list, what with refusing to sit on a chair without an additional chair at either side of him, so as not to fall into space.

In fact I now have to wonder if I did not mix up those two sentences as well, and that it was Pascal who wrote the one about wandering through an endless nothingness.

I have no explanation for my generally speaking of Pascal as Pascal, but of Friedrich Nietzsche as Friedrich Nietzsche, incidentally.

The question of the two dots over Dürer would appear to be basically the same as that of the two dots over Brontë, however.

In either case, that remark about Giovanni Bellini would have naturally also had to have been made before Dürer died from a fever he caught in a Dutch swamp, where he had gone to look at a stranded whale.

Although doubtless it was conversely made long after Bellini himself had become Andrea Mantegna's brother-in-law.

I am now perhaps showing off.

But where I truly did listen to Maria Callas singing *Medea*, on second thought, was in a Volkswagen van filled with picture postcards near a town called Savona, which is some distance from Florence although also in Italy.

I had not noticed the tape deck in the van either, as it happened, since it had not been playing while I was driving.

Only when the van went over an embankment and turned upside down in the Mediterranean did the tape deck begin to play.

I was not able to think of any explanation for why it did that.

Neither can I think of one now.

As a matter of fact the tape deck did not begin to play as soon as the van turned upside down either.

Actually I had already gotten out and was standing in the Mediterranean up to my waist before it started.

What I was doing was trying to get some of the dirt out of my hair, from where the rubber mat from the floor had fallen on top of me.

While I was doing that, I understood that my shoulder had gotten hurt.

Doubtless it was not until I became convinced that my shoulder had not gotten hurt badly, in fact, that I began to hear Maria Callas.

Which is to say that perhaps she had been singing before that after all.

Good heavens, here I have been driving a car which is now upside down in the Mediterranean and I am hardly injured at all, I was thinking, which is assuredly something else that would have kept me from hearing her more quickly.

In addition to which I was doubtless distressed over how wet I had gotten.

Perhaps I have not mentioned how wet I had gotten.

Well, doubtless I merely assumed it was unnecessary to mention that, already having mentioned being up to my bottom in the Mediterranean.

Too, I have never been on my hands and knees on the inside of the roof of a car before, being doubtless one more thing that I was thinking.

Though perhaps I had also noticed the sign by then, saying Savona.

I have no recollection as to whether the sign indicated that Savona was ahead of me or behind me, however.

As a matter of fact I have no recollection of ever having driven through any town with that name either, either in the vehicle which went over the embankment or in the one that I switched to subsequently.

Had I driven through it in the vehicle which went over the embankment, I would have had to have been there already, naturally.

Then again, considering how long the embankment appeared to have been deteriorating, perhaps there had been some sort of old detour around Savona altogether.

As a general rule I preferred to avoid detours, however.

Which is only to say that my sense of direction is sometimes less than extraordinary.

Given a choice between driving off immediately on a road which turned away from the embankment, for instance, or walking until it appeared safe to continue straight on, I would have walked.

Although as a matter of fact there was an identical Volkswagen van not a stone's throw from where I was standing.

That one was full of soccer equipment.

Some of the equipment turned out to be shirts, as it happened, with the name Savona on their fronts.

Being wet, as I have mentioned, I changed into one of those.

In fact I folded several others onto the seat, for the same reason.

Not that I would have been driving until this point without additional clothing of my own, of course, what with still possessing baggage in those days.

There it all was, upside down in the Mediterranean, however.

Along with the picture postcards.

Most of the postcards showed identical views of the

Borghese Gallery, in Rome, incidentally.

Although some few happened to be of the Via Vittorio Veneto, which is almost directly below the Borghese Gallery.

The reverse of that statement being equally true, obviously.

Modigliani was only thirty-five, by the way.

Now that I think about it, I may have worn that soccer shirt all the way to Paris, even.

Doubtless I stopped sitting on the other shirts after the rest of my own garments dried, however.

As a matter of fact I waited for them to become partly dry before I started driving.

What I did was take off my wraparound denim skirt and my cotton jersey and my underpants and leave them in the sunshine, and then put on the shirt that said Savona while I was waiting.

While I was waiting I also continued to listen to Maria Callas singing *Medea.*

The shirt was much too large, incidentally, hanging almost to my knees.

Still, for some reason I enjoyed wearing it.

In fact the shirt also had a numeral on it, although I have forgotten what numeral.

Doubtless this was because the numeral was on its back.

Where the shirt said Savona was across my breasts.

Although where it actually said that was all the way from under one arm to the other, because of how much too large the shirt was.

None of which answers the question as to whether I drove through Savona or not, meanwhile.

The fact that I do not remember doing so is in no way a verification that I did not, I do not believe.

One can drive through any number of towns without knowing the names of those towns.

Well, and especially in Russia, as I have perhaps even said, where even Fyodor Dostoievski could have driven right past St.

Petersburg without knowing it was St. Petersburg.

For that matter I myself had once wished to stop at Corinth, in Greece, but only some time later discovered that I had already been through Corinth and gone.

This was on a morning when I was driving counterclockwise, among mountains, from Athens toward Sparta, as it happens.

Which is to say that it was on the very morning after I had believed that somebody had called my name, beneath the Acropolis, and not far at all from the intersection of Katherine Hepburn Avenue and Archimedes Road.

How I nearly felt, in the midst of all that looking.

It was only the Parthenon, however, so beautiful in the afternoon sun, that had touched a chord.

Still, for a time, I had almost wished to weep.

But then looked into a guide to the birds of Southern Connecticut and Long Island Sound, for what it might tell me about seagulls.

Why I had wished to stop at Corinth was because of Medea herself, as a matter of fact, even if the opera had nothing to do with that at the time.

Although one doubts that there is any longer any evidence of her little boys' graves in either case.

Then again, very likely there had been a pharmacy or a movie theater with the name Savona on it, at the least, and I had simply not been paying attention.

Although I am now next to positive that the numeral on the back of the shirt was a seven.

Or a seventeen.

In fact it was a twelve.

Once, I was one hundred percent positive that I was in a town called Lititz, in Pennsylvania, without having any genuine reason for being positive about that at all.

As a matter of fact I had been equally positive, only moments earlier, that I was in Lancaster, Pennsylvania, until a name on a pharmacy or a movie theater indicated otherwise.

Even then, I also understood that there could easily be a pharmacy in Lancaster called the Lititz Pharmacy, just as there could be a movie theater in Savona called the Rimini. Or the Perugia.

Nonetheless I was one hundred percent positive that I was in Lititz, Pennsylvania.

I also believe that I was still wearing that same soccer shirt now and again at the Tate Gallery, in London, on chilly mornings when I was carrying in water from the Thames.

Or when I was enjoying Turner's own paintings of water.

I did not keep any of the additional shirts when I abandoned that particular Volkswagen van, however, which only this tardily has to strike me as thoughtless.

Obviously, since I so enjoyed wearing the one shirt, ordinary common sense ought to have told me to keep some of the others.

Then again, doubtless I had no idea that I was going to develop such a fondness for it, at the time.

For that matter it might just as easily have happened that I waited for my own garments to dry completely, in which instance I would have never developed any such feelings about the shirt to begin with.

What was to have prevented me from listening to Maria Callas singing *Medea* with nothing on at all, even, while I waited?

Actually it was quite warm, as I remember.

But now heavens.

Obviously it would have hardly been Maria Callas singing with nothing on, but only me myself listening that way.

What ridiculousness one's language still does insist upon coming up with.

And in either event I had already put on the shirt.

And had also incidentally listened long enough to understand that what Maria Callas was singing was not *Medea* by Luigi Cherubini after all, but was *Lucia di Lammermoor* by Gaetano Donizetti.

It was the famous mad scene in the latter which finally led me to understand this.

Gaetano Donizetti being still another person whom I otherwise might have mixed up with Vincenzo Bellini. Or with Gentile Bellini, who was also Andrea Mantegna's brother-in-law, being Giovanni Bellini's brother.

Well, I did mix him up. With Luigi Cherubini.

Music is not my trade.

Although Maria Callas singing that particular scene has always sent shivers up and down my spine.

When Vincent Van Gogh was mad, he actually once tried to eat his pigments.

Well, and Maupassant, eating something much more dreadful than that, poor soul.

That list becomes distressingly longer.

Even Turner, in his way, having such a phobia about not letting a single person ever see him at work.

As a matter of fact Euripides was said to have lived in a cave, for that identical reason.

Although Gustave Flaubert once wrote Maupassant a letter, telling him not to spend so much time rowing.

On my honor, Flaubert once wrote Maupassant that.

In fact the letter also told him not to spend so much time with prostitutes either.

Had he wished, Flaubert could have written this same letter to Brahms, come to think about it, although I know of no record of that.

Actually, he could have even written only part of the same letter to Brahms, and the earlier part to Alfred North Whitehead.

When Gertrude Stein first met Alfred North Whitehead, she said that a little bell rang in her head, informing her that he was a genius.

The only other time Gertrude Stein had ever heard the same bell was when she first met Picasso.

Doubtless it is generally more difficult than this to tell just who is mad and who is not, however.

In St. Petersburg, when he finally did find out how to get there, Dostoievski appeared to believe that everybody one met at all belonged in this category, or certainly that is the impression one is given.

Men are so necessarily mad, that not to be mad would amount to another form of madness, which happens to be one more sentence that I now remember I once underlined.

Where I underlined this one was in the identical book in which I underlined one of the others, and which was also the book that Jane Avril always kept right beside her bed, as a matter of fact.

This being the *Pensées,* by Pascal.

I believe I would have liked Jane Avril.

Well, and I certainly would have found it agreeable to tell Pascal how fond I am of his two sentences.

Don't bother to get up, I would have even been delighted to insist.

Actually, Euripides was finally forced to go into exile.

This was not because he did not have enough seclusion in his cave, however, but because of things he had said that certain people did not approve of.

Aristotle had to go into exile, too.

For that matter Socrates had to take poison.

One can be startled to remember that all of these things happened in Greece, I imagine, from where all arts and all freedoms came.

Although several of Andrea Mantegna's frescoes were destroyed by bombs during the second World War, and that was in Italy.

Still, many sorts of lists would appear to grow longer.

October twenty-fifth, Picasso's birthday was.

Even if I have no way of telling when it is ever October twenty-fifth.

Or any other date.

Simon's was July thirteenth.

In any event I do not believe I have heard Maria Callas again even once, since that day.

Well, I have scarcely been changing vehicles at all, lately.

Then again I have heard Joan Baez. And Kathleen Ferrier. And Kirsten Flagstad.

How I have heard these people is in much the same manner that Gertrude Stein heard her little bell, basically.

Although where I also heard Kirsten Flagstad was on a tape deck at the tennis courts.

Perhaps I have not mentioned the tennis courts.

The tennis courts are beside the road one takes to the town. The reason I have not mentioned them is that I have had no reason to mention them.

Nor would I have any reason to mention them now, were I not explaining about Kirsten Flagstad.

What happened was that one afternoon I decided to play tennis.

I did not decide to play tennis.

What I decided to do was to hit some tennis balls.

The tennis balls I decided to hit were not the same tennis balls that I once rolled down the Spanish Steps, incidentally. There is a small shed beside the tennis courts, which is where I had discovered these.

The tennis balls that I rolled down the Spanish Steps had been in a carton in the rear of a Jeep, I believe.

These tennis balls were in cans. Had they not been in cans, I am quite certain they would have lost their bounce some time before, and so doubtless I would not have decided to hit any to begin with.

One can hardly hit tennis balls which have lost their bounce, which I understood even when the idea first came into mind.

There were racquets in the shed also. The strings on most of those had become loose as well, but I selected one on which they had become less loose than on the others.

For perhaps an hour I opened cans and hit tennis balls across one of the nets.

There were no nets, those having been ruined by weather some time before as well.

Well, there were remnants of nets.

One pretends they are more than remnants.

Or that one of them is more than that, which is all that is required to hit tennis balls across.

Many of the tennis balls did not bounce very well in spite of having been in cans.

Or perhaps this was because of the grass, growing through the surface of the courts.

To tell the truth I had never been especially proficient at tennis in either case.

In fact I had almost never played tennis.

All of the balls are still at the side of the road, by the way. Frequently I notice them in going or coming from the town.

Well, I noticed them just the other day.

There are the tennis balls I hit that afternoon, was what I thought.

Happily, this is not the same thing as noticing smoke and thinking, there is my house, since what I am noticing in such instances are always real tennis balls.

One finds it agreeable to be positive as to what one is talking about at least part of the time.

I have not forgotten Kirsten Flagstad.

After I had stopped hitting the tennis balls I was quite sweaty.

There were several vehicles parked nearby.

Often, the air-conditioning in certain vehicles will still function.

Had I been at the beach, I would have gone into the ocean.

Not being at the beach, I started one of the vehicles.

Kirsten Flagstad was singing the *Four Last Songs,* by Strauss.

This will happen. One turns a key in an ignition, thinking only about starting the vehicle, or in this case about starting the air-conditioning, and one does not notice that the tape deck is set to the on position at all.

I have often been perplexed as to why they were called the *Four Last Songs,* by the way.

Well, doubtless they were called the *Four Last Songs* because that was what they were.

Still, one can scarcely visualize a composer sitting down and saying, now I am going to write my four last songs.

Or even lying down, and saying that.

Although perhaps this is not impossible. One finds it quite unlikely, but perhaps it is not impossible.

In either event it may have been Kathleen Ferrier singing.

And the songs may have been the *Four Serious Songs,* by Brahms.

Ever since *Lucia di Lammermoor* I have refused to make hasty decisions about such matters.

Brahms has never been my favorite composer, incidentally.

Granting that Brahms has been mentioned any number of times in these pages.

Though in fact Brahms has not been mentioned that great a number of times in these pages.

What has more frequently been mentioned is a life of Brahms, which is perhaps called *A Life of Brahms,* or *The Life of Brahms,* or possibly *Brahms.*

Among other alternatives.

In fact what has actually been mentioned are several lives of Brahms.

Lives of Beethoven and Tchaikovsky have been mentioned as well.

As has a history of music, written for children and printed in extraordinarily large type.

Additionally, I have mentioned listening to Igor Stravinsky while skittering from one end of the main floor of the Metropolitan Museum to the other in my wheelchair.

All of this has been purely happenstance.

The fact that I have also mentioned a book about baseball is surely not to be construed as implying that I possess any enthusiasm for baseball.

To tell the truth I do not believe I have a favorite composer.

Curiously, however, for a certain period not too long ago, all that I was ever able to hear was *The Seasons,* by Vivaldi.

Even when I would be positive I had something else in mind, *The Seasons* would be repeatedly what I heard.

Such things can happen.

They can happen with art just as readily.

Now and again I will be convinced that I am thinking about a certain painting, for instance, and what will come into my head will be a different painting altogether.

Just the other morning this happened with *The Descent from the Cross,* by Rogier van der Weyden.

Right at this moment I can see that painting.

Doubtless this is only natural, since I am again thinking about it.

Even if I had not been thinking about it, for that matter, certainly I would have had to begin to do so when I typed those last few sentences.

Nonetheless, when I was thinking about it just the other morning, I did not see *The Descent from the Cross* at all.

What I saw was that painting by Jan Vermeer of a young woman asleep at a table in the Metropolitan Museum.

There I go again.

Obviously, the young woman is no more asleep at a table in the Metropolitan Museum than Maria Callas was undressed at that embankment near Savona.

The young woman is asleep in a painting in the Metropolitan Museum.

There is something wrong with that sentence too, of course.

There being no young woman either, but only a representation of one.

Which is again why I am generally delighted to see the tennis balls.

But all I had started to say, in either case, was that I had not been thinking about that particular painting at all, even though that was the painting that came into my head.

Although what I was more specifically trying to solve was why I would keep on hearing *The Seasons,* by Vivaldi, even when I was thinking about *Les Troyens,* by Berlioz, say. Or about *The Alto Rhapsody.*

For that matter why am I now suddenly seeing an interior by Jan Steen when I would have sworn I was thinking about one painting by Rogier van der Weyden and still another by Jan Vermeer?

All of Vivaldi's music, including *The Seasons,* was totally forgotten for many years after he died, incidentally.

Well, and Vermeer was neglected for even longer.

In fact nobody ever bought a single painting by Vermeer when he was still alive.

Vivaldi also had red hair.

As did Odysseus.

The things one knows.

Even if, conversely, I cannot call to mind one solitary item about Jan Steen.

Or that all I am able to state categorically about Rogier van der Weyden is that one still cannot see the original of *The Descent from the Cross* the way it wants to be seen.

In spite of the windows having been washed nearby.

Or even if I also only now realize that everybody in it is as Jewish as everybody in *The Last Supper,* presumably.

There is nobody in the painting called *The Descent from the Cross* by Rogier van der Weyden, whatever any of them may believe in.

Shapes do not have religion.

And doubtless it was somebody else, later on, who decided to name them the *Four Last Songs.*

My favorite composer is Bach, as a matter of fact, whom I do not believe I have mentioned at all in these pages.

I have just realized something else.

On the front seat of the vehicle in which I turned on the air-conditioning, after having gotten sweaty from hitting the tennis balls, there was a paperback edition of *The Way of All Flesh,* by Samuel Butler.

Which presumably answers the question as to where I came upon the footnote about Samuel Butler having said that it was a woman who wrote the *Odyssey.*

Or perhaps the book contained some sort of preface, dealing with the life of Samuel Butler, which brought up this fact.

I am more than positive that I have never read a life of Samuel Butler, however, even in the form of a preface, what with knowing even less about Samuel Butler than I do about *The Way of All Flesh,* which I am just as positive I have never read.

And doubtless I would have scarcely looked into the book on that particular afternoon in either case.

If only because of having set fire to the pages of a life of Brahms not long before, in trying to simulate seagulls, surely I would have wished to devote my attention to the tape deck instead.

Even if there is still another life of Brahms somewhere in this house.

I have no idea why I have said somewhere when I know exactly where.

The life of Brahms is in the identical room into which I put the painting of this house, which until a few days ago had been on the wall directly above and to the side of where this type-writer is.

The door to that room is closed.

Sea air has contributed to that deterioration.

Hm. I would seem to have left something out, just then.

Oh. All I had meant to say, I am quite certain, was that the life of Brahms is standing askew, and has become badly misshapen.

Doubtless I was distracted for a moment, and then believed I had already put in that part.

As a matter of fact I was lighting a cigarette.

Sea air would have contributed to the deterioration of the tennis racquet as well, come to think about it.

Then again, one gathers that the strings on a racquet will generally come loose in any case.

When I say gathers, I mean used to, of course.

In fact one frequently seemed to gather all sorts of similar information about subjects one had less than profound interest in.

It is not even unlikely that I could name certain baseball players, should I wish.

I cannot imagine so wishing.

Babe Ruth and Lou Gehrig.

Sam Usual.

Actually, any number of the men in my life were greatly enraptured by baseball.

When my mother was dying my father watched games endlessly.

Well, perhaps I understood that at the time.

I understood it when he took away the tiny, pocket sort of mirror from beside her bed one evening, certainly.

One finds it difficult to conceive of Bach being enraptured by baseball, on the other hand.

Although perhaps they had not invented baseball at the time of Bach.

Vincent Van Gogh, then.

The black one, for Brooklyn. Well, and the other black one.

And Stan Usual, I perhaps meant.

None of which has answered the question as to how one can have one piece of music in mind and be hearing a different piece of music entirely, meanwhile.

When I say one can be hearing a different piece of music entirely, by the way, I scarcely mean that one will hear the entire piece of music. What I mean is that one hears an entirely different composition, obviously.

Possibly I did not need to make that explanation.

At any rate what is now in my head is that painting by Jan Vermeer again.

Although what I am more exactly thinking about is the sentence I typed just a few pages ago, in which I said that the young woman is asleep in the Metropolitan Museum.

Unquestionably, where the young woman is asleep is in Delft, which is in Holland, and which is where Jan Vermeer painted.

Well, Jan Vermeer of Delft being what he was generally called, in fact.

Nonetheless, what has now struck me is that there is undeniably a way in which the young woman is likewise asleep in the Metropolitan Museum after all.

Unless for some reason the painting itself is no longer in the museum, which one can sincerely doubt.

Even if I had had need of the frame, I would have nailed the painting back into place.

I always took the time to do that, by the way. No matter how chilly it happened to be at the moment.

Once, in the National Gallery, I did crack a canvas by Carel Fabritius, but not so badly that I was not able to wax it and tape the back.

But be that as it may, if I can sincerely doubt that the other painting is not not in the Metropolitan, then it is a fact that the young woman is asleep in the Metropolitan also.

As it is also a fact that in the painting by Rogier van der Weyden they are taking Jesus down from the cross at Calvary, but they are also taking him down on the top floor of the Prado, in Madrid.

Right next to the windows I washed.

I see no way of refuting either of those statements. Even if, as I indicated, there appeared to be something wrong with the first of them when I typed it before.

This is not something I intend to worry about, although I can fully understand how one might worry.

Well, perhaps I have already said that I actually do worry.

Although I have just now eaten a salad.

While I was eating the salad I thought about Van Gogh being mad again.

Lord above.

Van Gogh was not mad for a second time. It was I who was thinking about him once more.

And in any case it was Van Gogh trying to eat his pigments that I was more exactly once more thinking about.

Perhaps the fact that I was eating myself was what reminded me of this, although what I was eating myself were various sorts of lettuce, along with mushrooms.

When Friedrich Nietzsche was mad, he once started to cry because somebody was hitting a horse.

And Jackie Robinson was who, for Brooklyn.

Also Campy, was somebody called?

Actually, there were prostitutes in Van Gogh's life too, although I know of no record of Gustave Flaubert having written to Van Gogh either.

I scarcely mean to give any particular weight to this matter of prostitutes, incidentally, even if I would perhaps sometimes appear to.

Certain matters simply come up, being connected to the subject at hand.

Being sweaty after hitting tennis balls would hardly have appeared to be connected to the subject of Richard Strauss getting into bed to die, for instance, though it proved to be connected to that subject.

As a matter of fact even so trivial an item as Guy de

Maupassant eating his lunch every day at the Eiffel Tower is very likely connected to something, just as inevitably.

Even forgetting that I have just eaten my own lunch, or that Maupassant was even more mad than Van Gogh.

In fact I would almost be willing to wager that there is some way in which Maupassant is even connected to the soccer shirt with the name Savona on its front, should one wish to pursue such a question.

I cannot conceive of why anyone would wish to pursue such a question.

And actually I never really knew what it was, about wearing that soccer shirt.

Although Maupassant's rowing is now in my mind again, too.

Had I held onto the shirt, doubtless I might have worn it when rowing my own boat.

In fact it is perhaps unfortunate that I did not hold onto the lot of those shirts, in which case I might have worn a different one each time I rowed.

What I find interesting about this notion is that from the front it would have always looked as if I were wearing the same shirt.

Savona, it would have always said.

From under one arm to the other.

Assuredly the numerals on the back of each shirt would have been different, however.

So that possibly I could have even changed my back in sequence.

Although I am perhaps overlooking the question of sizes.

What with the one I did wear having already been too large, doubtless many of the others would have been even larger than that.

One is scarcely about to return to Savona to check on this, however.

And in any event I have practically never worn a shirt, while rowing.

Very likely I was not wearing anything on the day when I

played tennis either, to tell the truth.

I am still having my period, by the way.

Having my period is another matter I do not particularly mean to give any weight to.

In this case it is just something that happens to be happening.

Although I have lost track of how long it is now, actually.

Doubtless I could look back through what I have been writing, and try to calculate that. But I am fairly certain that I have not indicated all of the days.

Sometimes I indicate them and sometimes I do not.

Lately I have often merely stopped typing and then started again, without putting in that it is tomorrow.

I did not put in throwing away the lilacs either, which was at least yesterday.

And doubtless if I did look back I would be distracted by other things I have written anyhow.

In fact without looking back at all, but by merely thinking about doing so, I have now remembered that a prostitute with whom Van Gogh once lived was named Sien.

Something I doubtless did put in, somewhere, is that I once knew a great deal about many painters.

Well, I knew a great deal about many painters for the same reason that Menelaus must surely have known a great deal about Paris, say.

Even if I seem to have skipped Rogier van der Weyden and Jan Steen.

Somehow I would also appear to know that Bach had eleven children, however.

Or perhaps it was twenty children.

Then again it may have been Vermeer who had eleven children.

Though possibly what I have in mind is that Vermeer left only twenty paintings.

Leonardo left fewer than that, perhaps only fifteen.

Not one of these figures may be correct.

Fifteen paintings do not seem like very many, especially when several of them are not even finished.

Or are deteriorating.

Then again it is perhaps quite a lot if one is Leonardo.

Actually Vermeer left forty paintings.

Brahms had no children at all, although he was known for carrying candy in his pocket to give to the children of other people, when he visited people who had children.

And at least we have finally solved the question as to which life of Brahms it was that I read.

Surely a history of music written for children, and printed in extraordinarily large type, would place emphasis on the fact that somebody being written about in that very book was known for carrying candy in his pocket to give to children when he visited people who had children.

Even if Brahms had not done this very often, surely it would have been emphasized there.

In fact it is not even impossible that Brahms hardly ever carried candy in his pocket to give to children.

Very possibly Brahms did not even do this more than once in his life, and the entire legend was based on that single incident.

Helen ran off with a lover only once in her life herself, and for three thousand years nobody would ever let her forget it.

Here is some candy, children, Brahms doubtless said, once.

Brahms gave candy to children, somebody wrote.

The latter statement is in no way untrue. Any more than it is untrue that Helen was unfaithful.

Although when one comes right down to it, who is to say that Brahms may even have not liked children?

Or even disliked them, to the extreme?

As a matter of fact quite possibly the only reason Brahms ever gave candy to any of them, even the once, may have been so they would go away altogether.

Actually, Leonardo did not have children either, although

nothing appears to have been said about candy either way, in his instance.

Still, so much for your basic legend.

So much for solving the question as to which life of Brahms it was that I read, as well, since what I have also now just remembered is the affair that Brahms perhaps had with Clara Schumann.

I say perhaps, since it would appear that nobody has ever quite solved this, either.

Assuredly there would have been no hint of it in the history of music written for children, however.

Doubtless what Van Gogh wished was to reform Sien, when he invited her to live with him.

This was before he cut off his ear, I believe.

Often, in reading about Van Gogh, one gets the impression he must have been the first person to say hello to Dostoievski, in St. Petersburg.

Actually, it strikes me as quite agreeable to think of Brahms having had an affair with Clara Schumann.

Once, when I was a girl, I saw a film about music in Vienna, called *Song of Love.*

All I can remember about the film is that everybody took turns playing the piano.

But also that Katherine Hepburn had the part of Clara Schumann.

So perhaps it is the notion of Brahms having had an affair with somebody like Katherine Hepburn which strikes me as so agreeable.

Especially if his affair with Jane Avril did not last.

And even if I have no idea what I have been saying that has now reminded me that Bach was almost blind, before he died.

This was from copying too many scores late at night, if I remember.

Homer was blind too, of course.

Although possibly this was only something that was said,

insofar as Homer was concerned.

I believe I have already mentioned that there were no pencils, then.

Which is to say that when people said Homer was blind, it was because what they really did not wish to say was that Homer did not know how to write.

Emily Brontë was one more person who did not have children.

Well, doubtless it would have been extraordinarily interesting if Emily Brontë did, what with the considerable likelihood that she never even once had a lover.

Still, I would perhaps find it difficult to think of anybody I would rather be descended from than Emily Brontë.

Unless Sappho, of course.

Well, or Helen.

To tell the truth, I may even have made believe that I *was* Helen, once.

At Hisarlik, this would have been. Looking out across the plains that once were Troy, and dreaming for a while that the Greek ships were beached there still.

Or that one could even see the evening's watchfires, being lighted along the shore.

Well, it would have been a harmless enough thing to make believe.

Even if Troy itself was disappointingly small. Like little more than your ordinary city block and a few stories in height, practically.

Although now that I remember, everything in William Shakespeare's house at Stratford-on-Avon was astonishingly tiny, too. As if only imaginary people had lived there then.

Or perhaps it is only the past itself, which is always smaller than one had believed.

I do wish that that last sentence had some meaning, since it certainly came close to impressing me for a moment.

There is a great deal of sadness in the *Iliad* in either case, incidentally.

Well, all that death. Wrist deep in that, and in loss, so many of them so often being.

But too, with all of it so long ago, and forever gone.

On the way to certain of his own conquests, Alexander the Great once stopped at Troy himself, to lay a wreath at Achilles's grave.

That older war seeming so much closer to then than to now, of course.

Still, even by the time of Alexander, it was almost a thousand years.

I can almost not conceive of that, come to think about it.

Julius Caesar laid a wreath at Achilles's grave, as well. Although that was only about three hundred years after Alexander.

When I say only, what I imagine I mean is that it was practically as close as between Shakespeare and today, for instance.

In which case I have unquestionably now lost track of what I was trying to conceive of altogether.

Bertrand Russell was born fifteen years before Rupert Brooke, and was still alive more than fifty years after Brooke had died on Scyros, if that is perhaps connected to anything?

If I have not mentioned having been at Stratford-on-Avon before, by the way, this is only because I assume it is taken for granted that everybody who goes to London will sooner or later also go to Stratford-on-Avon.

London and Stratford-on-Avon always remaining equidistant from each other too, as it happens.

Whatever the people who wrote the instructions in Japanese about situating phonograph speakers may have believed.

And in the meantime I would appear to have let still another day pass without putting that one in, either.

As a matter of fact I did not sit here at all, yesterday.

For some reason, what I felt like doing yesterday was dismantling.

Although after that I went for a ride in the pickup truck, as far as to the garbage disposal area.

The tires on the pickup truck are getting a little soft.

Have I said that on certain mornings, when the leaves are dewy, some of them are like jewels where the earliest sunlight glistens?

It is what I sometimes have instead of a rosy-fingered dawn, possibly.

Possibly the garbage disposal area is one more thing that I have never mentioned before, as well.

One would have little reason to do so, however, it being nothing more extraordinary than a hole in the ground.

It is quite a huge hole, but still.

One follows a sign, to get there.

To the Garbage Disposal Area, the sign says.

In a manner of speaking, one follows the sign.

What one is actually following is a road, of course.

Possibly I did not need to make that explanation.

My own garbage is always meager enough to be disposed of by being buried on the beach, incidentally.

I do this while taking my walks, perhaps every third time I take one.

And doubtless it goes without saying that any such garbage as had once been disposed of at the hole has long since decomposed.

So that the hole is just a hole, as I have said.

Although there is an enormous heap of broken bottles nearby.

Perhaps the latter is somewhat extraordinary, after all.

Certainly the bottles are extraordinarily pretty, being of various colors.

Too, they glisten much more dramatically than do my wet morning leaves.

In fact the entire mound of them is sometimes like a kind of glistening sculpture.

Michelangelo would not have thought so, but I think so.

Sculpture is the art of taking away superfluous material, Michelangelo once said.

He also said, conversely, that painting is the art of adding things on.

Although doubtless he would not have thought that the heap of added-on bottles is like a painting, either.

Yet it is not one hundred percent unlike a painting by Van Gogh at that, when one comes right down to it.

If one squints just a little, it is even very like a painting by Van Gogh.

It is all of those swirls in Van Gogh that I am no doubt thinking about. Such as for instance in his painting called *The Starry Night.*

As a matter of fact, at night is exactly when Van Gogh would have most probably chosen to paint such bottles.

Assuming there was a moon, obviously.

El Greco was fond of painting at night also, but only indoors. And one seriously doubts that El Greco would have been given inspiration by a garbage disposal area, in either case.

Actually, the bottles could be effectively done by the light of a fire, as well.

Even if it would have to be quite a large fire.

Now and again I have built fires along the beach, by the way.

This is always a pleasant diversion.

This is also not including when I have built other sorts of fires along the beach. Such as out of entire houses.

Doubtless it has generally been on an unexpectedly chilly evening in summer, when I have built the former.

Or on the first evenings when one senses that winter is finally almost ending.

Along the sand there will be frisky shadows, that will dance and fall away.

Or, if there is snow, the flames will write a strange calligraphy against the whiteness.

For the life of me, I cannot remember what I had been trying to get that nine-foot canvas up the main stairway in the Metropolitan Museum for.

Doubtless my ankle was only sprained. Though it was swollen to twice its normal size.

One never does solve what it is about watching fires, really.

Although probably where I should build my next one is at the garbage disposal area after all.

One would have never created a painting by merely lighting a match and then squinting, before.

El Greco did not care very much for Michelangelo as a painter, by the way.

For that matter Picasso did not care very much for him, either.

A good deal of Michelangelo reminded Picasso of Daumier, as a matter of fact.

One doubts that Alfred North Whitehead's little bell would have rung if he had heard Picasso saying that.

Daumier was somebody else who went blind, incidentally.

Well, as did Degas. And Monet.

And Piero della Francesca.

Although Piero della Francesca is again not to be confused with Piero di Cosimo, the latter having been the one who would hide under a table when there was thunder.

In fact the other Piero had an even worse phobia than Turner about not letting a single person ever see him at work, too.

And frequently would cook as many as fifty eggs at one time, in the same pot in which he was boiling his size, so as not to have to fret over meals.

When Maurice Utrillo was mad, he once tried to commit suicide by repeatedly hitting his head against a wall in a jail.

And in the same period when he was trying to reform Sien, Van Gogh was known to give away all of his clothes to the poor. Or to start to cry in front of churches.

Although Piero di Cosimo did have one pupil, who turned out to be Andrea del Sarto. So doubtless he was at least sometimes agreeable enough to share some of the eggs.

Don't bother to get up, doubtless Andrea said in his turn, if it stormed during lunch period.

What Sien shared with Van Gogh was her venereal disease.

Turner grew up as the son of a barber. In a street called Maiden Lane, near Covent Garden.

Utrillo's father may have been Renoir.

Although he could just as well have been Degas.

Suzanne Valadon, who was Utrillo's mother, evidently never knew.

If Renoir or Degas knew, they evidently never said.

Andrea del Sarto has such a poetic sound for a name, when one reads it.

Although all it actually means is that his own father was a tailor.

Andrea senza errori, he was also called. What that means is that he never made a single mistake, when he was drawing.

Naturally I had to look that up too, whenever it was that I memorized it.

It saddens me to also happen to know that how Andrea died was during a plague, poor and neglected.

Although Titian died during a plague, as well. If in his case at the age of ninety-nine.

Jackson Pollock crashed his car into a tree, no more than ten minutes away in the pickup truck from where I am sitting right at this moment, on August eleventh, 1956.

I forget Pollock's birthday, on the other hand. Although doubtless it is not something I ever knew.

I had also forgotten Renoir's arthritis.

My own left shoulder has not troubled me at all lately, however.

Gauguin was one more painter who had syphilis.

Even if, had he lived during the Renaissance, he would have had to belong to the guild of pharmacists.

All painters did. This was because they compounded pigments.

On my honor, that was how things worked, then.

So possibly the drugstore I forgot to notice in Savona was not called the Savona Drugstore to begin with, but was named after Gauguin.

In Madrid, I once lived in a hotel named after Zurbarán.

Unless perhaps it was named after Goya.

And was in Pamplona.

Although what I would more seriously wish to know is why any of this is now making me think about seagulls.

Aha. Seagulls being scavengers, of course.

When I say being, I mean having been, naturally.

But which in either case was only to suggest that there surely once would have been any number of seagulls at the garbage disposal area.

One has no idea how great a number, but surely a considerable number.

Doubtless other creatures would have come and gone also, of course.

Such as dogs and cats, one imagines.

Then again, perhaps even large dogs would have been leery of that many seagulls.

Certainly cats would have been.

Unless of course there were a considerable number of cats, basically approximating the considerable number of seagulls, which one sincerely doubts.

Actually all I had in mind was a house cat or two, put out for the night.

Once, when I was painting in Corinth, New York, for a summer, I put my own cat out each night.

I remember this because the cat was a city cat and had never been put out before.

Every night for weeks, I worried about that cat.

As a matter of fact I felt quite guilty as well, even though I was never quite certain what it was that I was feeling quite guilty about.

Surely a cat which has been locked up in a loft in SoHo for all of its life will find it agreeable being outside at night, I attempted to convince myself.

Possibly it will even find other cats to associate with, which it has likewise never done before, I additionally rationalized.

Nonetheless my condition of feeling quite guilty continued for the longest time.

Even after I had become reassured that the cat would always come back, so that eventually it would often be as late as noon before I even remembered to look, my condition of feeling quite guilty continued.

Except that by then what I was feeling quite guilty about was having forgotten to let the cat back in.

Frequently I suspected that the cat had done little more than sleep under the porch all night in any event.

Nor have I the slightest notion what this might have to do with the garbage disposal area, since I do not remember a garbage disposal area from the summer when I painted in Corinth, New York.

That summer's garbage was collected at the door.

There is likewise no connection between the cat I am talking about and the cat I saw at the Colosseum, incidentally.

The cat I saw at the Colosseum was gray, and appeared to be playing with something, such as a ball of yarn.

My own cat was russet colored, and was basically slothful.

There is also obviously no connection between my russet cat and the cat which scratches at the broken window here.

Even if for the life of me I cannot remember having put that tape on.

Possibly there was no cat at the Colosseum either.

If one wishes to see a cat badly enough, one will doubtless see one.

Though possibly there was a cat. Possibly it was only the floodlights, when I rigged up floodlights, which made it leery.

Naturally I would have had no way of knowing if it had

nibbled at anything behind my back either, since most of the cans I had set out were half emptied by rain in no time.

Before I ever saw one, I would have supposed that castles in Spain was just a phrase, too.

Was it really some other person I was so anxious to discover, when I did all of that looking, or was it only my own solitude that I could not abide?

In either event people continually looking in and out of windows is doubtless not such a ridiculous subject for a book, after all.

Even though Emily Brontë once struck her dog so angrily that she knocked it out, simply because it had gotten onto her bed when she had told it not to get onto her bed, which is the one thing Emily Brontë did that one wishes she hadn't.

Even if, as I have perhaps said, there are also things Emily Brontë did not do that one wishes she had.

Although which may well be none of one's business either, it finally occurs to me.

And meantime I would appear to have completely forgotten my russet cat's name.

Although what I called the cat at the Colosseum, I am fairly certain, was Pintoricchio, after a minor painter from Perugia who did some frescoes in the Sistine Chapel some time before Michelangelo put in the parts that look like Daumier.

Possibly I will think up a name for the cat outside of my broken window, too.

Then again, I should also perhaps indicate that there is no connection between any of these cats and the cat which Simon once had, in Cuernavaca, and which we never could seem to decide on a name for at all.

Cat, having been all we ever called that one.

Well, and additionally none is connected to the cat which was intelligent enough to ignore the gold coins that his students had painted onto the floor of Rembrandt's studio, either.

Though by stating that, it so happens that I have now simultaneously solved the question of my russet cat's name after all.

In fact now that it has come back to me, it could not have come back more vividly.

Practically every single day at Corinth, for instance, when I did remember to let the cat back in, I said good morning to it.

Good morning, Rembrandt, being exactly how I said it practically every single time.

Russet as a color that one automatically associates with Rembrandt having been the origin of this, naturally.

Even if russet is perhaps not a color.

In any case it is surely not a color that has anything to do with painting, although admittedly it may be a color that has something to do with bedspreads. Or with upholstery.

Although not being a painting a cat can be russet too.

And being russet is apt to be named Rembrandt.

Which in fact no less an authority than Willem de Kooning found to be a perfectly suitable name, on an afternoon when the identical cat happened to climb into his lap.

Perhaps I have not mentioned that my russet cat climbed into Willem de Kooning's lap.

My russet cat once climbed into Willem de Kooning's lap.

The cat did this on an afternoon when Willem de Kooning was visiting at my loft, in SoHo.

I have forgotten the date of this visit, but I do believe it was not long after the afternoon on which Robert Rauschenberg had also visited, and I had hastily hidden my drawings.

Then again, the reason for Willem de Kooning having approved of the cat's name may have actually had less to do with the cat being russet than with Rembrandt having been Dutch, when one stops to think about it.

Being Dutch himself, de Kooning would have naturally felt certain ties to Rembrandt.

One scarcely means family ties, of course, since one would have surely known about this, had any existed.

Willem de Kooning is descended from Rembrandt, one

would have heard.

Then again, who is to argue that he might not have been descended from somebody who had at least once met Rembrandt, on the other hand, which even de Kooning himself would have doubtless not been aware of?

Or from somebody who had been a pupil of Rembrandt, even?

Surely it would have been easy to lose track, after so many years.

How many people would have ever guessed that Maria Callas could be traced all the way back to Hermione, for instance?

Actually, something like this could have been all the more likely if the pupil de Kooning was descended from had never become famous himself, which is generally what happens in any event.

Many pupils not only fail to become famous, in fact, but eventually even go into a different line of work altogether.

Why couldn't Willem de Kooning have been descended from a pupil of Rembrandt who had decided he did not have any future as a painter and had become a baker instead, let us say?

Sooner or later, surely, the man's descendants would have had no idea that anybody in the family had ever been a pupil of Rembrandt at all.

Father was a pupil of Rembrandt before we opened the pastry shop, one can imagine being said. Or even, grandfather was a pupil of Rembrandt.

Certainly it would have stopped being passed down long before Willem de Kooning himself was alive, however.

As a matter of fact Claude Lorrain was actually a pastry cook who decided to become a painter, and one would wager that hardly any of his descendants could have named the man who taught him to bake, either.

Then again, what I have been saying about pupils is not necessarily always the case, as it happens.

Merely from among those who have been mentioned in these pages, Socrates's pupil Plato and Plato's pupil Aristotle and Aristotle's pupil Alexander the Great are three who certainly did become famous.

Even if one does sometimes stop to wonder just exactly what Aristotle might have happened to call Alexander, in those days.

This morning we are doing geography. Will you kindly go to the map and point out where Persepolis is, Alexander the Great?

Who will now recite the passage in the *Iliad* about Achilles dragging Hector's body through the dust for us? Is that your hand I see, Alex?

But be that as it may, it furthermore strikes me that Andrea del Sarto is another famous pupil who was only recently mentioned.

Well, and a pupil of Bertrand Russell's not too long ago, either.

As a matter of fact, many more pupils than one had suspected may well become equally as famous as their teachers.

Or even more so.

Ghiberti had a pupil named Donatello, for instance.

And Cimabue once made a pupil out of a boy he found doing drawings of sheep, in a pasture, and the boy turned out to be Giotto.

As a matter of fact Giovanni Bellini had one pupil named Titian, and still another named Giorgione.

Although to tell the truth certain teachers were never really too happy about this sort of thing.

After Titian had become equally as famous as Giovanni Bellini he took in a pupil of his own, but then kicked him out when it looked as if the pupil might become as famous as he was.

Which Tintoretto did anyhow.

I happen to believe the story about Giotto and the sheep, by the way.

I would also suddenly seem to remember that Rogier van der

Weyden had a pupil named Hans Memling, even though I would have sworn categorically that I knew no such thing about Rogier van der Weyden.

In any event almost every one of these is a pupil I am sure Willem de Kooning would have found it agreeable to have been descended from.

Well, doubtless he would have found it agreeable to have been descended from Vincent Van Gogh as well, even if he was born less than fifteen years after Van Gogh shot himself.

I am not quite certain how the second part of that sentence is connected to the beginning part, actually.

Perhaps all I was thinking about was that Van Gogh was Dutch too.

One of the things people generally admired about Van Gogh, even though they were not always aware of it, was the way he could make even a chair seem to have anxiety in it. Or a pair of boots.

Cézanne once said that he painted like a madman, on the other hand.

Still, perhaps I shall name the cat that scratches at my broken window Van Gogh.

Or Vincent.

One does not name a piece of tape, however.

There is the piece of tape, scratching at my window. There is Vincent, scratching at my window.

Well, it is not impossible. I suspect it is not very likely, but it is not impossible.

Good morning, Vincent.

Van Gogh sold only one painting in his lifetime, incidentally.

Although that did put him one ahead of Jan Vermeer, at least.

Conversely I have no idea how many Jan Steen sold.

I do know that at the end of his life Botticelli was lame, and had to live off charity.

Frans Hals had to live off charity, as well.

Well, and again Daumier.

Too, Paolo Uccello was another who died poor and neglected.

As did the Piero who did not hide under tables.

So many lists keep on growing, and are saddening.

Even though the work itself lasts, of course.

Or does thinking about the work itself while knowing these things somehow sadden one even more?

Even Rembrandt went bankrupt, finally.

This was in Amsterdam, which I make note of because it was only a few short blocks away from where Spinoza was excommunicated, and in the very same month.

I am assuming it will be understood that I hardly know that because of knowing anything about Spinoza.

Assuredly, this was a footnote I did once read.

Although what I do only this instant realize is why Rembrandt was always so easily fooled by those coins, of course.

Certainly if I myself were going bankrupt I would keep on bending to pick up every coin I happened to notice, too.

Considering the circumstances, one would scarcely stop to remember that one's pupils had contrived such illusions before.

Merciful heavens, there is a gold coin, one would surely think. Right on the floor of my studio.

Let us hope it does not belong to some troublemaker who will dash up to claim it either, one would think just as readily.

Doubtless Rembrandt's pupils found this endlessly amusing.

Well, unquestionably they did, or they would have scarcely kept on playing the same trick.

Doubtless not one of them ever stopped to give a solitary thought to Rembrandt's problems either, such as the very bankruptcy in question.

I find this sad too, in its way, even though there was never any way to prevent schoolboys from being schoolboys.

Very probably Van Dyck played tricks on Rubens, too. Or Giulio Romano on Raphael.

Although in the case of Rembrandt it might at least explain why his pupils generally failed to become famous, or even went into different lines of work, what with the lot of them being so insensitive.

In fact it was no doubt equally insensitive on my own part to suggest that Willem de Kooning could have been descended from anybody in such a bunch.

I had simply failed to carry my thinking far enough when I made such a suggestion.

Oops.

Carel Fabritius was a pupil of Rembrandt.

Granting that Carel Fabritius was hardly as famous as Rembrandt himself. Still, he was surely famous enough so that Willem de Kooning doubtless could not have minded having been descended from him after all.

As a matter of fact I believe that I myself have even mentioned Carel Fabritius at least once, in some regard or other.

I suppose all one can now do is hope for Willem de Kooning's sake that Carel Fabritius was not one of the pupils who played that mean trick.

Well, presumably he would not have been able to become Rembrandt's best pupil to begin with, if he had wasted his time in such a way.

Then again, quite possibly in being the best he was the only pupil who had such time to waste.

Quite possibly whenever Rembrandt gave a quiz, for instance, it was always Carel Fabritius who finished first, and then devoted himself to mischief while everybody else was still laboring to catch up.

Many questions in art history remain elusive in this manner, unfortunately.

As a matter of fact Carel Fabritius may have had a pupil of his own, named Jan Vermeer, but nobody was ever able to verify that for certain, either.

Carel Fabritius died in Delft, however, which was one factor that led to such speculation.

I have pointed out Vermeer's own connection with Delft elsewhere, I believe.

But as I have also pointed out, practically two hundred years would have to pass before anybody would become interested enough in Vermeer to look into such matters, and thus a great deal would have already been lost track of.

Well, I have more than once noted how easily that can occur, too.

One thing that does happen to be known is that Vermeer was another painter who went bankrupt, however.

Although it was actually his wife who did that, not long after Vermeer died.

As a matter of fact she owed a considerable bill to the local baker.

This baker was also in Delft, of course, so one is willing to assume it was not the same baker who had himself once been a pupil of Rembrandt.

Then again this is perhaps not so certain an assumption after all.

What with Carel Fabritius having recently moved from the one city to the other, who is to argue that his old classmate might not have done so, as well?

In addition to which, two of Vermeer's paintings had actually been given to this same baker, as a kind of collateral.

Surely your ordinary baker would have been less than agreeable about such an arrangement, and especially in the case of a customer who had never sold a single painting in his life.

Unless of course the baker happened to be somebody who knew something about art himself.

Or at any rate knew enough to go to somebody who was still in the same line of work, for advice.

Tell me, Fabritius, what am I to do about this pupil of yours, who keeps on buying pastry for his eleven children? How long must I wait before any of these paintings become worth anything?

Unfortunately there would appear to be no record of Carel Fabritius's answer, here.

Neither is there any in regard to the connection between Rembrandt and Spinoza, actually, which it occurs to me I had not intended to leave hanging as I did.

Even if there was no connection between Rembrandt and Spinoza.

The only connection between Rembrandt and Spinoza was that both of them were connected with Amsterdam.

Although on the other hand Rembrandt may have painted a portrait of Spinoza.

People often made what they called an educated guess that he had painted such a portrait, in any event.

Most of the subjects of Rembrandt's portraits being unidentified to begin with, naturally.

So all that people were really doing was guessing that one of them may as well have been Spinoza.

In the end this is one more of those questions in art history that has always had to remain elusive, however.

On the other hand it is probably safe to assume that Rembrandt and Spinoza surely would have at least passed on the street, now and again.

Or even run into each other quite frequently, if only at some neighborhood shop or other.

And certainly they would have exchanged amenities as well, after a time.

Good morning, Rembrandt. Good morning to you, Spinoza.

I was extremely sorry to hear about your bankruptcy, Rembrandt. I was extremely sorry to hear about your excommunication, Spinoza.

Do have a good day, Rembrandt. Do have the same, Spinoza.

All of this would have been said in Dutch, incidentally.

I mention that simply because it is known that Rembrandt did not speak any other language except Dutch.

Even if Spinoza may have preferred Latin. Or Jewish.

Come to think about it, Willem de Kooning may have spoken to my cat in Dutch too, that afternoon.

Although what I am actually now remembering about that cat is that it climbed into certain other laps beside de Kooning's, as it happens.

As a matter of fact it once climbed into William Gaddis's lap, on an occasion when Lucien brought William Gaddis to my loft.

I believe there was an occasion when Lucien brought William Gaddis to my loft.

In any event I am next to positive that he did bring somebody, once, who made me think about Taddeo Gaddi.

Taddeo Gaddi scarcely being a figure one is otherwise made to think about that frequently, having been a relatively minor painter.

One is made to think about Carel Fabritius much more frequently than one is made to think about Taddeo Gaddi, for instance.

Even if one is rarely made to think about either of them.

Except perhaps when slightly damaging a painting by the former in the National Gallery, say.

Which happened to be a view of Delft, in fact.

Well, fame itself being basically relative in any case, of course.

An artist named Torrigiano having once been much more famous than many other artists, for no other reason than because he had broken Michelangelo's nose.

Well, or ask Vermeer.

And to tell the truth William Gaddis was less than extraordinarily famous himself, even though he wrote a novel called *The Recognitions* that any number of people spoke quite well of.

Doubtless I would have spoken quite well of it myself, had I read it, with what having gathered that it was a novel about a man who wore an alarm clock around his neck.

Although what I am now trying to recall is whether I may have asked William Gaddis if he himself were aware that there had been a painter named Taddeo Gaddi.

As I have suggested, certainly many people would not have been aware of that.

Then again, if one were named William Gaddis, doubtless one would have gone through life being aware of it.

As a matter of fact people had probably been driving William Gaddis to distraction for years, by asking him if he were aware that there had been a painter named Taddeo Gaddi.

Possibly I was sensible enough not to ask him.

In fact I hope I did not even ask him if he knew that Taddeo Gaddi had been a pupil of Giotto.

Well, doubtless I would not have asked him that, having not even known I remembered it until the instant in which I started to type that sentence.

And in any event the cat may not have climbed into William Gaddis's lap after all.

The more I think about it, the more I seem to remember that Rembrandt rarely went anywhere near strangers.

Even if he and William Gaddis would have remained equidistant from each other at all times, of course.

Well, as any other cat and any other person.

Or even as the cat I saw in the Colosseum and each of those cans of food I put out, also.

Even though there were as many cans as there must have been Romans watching the Christians, practically.

In fact each Christian and each lion would have always remained equidistant from each other, too.

Except when the lions had eaten the former, naturally.

Although I can now actually think of another exception to this rule, as well.

I myself and the cat which is presently scratching at my broken window again might both normally be presumed to be equidistant from each other, too.

Except when the tape happens to stop scratching, at which time there is no cat.

And surely one cannot be equidistant from something that does not exist, any more than something that does not exist can be equidistant from whatever it is supposed to be equidistant from either.

Or can any donkey see that?

It is easier to think about the cat as not existing than about Vincent as not doing so, incidentally.

And meanwhile for some reason I am extraordinarily pleased to have remembered that, about Taddeo Gaddi and Giotto.

Well, and it makes for an interesting connection from Cimabue to Giotto to Taddeo Gaddi, also.

Like the connection from Perugino to Raphael to Giulio Romano.

Even if I have perhaps not mentioned that Raphael had been a pupil of Perugino. Or for that matter that Perugino in turn had been a pupil of the Piero who did not hide under tables, which connects everything even farther than that.

In fact I have now suddenly solved the entire question as to whom Willem de Kooning was descended from.

Willem de Kooning was not descended from anybody. Willem de Kooning's teacher was.

Now heavens. Or should I perhaps give up troubling to correct such nonsense altogether, and simply let my language come out any way it insists upon?

In fact even before I just wrote that Willem de Kooning was not descended from anybody, which was obviously hardly what I meant, I happened to be thinking about *Les Troyens* again.

What I would have written about *Les Troyens,* if I had stopped to put that in, was that nobody ever pays attention to a word Cassandra says in the opera any more than they do in the plays.

√ Except that if nobody ever pays attention to a word Cassandra says, how can anybody know that nobody pays attention to her to begin with?

Now I suspect I have put that badly, as well.

Certain things can sometimes be almost impossible to put, however.

Once, when I was in the seventh grade, the teacher told us Archimedes's paradox about Achilles and the tortoise.

How the paradox went was that if Achilles was trying to catch the tortoise, but the tortoise had a head start, Achilles could never catch it.

This was because by the time Achilles had caught up the distance of the head start, the tortoise would have naturally gone another distance. And even though each new distance the tortoise could go would keep on getting smaller and smaller, Achilles would still always be that new distance behind.

Now I knew, knew, that Achilles could certainly catch that tortoise.

Even when Achilles was only the tiniest fraction behind, however, and the tortoise could go only the tiniest fraction past that, what the teacher showed on the blackboard was that there would still always be more fractions.

This finally almost made me want to cry.

So now I know that nobody ever pays attention to a word Cassandra says in the opera, but I also know, know, that the way I know it is by having paid attention.

Philosophy is not my trade.

And in fact it was not Archimedes who had the paradox but was Zeno.

Archimedes was killed by soldiers during some war at Syracuse while he was doing his geometry in the sand. With a stick.

Or have I now just done it all over again?

Oh, well, I suppose it is not one hundred percent impossible that Archimedes was killed with the same stick I was trying to say he was writing with.

I have not forgotten Willem de Kooning's teacher.

What I had meant to write about Willem de Kooning's

teacher, however, was not that I had suddenly realized whom he was descended from, but whom he was connected to.

As in the connection from Rembrandt to Carel Fabritius to Vermeer, this obviously is.

Except that what I am now thinking about is the person who was next in line, as a pupil of Vermeer. And then the person who was a pupil of the pupil of Vermeer.

And after that all the way down until the next to last pupil of a pupil had a pupil of his own named Willem de Kooning.

Surely this is much more likely than Willem de Kooning himself having been descended from the man who taught Claude Lorrain how to make pastry?

Ralph Hodgson was born fifteen years before Rupert Brooke, and was still alive almost fifty years after Brooke had died on the same island where Achilles had made one of the women pregnant.

And when Bertrand Russell was more than ninety years old, he could still remember hearing his grandfather talk about remembering the death of George Washington.

As a matter of fact, suppose one day when Willem de Kooning was a pupil, his teacher told him something.

Suppose this was something quite simple, even, such as that russet is not a name one gives to a color.

But also suppose that when Willem de Kooning's teacher said that, he was really repeating something he had been told when he himself was a pupil.

And suppose that the teacher who told it to Willem de Kooning's teacher had been told the same thing when he himself was a pupil.

And so on.

So who is to argue that one day Rembrandt might not have been standing next to Carel Fabritius's easel, and Carel Fabritius said he was going to paint something russet, and Rembrandt said that russet is a color one calls a bedspread?

So in a manner of speaking Willem de Kooning was actually

√ [148]

The imagination = put things together; takes things apart. n: remove signs, subtract signs, rearrange! change signs —

a pupil of Rembrandt.

This is scarcely to suggest that it was Willem de Kooning who painted the gold coins on the floor of Rembrandt's studio, of course.

Although who is to additionally argue that he might not have finished that quiz even more quickly than Carel Fabritius did?

Come to think about it, however, why is it not possible that all of this might go back even farther still?

Why couldn't it just as readily have been Cimabue who told Giotto about bedspreads, for instance, even long before Gilbert Stuart happened to mention it in passing to George Washington?

 This is scarcely to suggest that Willem de Kooning was anywhere in the vicinity when Giotto was drawing the perfect circle freehand either, of course.

Unless, on the other hand, I suddenly make up my mind to imagine that he was.

This very sort of imagining being the artist's privilege, obviously.

Well, it is what artists *do*.

There is a famous canvas in the National Gallery, of Penelope weaving, and nobody stopped the painter from putting everybody from Ithaca into clothes that people did not wear until practically three thousand years later, during the Renaissance.

In fact it was similarly Leonardo's own doing when he made the table in *The Last Supper* far too small for all of those Jewish people who are supposed to be eating at it.

Or Michelangelo's, when he took away superfluous material on his *David* but left the hands and feet too big.

I have now made up my mind to imagine Willem de Kooning in Giotto's studio.

In fact Giotto is wearing clothes from the Renaissance, but Willem de Kooning is in a kind of sweatshirt.

Actually I have just made the sweatshirt into a soccer shirt. With the word Savona across its front.

Giotto and Willem de Kooning are both equidistant from each other, naturally.

Well, and from the circle.

In fact all points on the circumference of the circle are equidistant from the center of the circle as well, as Zeno proved.

And now Cimabue and Rembrandt and Carel Fabritius and Jan Vermeer are in the studio also.

There is nothing astonishing in my ability to arrange any of this, of course, although in certain ways it is perhaps interesting.

What is especially interesting is that I do not have any idea what Giotto or Cimabue or Jan Vermeer look like.

In the case of Rembrandt and Carel Fabritius I have seen self-portraits. Even if it does not appear necessary for me to visualize which of the many of those on Rembrandt's part happens to apply at the moment.

Willem de Kooning is a special case as well, having once visited my loft.

As a matter of fact I have now put my russet cat into Giotto's studio, also.

Even if russet is traditionally not a name anybody present would give to a color.

I think I will put the cat that scratches at my broken window in, too.

Both cats are now in Giotto's studio.

I suspect I would prefer that Rembrandt not discover what the first of these cats is named, however.

Although in fact Willem de Kooning is aware of the name of that one.

I have no way of telling whether Willem de Kooning might mention to Rembrandt what that cat's name is.

Even though it is I who am imagining Willem de Kooning and Rembrandt in the same studio, I would appear not to have any control over this.

Then again it is quite possible that Willem de Kooning does not remember the cat's name in either case, it being some years since the cat may or may not have climbed into his or William Gaddis's lap.

Now Vincent Van Gogh is in Giotto's studio.

This would be Vincent Van Gogh the painter, naturally, since Vincent Van Gogh the cat is there already.

The newer Vincent's ear is bandaged.

I have just decided to put El Greco into the studio, as well.

Which is perhaps why everything now appears slightly elongated, or even astigmatic.

The number on the back of Willem de Kooning's soccer shirt would appear to be an eleven, however.

Unless it is a seventeen.

As a matter of fact Willem de Kooning now looks a good deal like Jackson Pollock.

I had also just thought to make Rembrandt bend over as if to pick something up from the floor, and to have Carel Fabritius find this extremely amusing, but I am not certain whether that happened.

Things are actually getting cluttered, to tell the truth.

Especially now that there are sheep.

Still, any one of these figures remains indisputably equidistant from any other.

Well, as I myself do from each, in turn.

Although perhaps I am not equidistant from a single one of them, come to think about it, since they are all only in my head.

Which would again be somewhat like the Christians after they had been eaten by the lions, doubtless.

Then again it is doubtless not like that at all.

Meanwhile the artist who painted the painting of this very house has just come into my head in place of all that, and in this instance I not only do not know what she looks like, but I do not even know her name.

For that matter her painting itself is now in my head as well, even though I have not given that a thought for a week or more.

The reason I have not given that a thought for a week or

more, as it happens, is because it is in the room with the life of Brahms, and the atlas, and to which the door is closed.

But which has therefore now brought the life of Brahms and the atlas into my head, likewise.

Although what I am next forced to wonder is what might happen if I were to decide that I have Brahms himself in my head.

Would it be the real Brahms, or the Brahms from the life of Brahms?

And which one of them wrote *The Alto Rhapsody,* then?

Or do I perhaps have no idea what on earth I mean by this distinction?

At least it has suddenly occurred to me that the Achilles from the seventh grade who could not catch the tortoise is the same Achilles I have been writing about for all of this time.

Well, it had simply not struck me that way before, is all.

Even if I now realize that this means the tortoise was faster than Hector was too, since Achilles did finally catch Hector, even though Hector ran and ran.

Then again, I doubt that the tortoise was the same tortoise that an eagle was said to have dropped on Aeschylus's bald head, which is how Aeschylus was said to have died.

There is an explanation for the eagle having done this, incidentally.

The explanation being that presumably the eagle wished to crack the shell of the tortoise, and believed that Aeschylus's bald head was a rock.

On my honor, it was said that this was how Aeschylus died.

When Aeschylus wrote about all of that bloody business in the bath with Agamemnon and Clytemnestra and the net, by the way, he put in a terribly sad part for while Cassandra is waiting to die herself.

What Cassandra thinks about is how lovely everything had been when she was a little girl, at Troy, and used to sit and play.

Beside the banks of the Scamander.

This being another sort of thing that artists do.

Then again Cassandra is not carried off to Greece at all, in *Les Troyens.*

What Berlioz does, instead, is have her kill herself, once Troy falls.

Perhaps Hector Berlioz was named after the same Hector also, come to think about it.

I do not remember anything in the opera about anybody lurking at windows, on the other hand.

Although it was Herodotus who wrote the line about the entire war having been because of a single Spartan girl, which I do believe I was trying to remember a good number of days ago.

Raphael and Giulio Romano were two more artists who painted versions of Helen being abducted, incidentally, just as Rubens and Van Dyck both painted versions of Achilles hiding among the women.

I find it interesting, when teachers and pupils do that.

Although Rubens was sometimes not very much happier about Van Dyck than Titian was about Tintoretto, actually.

Even if he did not kick Van Dyck out, what he did was always give him just faces to do, so that he himself could keep on being the best at the parts where everybody is always touching everybody else.

Rubens also spoke five languages, which I mention only because of having mentioned that Rembrandt could speak only one.

Have I said that I brought in an armful of red roses, earlier this morning?

Or that Utrillo actually painted certain canvases by copying scenes he found on picture postcards?

Meantime that question of things existing only in one's head may still be troubling me slightly, to tell the truth.

Basically this is because it has just now come to mind that the fire I am perhaps going to build at the garbage disposal area, in order to watch it glisten on the broken bottles, is something else that exists only in my head.

Except that in this case it is something that exists in my head even though I have not yet built the fire.

In fact it exists in my head even if I may possibly never build the fire.

Moreover, what is really in my head is not the fire either, but that painting by Van Gogh of the fire.

Which is to say the painting by Van Gogh that one can see if one squints just a little. With all of those swirls, as in *The Starry Night.*

And with anxiety in it, even.

Even if a certain amount of the anxiety may be simply over the likelihood that the painting will not sell, of course.

Although as a matter of fact what has now suddenly happened is that I am not actually seeing the painting itself, but am seeing a reproduction of the painting.

In addition to which the reproduction even has a caption, which says that the painting is called *The Broken Bottles.*

And is in the Uffizi.

Now obviously there is no painting by Van Gogh called *The Broken Bottles* in the Uffizi.

There is no painting by Van Gogh called *The Broken Bottles* anywhere, in fact, including even in my head, since as I have said what is in my head is only a reproduction of the painting.

I suspect I am getting mixed up.

All I had started to say, I think, is that I am seeing a painting that Van Gogh did not paint, and which has now become a reproduction of that painting, and which to begin with is of a fire that I myself have not built.

Although what I have entirely left out is that the painting is not actually of the fire either, but of a reflection of the fire.

So in other words what I am ultimately seeing is not only a painting which is not a real painting but is only a reproduction, but which is also a painting of a fire which is not a real fire but is only a reflection.

On top of which the reproduction is hardly a real reproduction itself, being only in my head, just as the reflection is not a real reflection for the same reason.

No wonder Cézanne once said that Van Gogh painted like a madman.

At this rate the next thing I am going to ask is if my roses will still be red after it gets dark.

On second thought I am not going to ask if my roses will still be red after it gets dark.

Or even if Cézanne ever happened to talk to anybody about Van Gogh personally, before he said that.

Which would naturally make his insight rather less than memorable, if he had.

I mean if Gauguin had taken Cézanne off into a corner somewhere and muttered a thing or two, for instance.

Or if Dostoievski did.

The dog which would not stay off Emily Brontë's bed was named Keeper, incidentally.

And the way Euripides was said to have died was by having been attacked by dogs, in fact, although I mention this only because of having mentioned Aeschylus and the eagle.

But what this reminds me of is that how Helen died, according to one old legend, was by being hanged from a tree, by jealous women.

Then again, another story insisted that she and Achilles became lovers, and lived forever on a magic island.

Although the identical story was sometimes told about Medea and Achilles.

Well, doubtless both of those stories arose because people were distressed at the notion of Achilles being left in Hades, as when Odysseus visits him there, in the *Odyssey.*

This does not occur until after Achilles is killed by Paris, of course, by being struck in the heel with an arrow.

In fact Paris himself has gone to Mount Ida to die by then, as well, because of still another arrow.

Even if one is forced to read books by people with names like

Dictys of Crete, or Dares the Phrygian, or Quintus from Smyrna, to learn such things, since the *Iliad* does not go that far.

I dropped the pages from those books into the fire after reading the reverse sides of each too, as I recall.

In the Louvre, this would have been, which is perhaps three bridges away from the Pont Neuf.

Once, that same winter, I signed a mirror. In one of the women's rooms, with a lipstick.

What I was signing was an image of myself, naturally.

Should anybody else have looked, where my signature would have been was under the other person's image, however.

Even in late spring, from the ruins at Hisarlik, one can still see snow on Paris's mountain.

There is a painting in the Louvre of Helen and Paris, by the way, by Jacques Louis David, which is perhaps the only convincing representation of Helen that I have ever seen.

As a matter of fact the painting itself is silly, since Helen has all her clothes on while Paris is wearing only sandals and a hat.

Still, there is a wistfulness in Helen's face, that suggests that she has been thinking about a good many things.

I am quite taken by the idea of Helen having been thinking about a good many things.

Doubtless I would never have signed that mirror had there been anybody else to look, on the other hand.

Though in fact the name I put down was Jeanne Hébuterne.

I am also still staining, incidentally.

At a guess, I would say it is nine or ten days, now.

I would appear to have been failing to indicate a good many more of the latter too, as it happens.

Even if that has nothing to do with the staining, which as I have said is scarcely unusual.

Any more than would be waiting for some months without getting my period at all.

Although I have had to go to the spring again, to wash fresh underpants.

Ah, me.

Naturally I did not wash fresh underpants. Naturally the underpants were not fresh until after I had washed them.

In either case I have also left everything outside once more, since there is always something pleasurable about changing into garments that are still warm from the sun.

Conversely I am not extraordinarily happy about this new habit of skipping days so frequently, to tell the truth, even if I am less than positive why.

Although possibly it has something to do with the question I was writing about yesterday.

By which I perhaps mean a day or two before yesterday.

Nor am I certain that I remember the question very clearly.

Or perhaps I did not define it that well.

Although doubtless all I have in mind is that if so many things would appear to exist only in my head, once I do sit here they then turn out to exist on these pages as well.

Presumably they exist on these pages.

If somebody were to look at these pages who could understand only Russian, I have no idea what would exist on these pages.

Not speaking one word of Russian myself, however, I believe I am able to state categorically that the things which had existed only in my head now also exist on these pages.

Well, some of such things.

One can hardly put down everything that exists in one's head.

Or even begin to be aware of it, obviously.

In fact I have no doubt that I have more than once written things that I did not even remember I remembered until I wrote them.

Well, I have commented on that.

Though as a matter of fact there are also certain things that one remembers while one is writing that one did not remember one remembered but does not happen to put down, either.

For instance when I was writing about the fact that Rembrandt and Spinoza had lived in Amsterdam at the same time, which I had learned from a footnote, I suddenly remembered from a different footnote entirely that when El Greco had lived in Toledo such people as St. Teresa and St. John of the Cross had lived there, too.

Even though I remembered that, however, I did not put it down.

Basically my reason for not doing so may have been because I do not know one solitary thing about either St. Teresa or St. John of the Cross.

Except obviously that they were both in Toledo when El Greco was in Toledo.

Although there is more to what I am talking about than this.

Still another person who lived in Toledo when El Greco lived in Toledo was Cervantes, except that I had a different sort of reason for not bringing up Cervantes just now when I brought up St. Teresa and St. John of the Cross.

When I brought up St. Teresa and St. John of the Cross it was because, as I said, I had thought about them in connection with El Greco at the time when I was thinking about Rembrandt in connection with Spinoza.

As I also said, however, the fact that El Greco may have known St. Teresa and St. John of the Cross was something I did not remember I remembered until the very moment in which I was writing what I wrote about Rembrandt and Spinoza.

The fact that El Greco may have also known Cervantes, on the other hand, is something I did not remember I remembered until all of these pages later, when I was finally writing what I had remembered but had not put down about El Greco earlier.

This is not really that complicated, although it may seem to be.

All it actually means is that even when one remembers something one did not remember one remembered, one may have still no more than scratched the surface in regard to things one does not remember one remembers.

Although as a matter of fact I believe I did remember Cervantes before too, even if in that case it may have only been in connection with that castle.

Then again, perhaps it was Don Quixote I remembered, what with the castle having been in La Mancha.

The title of the book about Don Quixote being *Don Quixote de La Mancha,* of course.

Anything that El Greco and Cervantes may have said to each other in Toledo would have been said in the same language as the title also, presumably.

Even if El Greco may have preferred Greek. Or whatever language they spoke on Crete, which was where he was actually from, in fact.

This is of course assuming that even if El Greco and Cervantes did not know each other very well, certainly they would have at least begun to nod in passing, after a time.

And naturally next to exchange amenities.

Buenos días, Cervantes.

Buenos días a usted, Theotocopoulos.

Well, and doubtless they would have exchanged similar amenities with St. Teresa and St. John of the Cross eventually, too.

Possibly all of this would have happened in some local shop or other, such as the neighborhood pharmacist's, say.

Even if one doubts that either of the latter two would have been called Saint yet, naturally.

Well, or that St. John of the Cross would have been called of the Cross by then, either.

Buenos días, Saint Teresa, or, *Buenos días,* John of the Cross, surely being a little clumsy for in a drugstore in either event.

Or for while waiting on line at the cigarette counter, certainly.

Still, all of these people always remaining just as equidistant from each of the others as everybody in Taddeo Gaddi's studio was, of course.

Except that they are now undeniably equidistant from me as well, because of being on these pages as opposed to being only in my head.

I think.

So that even if I were to unexpectedly think about somebody else I had not thought about for the longest time, such as, oh, Artemisia Gentileschi, let me say, the same rule would apply.

Although something I have also just incidentally realized is that I was probably wrong, a little while ago, when I said it was Zeno who had proved the other rule, about the hypotenuse of a circle.

Possibly it was Archimedes who proved that. Or Galileo.

Although what now more truthfully surprises me is that I could have written this many pages without having mentioned Artemisia Gentileschi to begin with.

Or that any woman artist could.

In fact Artemisia is perhaps the one person one would call Saint at a cigarette counter or anyplace else without feeling clumsy in the least.

So she was raped too, naturally.

At only fifteen.

But heavens, what a painter. In spite of what kind of a world she had to face, that many years ago.

Well, in spite of even having been tortured, to test her word, when the rape came to trial.

Although of course one of the popes made Galileo take back every word he had said, as well.

Meantime my period and I still remain no distance at all from each other, presumably.

Well, or the pain in my left shoulder and I, similarly.

Perhaps I have not mentioned the pain in my left shoulder.

I have mentioned it.

When I have done so up until now, however, it would have only been as one more thing I was remembering, since I had not actually felt it for quite some time, lately.

Which is to say it would have been still another instance of
something which existed only in my head or on the pages where
I was writing about it.

Although now it would appear to exist not only in both of
those places, but in my shoulder again also.

Even if I am perhaps somewhat perplexed as to how a pain
can exist in two other places as well as where it actually hurts.

One would appear to have just expended a great deal of effort
in verifying exactly that likelihood, however.

In either event I woke up with it this morning.

This can happen. It does not happen frequently, but it can
happen.

Basically, I believe that the pain is arthritic.

Then again, I have sometimes been tempted to connect it to
the afternoon on which I drove a Land Rover filled with picture
postcards into the Mediterranean, even though I did not believe
I had hurt myself badly at the time.

Many of the postcards in the Land Rover happened to show
reproductions of certain familiar paintings, by the way.

Mostly by Maurice Utrillo.

Somehow I have the feeling I would like to make a comment
about that, but whatever the comment is is eluding me.

Although on third thought the other question may be in no
way connected to my arthritis or to that incident near Savona
after all.

Or at least in this present instance.

I make that suggestion because it is quite possible that I
strained certain muscles, yesterday.

How I might have done that was by moving the rusted lawnmower, when I was downstairs in the basement.

Perhaps I have not mentioned having been downstairs in the
basement.

I was downstairs in the basement. Yesterday.

Naturally I did other things besides moving the rusted lawnmower. One would hardly go downstairs into a basement one

rarely otherwise goes into simply to move a rusted lawnmower.

Moving the lawnmower remains the most strenuous thing I did while I was down there, however.

I did not move any of the bicycles, or the hand truck.

I believe I have mentioned that there are several bicycles in the basement, as well as a hand truck.

There are also a number of baseballs, on a ledge.

I did not move any of the baseballs either, although I am quite certain one would have hardly injured one's shoulder in moving those.

In fact it was silly of me to have brought up not having moved the baseballs.

Then again, perhaps moving the lawnmower did not really have anything to do with anything, either.

The basement of this house is extremely damp, even at this time of year, as I have also perhaps mentioned.

One can smell the dampness, in fact.

And to tell the truth I was down there for quite some time.

So perhaps the pain is arthritic after all, and it was the dampness in the basement which aggravated this.

Although on yet another hand the whole business could have actually gotten started at the spring, when I was washing my underpants on the day before I ever even gave a thought to the basement.

In any case one generally feels wisest in enumerating all such possibilities where an injury is concerned.

Meanwhile the way one reaches the basement is down a sandy embankment at the rear of the house, which I do not remember if I have mentioned or not.

The reason I mention it now is that I would have been confronting that part of the house in returning from the spring, this doubtless having been what brought the basement into mind to begin with.

Even if I have confronted that identical part of the house any number of times without having thought to go down to the basement at all.

So that to tell the truth I have no real idea why I went down there yesterday either, when one comes right down to it.

What I did, after I did happen to get there, was to look at the eight or nine cartons of books.

What one does after having happened to get someplace often having very little to do with why one may have gotten there, however.

So that perhaps I had no reason whatsoever for having gone to the basement yesterday.

Although I do believe I have mentioned the eight or nine cartons of books.

These being the eight or nine cartons of books which have more than once perplexed me by being in the basement rather than in the house, especially since there is adequate room for them, up here.

In fact many of the shelves up here are half empty.

Although doubtless when I say they are half empty, I should really be saying they are half filled, since presumably they were totally empty before somebody half filled them.

Then again it is not impossible that they were once filled completely, becoming half empty only when somebody removed half of the books to the basement.

I find this second possibility less likely than the first, although it is not utterly beyond consideration.

In either event the present state of the shelves is even an explanation for why so many of the books in the house are so badly damaged.

Such as the life of Rupert Brooke, for instance. Or the poems of Anna Akhmatova, or of Marina Tsvetayeva.

Perhaps if there were more books on the shelves, so that so many of them were not standing askew, there would have been less opportunity for the sea air to have ruined as many as it has.

The person who left the additional books in the basement would not appear to have thought of this, however.

Still, perhaps there was some equally important reason for the additional books having been left there.

Perhaps it was my curiosity about this very reason which finally led me to go down to the basement yesterday to look at the eight or nine cartons after all, in fact.

Even if I did not actually look at the eight or nine cartons of books.

What I looked at was one of the eight or nine cartons.

Although as a matter of fact I have no idea why I keep on speaking about eight or nine cartons, either.

There are eleven cartons of books in the basement.

One being able to make this sort of incorrect estimate in many such situations, of course.

And which in fact will then remain in one's head for some time even when one knows better.

Well, as I have just been illustrating.

All of the books in the basement have their own peculiar odor of dampness, incidentally.

I have no idea how one would describe this, but it is an odor of dampness that is peculiar to books.

Or in any event this was undeniably the case with the books in the one carton I had opened before, which was the same one I opened again yesterday.

Possibly I have not mentioned having opened one of the cartons before.

One would scarcely be speaking about eleven cartons in the basement of a house on a beach as containing books without having opened at least one of the cartons to discover this, however.

As a matter of fact one should have doubtless opened all eleven of the cartons before speaking about them in that manner.

So I am still operating on the basis of very limited evidence, actually.

Although to tell the truth the entire question has never interested me very deeply.

In fact moving the rusted lawnmower to open even that same single carton again may have been little more than a way of passing my time, yesterday.

Once I had found myself downstairs in the basement with no reason whatsoever for finding myself there, as I have indicated.

Had I been in a different frame of mind I might have moved the baseballs after all.

And in which instance very likely my shoulder would not feel the way it does, either.

Actually I did look through the books this time, however, which I had not done on the other occasion when I had opened the carton.

Well, the other time I had not moved the lawnmower first in any event, so that it would have been difficult to look through the books even if I had wished to.

All I had wished to do on that occasion was to discover what the carton contained, however.

Yesterday I took the books out of the carton.

With only one exception, every single one of them was in a foreign language.

Most were in German, in fact, although not all.

The one book not in German or in another foreign language was an edition of *The Trojan Women,* by Euripides, which had been translated from Greek into English.

By Gilbert Murray.

I believe the person who had translated it was Gilbert Murray.

As a matter of fact I am not now certain I looked.

One finds that many of the Greek plays have been translated by Gilbert Murray, however.

In fact I suspect I have even once discussed this subject.

Then again it is perhaps surprising that I did not devote more attention to the translation after all, that being the only book from the carton that I would have been able to read one word of.

Although actually I can read Spanish, too.

Or perhaps I should say I was once able to read Spanish, not having tried to do so for years.

And to tell the truth I never read Spanish very well when I did read it.

Two of the books from the carton were in Spanish.

One of these was a translation of *The Way of All Flesh.*

In fact I did have a certain amount of difficulty in recognizing that one, come to think about it.

Basically, this was because the word *carne* was used in the title, and for some moments I kept thinking of *carne* as meaning meat.

Certainly *The Way of All Meat* did not seem like the sort of title that anybody would give to a book.

The difficulty persisted only until I noticed that the book had been written by Samuel Butler, however.

Naturally one would sincerely doubt that anybody one believed had already written one book called *The Way of All Flesh* would have then written another book called *The Way of All Meat.*

Or that the reverse of that statement would have been very likely true, either.

Still, I must admit that the confusion did briefly exist.

The other book in Spanish was not a translation, but had been written in that language. This was a volume of poems by Sor Juana Inés de la Cruz.

Well, Sor Juana Inés de la Cruz being still another person I suspect I have mentioned.

My reason for suspecting this is that Sor Juana Inés de la Cruz was Mexican, and I am quite positive I have spoken of having once lived in Mexico.

Living in Mexico one would naturally have become familiar with the names of certain Mexican poets, even if one did not read the language they wrote in very well.

If one does not read a language very well, one generally reads poetry in that language even less well than that, as a matter of fact.

Although I do believe I once did make an effort to read certain poems by Marco Antonio Montes de Oca, even if the chief reason I did so may have only been because of how taken I was with his name.

Certainly it has a memorable resonance, when one says it out loud.

Marco Antonio Montes de Oca.

Mountains of Goose being what the second half of it would curiously appear to mean, on the other hand.

Although Sor Juana Inés de la Cruz certainly has a resonance of its own.

Sor Juana Inés de la Cruz. Sister Juana Inés of the Cross being the translation here, obviously.

The sister part also making her a nun, of course. Even if I had not thought of the other connection until this very instant.

Which is to say the connection between Sor Juana Inés of the Cross and St. John of the Cross.

Well, possibly there is a connection. Then again, possibly all sorts of people who had something to do with the Catholic Church were called of the Cross, and it is no more than a coincidence that I have suddenly been thinking about two of them.

Doubtless if I were more interested in such matters I would have been thinking about any number of them.

For that matter I have no idea what I have been saying that has now made me think about Artemisia Gentileschi again, either.

Even if as I said a few pages ago I was surprised that I could have written as many pages as I already had without having thought about her long before that.

Well, Artemisia perhaps being the one person who, if one could have been positive of a life after death, almost any woman artist would have happily hanged herself to see.

Even if nobody had ever even taught her to read or write.

Or were the paintings themselves perhaps enough, if one was Artemisia?

That was a ridiculous question to have asked.

Still, it is perhaps an indication of how one feels about Artemisia Gentileschi.

Of the Brush.

Although for the life of me I now additionally have no idea why I have just remembered that Galileo was one more person who went blind.

In Galileo's case this would have been from looking at the sun too many times through his telescopes, or so it was said.

But so how in heaven's name has this in turn reminded me of that cracked old oblong of plate glass that I used to use as a pallet, all of those years ago in SoHo, and which before that had been the top of my aunt Esther's coffee table?

Or that they actually named a disease after one of those baseball players?

One would certainly give almost anything to understand how one's head sometimes manages to jump about the way it does.

Esther was from my father's side of the family, actually.

I have just made some souchong tea.

Before I came back to the typewriter I went upstairs and took the framed snapshot out of the drawer in the table beside my bed, for just a moment.

I did not put it back on the table itself, however.

There was no book by Marco Antonio Montes de Oca in the carton either, if I happen to have given that impression.

On the other hand there were no less than seven books by Martin Heidegger.

I have no way of indicating the titles of any of these, of course, short of returning to the basement and copying out the German, which it would certainly seem pointless to trouble myself with.

When I say it would seem pointless, naturally what I mean is that I would still not understand one word of the German in any event.

A word that certainly did catch my attention was the word

Dasein, however, since it seemed to appear on practically every page I opened to.

Martin Heidegger himself remaining somebody I know no more about than I know about Sor Juana Inés de la Cruz, on the other hand.

Except for now knowing that he was certainly partial to the word *Dasein,* obviously.

Then again as I believe I have said one is frequently apt to come upon a name such as Martin Heidegger's in one's reading, even if one is scarcely apt to be reading any books by Martin Heidegger himself.

At least this would presumably remain the case if one happened to ever do any reading, which as I have also said I have stopped doing.

In fact I cannot remember the last book I read, even if it may on occasion have appeared to have been a life of Brahms.

All things considered I still do not believe it has ever been verified that I did read a life of Brahms, however.

As a matter of fact it has only at this moment struck me that every solitary thing I know about Brahms could have been learned by reading the backs of the jackets on phonograph records.

Possibly I have not mentioned reading the backs of the jackets on phonograph records before.

It is a thing one does, however.

Well, or did, in any event, since it can now also be fairly definitely stated that I have not read the back of the jacket on a phonograph record for basically as many years as I have not read a book.

In fact there are no phonograph records in this house.

Well, there is no phonograph either, when one comes down to that.

Actually, this may have surprised me when I first came to the house, although it is not something to which I have given any thought since I perhaps first gave it some thought.

Well, as I have furthermore said, I have not played any music since having gotten rid of my baggage in any case, said baggage having naturally included such things as generators for operating such things as phonographs.

None of this is counting whatever music I hear in my head, conversely.

Well, or even in certain vehicles when I have turned on the ignition and it has happened that the tape deck has been set to the on position.

Hearing Kathleen Ferrier singing Vincenzo Bellini under either of those circumstances being hardly the same thing as making a deliberate decision to hear Kathleen Ferrier singing Vincenzo Bellini, obviously.

Although what I am now suddenly forced to wonder is if certain things I do know about Brahms would have appeared on the backs of the jackets on phonograph records after all.

Such as about his affairs with Jane Avril or with Katherine Hepburn, for instance.

Or for that matter how do I know that Beethoven would sometimes write music all over the walls of his house when he could not get his hands on any staff paper quickly enough?

Or that George Frederick Handel once threatened to throw a soprano out of a window because she refused to sing an aria the way he had written it?

Or that the first time Tchaikovsky ever conducted an orchestra he was positive that his head was going to fall off, and held on to his head with one hand through the entire performance?

Well, or on another level altogether, would anybody writing the information for any of such jackets have actually troubled to put down that Brahms was known for carrying candy in his pocket to give to children when he visited people who had children?

Certainly nobody writing such information would have put down that one of the children to whom Brahms now and again gave some of that candy might very well have been Ludwig Wittgenstein.

Perhaps I have not mentioned that one of the children to whom Brahms now and again gave some of that candy might very well have been Ludwig Wittgenstein.

On my honor, however, Brahms frequently visited at the home of the Wittgenstein family, in Vienna, when Ludwig Wittgenstein was a child.

So if it is a fact that Brahms was known for carrying candy in his pocket to give to children when he visited people who had children, then surely it is likely that Ludwig Wittgenstein was one of the children he gave candy to.

Very possibly this was what was in Wittgenstein's own mind all of those years later, in fact, when he said that you do not need a lot of money to give a nice present, but you do need a lot of time.

By which I mean that if the person Wittgenstein had wished to give a present to had been a child, he could have naturally taken care of the problem exactly the way Brahms generally did.

Doubtless one does not stroll about Cambridge carrying candy in one's pocket to give to Bertrand Russell or to Alfred North Whitehead, however.

Although what one might now wish one's self is that Wittgenstein had been in the basement with me yesterday, so as to have given me some help with that *Dasein.*

Well, or perhaps even with that other word, *bricolage,* that I woke up with in my head, that morning.

Or likewise with the whole sentence that I also must have said to myself a hundred times, a little later on, about the world being everything that is the case.

Surely if Wittgenstein was as intelligent as one was generally led to believe he ought to have been able to tell me if that had meant anything, either.

Then again, something else I once read about Wittgenstein

was that he used to think so hard that you could actually *see* him doing it.

And certainly I would have had no desire to put the man to that sort of trouble.

Although what this for some reason now reminds me of is that I do know one thing about Martin Heidegger after all.

I have no idea how I know it, to tell the truth, although doubtless it is from another one of those footnotes. What I know is that Martin Heidegger once owned a pair of boots that had actually belonged to Vincent Van Gogh, and used to put them on when he went for walks in the woods.

I have no doubt that this is a fact either, incidentally. Especially since it may have been Martin Heidegger who made the very statement I mentioned a long while ago, about anxiety being the fundamental mood of existence.

So that what he surely would have admired about Van Gogh to begin with would have been the way Van Gogh could make even a pair of boots seem to have anxiety in them.

Even if there was only the smallest likelihood that a pair of boots Van Gogh used to wear were the same pair he also once painted a painting of, obviously.

Unless of course he had painted with only his socks on, that day.

Or had borrowed a second pair of boots.

And on third thought it may have been Kierkegaard's boots that I was thinking about, and Van Gogh who had owned those.

Actually I rarely read footnotes.

Although doubtless it is also partly age, which will sometimes blur certain distinctions.

And by now there could well be a question of hormones too, and of change of life.

In fact the entire story may have had something to do with somebody sitting in one of Pascal's chairs.

And what I had really intended to have said by now was that I was familiar with the names of the writers on certain other of the books from the carton as well, besides the seven by Martin Heidegger.

Such as Johannes Keats, for instance.

Although there was also a translation of *Anna Karenina* in which case it was the title itself that I was able to recognize.

This simply being because the title in German appeared to be virtually identical with the title in English, as it happened.

But what I find interesting about this is that if the copy of that book had been the original book itself, and had not been translated, I would not have been able to make sense out of the title at all.

When one says that one does not read one word of Russian one is saying so even more truthfully than when one says that one does not read one word of German, obviously.

In spite of practically every other word in the latter looking like Brontë. Or Dürer.

Though there were also several items in the carton that I was not able to identify in any way whatsoever.

By which I mean that there were certain volumes on which I could not make sense out of the titles and did not recognize the names of the writers either.

Doubtless none of these was a book which had been translated from English, however, where I have the largest familiarity with writers, but had been written in German to begin with.

Which is scarcely to say that I am not familiar with certain German writers also, on the other hand.

Certainly I am familiar with Friedrich Nietzsche, for instance.

Well, or with Goethe.

Although by saying that I am familiar with either of these writers I do not necessarily mean that I am extraordinarily familiar with them.

As a matter of fact by saying that I am familiar with them I do not even necessarily mean that I have read a solitary word that either one of them ever wrote.

Actually the sum total of that familiarity may well extend no farther than to my reading of the backs of the jackets on phonograph records.

Such as the back of the jacket on *Thus Spake Zarathustra,* by Richard Strauss, for instance.

Or the back of the jacket on *The Alto Rhapsody.*

Possibly my including the back of the jacket on *The Alto Rhapsody* would appear to be less relevant than my including the back of the jacket on *Thus Spake Zarathustra.*

Certainly if I had never read the back of a jacket on *The Alto Rhapsody* I would not be familiar with the fact that what Brahms had based *The Alto Rhapsody* on was a poem by Goethe, however.

Neither am I forgetting *The Damnation of Faust,* by Berlioz, on the other hand.

Or Gounod's *Faust.*

Or Liszt's *Faust Symphony.*

Even if I am perhaps now showing off again.

In either event it was certainly not my intention to demean any German writers by remarking that I did not recognize their names.

Possibly any number of these writers were quite famous in Germany and the news had simply not reached me by the time I stopped reading.

Doubtless I would have heard of many of them within a few more years.

Then again, perhaps some of the writers whose books I took from the carton were not German writers after all. Quite possibly there were just as many French writers whose names I did not recognize. Or Italian writers.

In fact this could have been just as true of certain writers who wrote in Spanish.

Surely it is no more than chance that I had ever heard of Sor Juana Inés de la Cruz herself, actually. Or of Marco Antonio Montes de Oca.

Moreover even after having heard of them I might very well have forgotten about them again entirely, if their names had not had a certain resonance.

So perhaps it was not necessary for me to have apologized to any German writers after all.

Franz Liszt was one more person who was in the movie *Song of Love* with Bach and Clara Schumann, by the way.

I bring this up just in passing.

Well, or because of just having mentioned Liszt.

And Rainer Maria Rilke was another German writer I could have said I was similarly familiar with, had I wished.

Although what I am really still thinking about is how you could actually *see* Wittgenstein thinking, that way.

Even if thinking is what philosophers obviously *do,* on the other hand.

So quite possibly the lot of them were like that. Possibly every single philosopher from all the way back to Zeno used to walk around letting people see that they were thinking.

Possibly they even did this when they did not have a single thing more on their minds than the most inconsequential perplexities, as a matter of fact.

Not that inconsequential perplexities cannot now and again become the fundamental mood of existence too, of course.

Still, all I am suggesting is that quite possibly the only thing that Wittgenstein himself had on his mind when people believed he was thinking so hard may very well have been a seagull.

This would be the seagull which had come to his window each morning to be fed, that I am speaking about. One time when he lived near Galway Bay, in Ireland.

Possibly I have not mentioned that Wittgenstein had a pet seagull which came to his window each morning to be fed.

Or even that he ever lived in Ireland.

Or rather what occurs to me is that I may have said it was somebody else who had the pet seagull. And in another place altogether.

On my honor, it was Wittgenstein who had it. At Galway Bay.

Wittgenstein also played an instrument, incidentally.

And sometimes did some sculpture.

I enjoy knowing both of those things about Wittgenstein.

In fact I also enjoy knowing that he once worked as a gardener, in a monastery.

And inherited a good deal of money, but gave it all away.

In fact I believe I would have liked Wittgenstein.

Especially since what he did with the money, once he did decide to give it away, was to arrange to have it be used to help other writers who did not have any.

Such as Rainer Maria Rilke.

Actually, the next time I am in a town where there is a bookstore to let myself into, perhaps I will try to find something to read by Wittgenstein after all.

Galway Bay has a much lovelier sound when one says it out loud than when one merely looks at it on the page, by the way.

Well, doubtless it has no sound at all, when one merely looks at it on the page.

In fact even such words as Maria Callas do not have any sound when one is merely looking at them on the page, come to think about it.

Or *Lucia di Lammermoor.*

Hm. So what color were my red roses when I typed those words also, then?

In any case it had never crossed my mind that one might actually name a seagull before, I do not believe.

Galway Bay. Cádiz. Lake Como. Pamplona. Lesbos. Bordeaux.

Shostakovitch.

Oh, well. Meanwhile I have just been out to the dunes.

While I was peeing, I thought about Lawrence of Arabia.

This is scarcely to suggest that there is any particular connection between taking a pee and Lawrence of Arabia, however.

The reason I thought about Lawrence of Arabia, as a matter of fact, was simply because there was only one other book from the carton that I was able to recognize, and that happened to be a life of Lawrence of Arabia.

The reason I recognized that one, as it happened, was because the name Lawrence of Arabia had been kept in English in the title, in quotation marks.

Actually, I might have recognized it as a life of Lawrence of Arabia at any rate, since the book also contained several photographs of Lawrence of Arabia, but I had already made the assumption that it was a life of Lawrence of Arabia before noticing these.

Once I did notice the photographs I was delighted to accept this as a verification of my assumption, however.

Lawrence of Arabia did not look very much like Peter O'Toole, by the way, even though in some of the photographs he was dressed like Peter O'Toole.

This would be Peter O'Toole the way he was dressed in the film about Lawrence of Arabia, naturally.

I believe I have mentioned having seen Peter O'Toole in the film about Lawrence of Arabia.

Although on the other hand when I say that Lawrence of Arabia did not look very much like Peter O'Toole, I should perhaps also say that I am in no way certain of what Lawrence of Arabia actually looked like.

Granting, I have just said it was only yesterday that I saw certain photographs of Lawrence of Arabia.

Still, when I say that the photographs I saw yesterday were of Lawrence of Arabia, this itself may very well be no more than one additional assumption.

Naturally I could not make sense out of the captions that went along with the photographs.

What I was basically basing this assumption on, therefore, was the fact that the person in the photographs was dressed in some of them the way Peter O'Toole was dressed in the film about Lawrence of Arabia.

Nonetheless one is still forced to allow for the possibility that the photographs may not have been photographs of Lawrence of Arabia after all.

Or even that the book itself may not have been a life of Lawrence of Arabia.

One doubts that either of these possibilities would be particularly extreme, but they remain possibilities nonetheless.

Certainly with the remainder of the title and every single word in the actual book being in German, there is no denying that some small margin for error must continue to exist.

Even if on second thought every single word in the book was not actually in German.

In addition to Lawrence of Arabia's name, certain other names similarly appeared in English.

Although doubtless when one says that certain other names appeared in English, one is really only saying that in a manner of speaking.

Surely somebody who was reading the book in German would not stop on such occasions as when he came to the name Winston Churchill, say, or to the name T. E. Shaw, and say to himself, this book I am reading is in German but the names Winston Churchill and T. E. Shaw are in English.

Even if it is perhaps amusing to think of Winston Churchill as not being an English name.

Still, this is not basically a thing one does.

Any more than when I myself was reading a translation of a Greek play I did not stop on such occasions as when I came to the name Clytemnestra, say, or to Electra, and say to myself, this play I am reading is in Gilbert Murray but the names Clytemnestra and Electra are in Greek.

Even if on another level altogether that other name has had to begin to trouble me again, naturally.

Or at least to the extent that after having thought about somebody called T. E. Shaw this often I do wish that the man might have done something more that I knew about than simply having translated the *Odyssey*.

Although one can now safely assume he was in some way connected to Lawrence of Arabia also, of course.

Had his name appeared in any of the captions I might have at least had a look at him as well, even if that would have hardly eliminated the problem.

Each of the photographs was only of Lawrence of Arabia, however.

Still, it undeniably does remain an interesting coincidence to have been thinking about somebody one knows so little about and then to have noticed his name in a book not that long afterward, even if one has no way of making sense out of the book in which his name happened to be noticed.

And at least it would now appear fairly certain that he was not a baseball player, as I had perhaps once thought.

Certainly there was no connection between Lawrence of Arabia and baseball in the movie, at any rate.

All things considered, most likely T. E. Shaw was somebody Lawrence of Arabia once fought with in Arabia, which I do remember many scenes of in the movie.

Although when I say fought with, I should perhaps point out that I mean fought on the same side as, incidentally.

Frequently when one says that somebody fought with somebody one could just as readily mean that the person was fighting against that person, as it happens.

So that when Marlon Brando and Benito Juárez were in Mexico, for instance, as in another movie I once saw, one could say that one side was fighting with the other side and mean exactly the opposite from what one means when one says that T. E. Shaw most likely was somebody that Lawrence of Arabia was fighting with in Arabia.

For some curious reason one's meaning would generally appear to be understood in such cases, however.

Naturally Lawrence of Arabia would not have been called of

Arabia until some time after he had gotten to Arabia either, by the way.

And what has also only now struck me is that when one is reading certain translations in which what one keeps coming to is a name like Rodion Romanovitch, on the other hand, possibly one does stop and say that the name one has just come to is not an English name after all.

Well, or when the people who do the translations make use of peculiar spellings, as well. Such as for Klytaemnestra.

Or Elektra.

But in the meantime something I believe I may not have indicated, when I indicated that the life of Lawrence of Arabia was the only other book from the carton I was able to recognize, was that it was also the last book from the carton.

Why I find this worth pointing out, as it happens, is that when one says that a certain book was the last book from a carton, what one almost always happens to be saying at the same time is that it was also the first book to have been put into that carton.

And the reason for any particular book being the first book to have been put into a carton, generally, is because it also happens to have been the largest book among those being put in.

As a matter of fact this can practically be taken as a general rule. Almost categorically, if the other books are put into the carton before the largest book there will scarcely ever be any way to fit in the largest book when one finally gets to the largest book.

So what I actually ought to have said that I find worth pointing out is that I have never been able to understand this at all.

Surely there has got to be the identical amount of space in the carton no matter which way the books go in.

Just go try putting books into a carton without putting the largest book in first, however.

In fact now that I think about it, either Archimedes or Galileo may have once proved something quite extraordinary in regard to this, even if for some reason how they proved it was by putting books into a bathtub instead of into a carton.

Well, doubtless the reason they put the books into a bathtub was because their own edition of the life of Lawrence of Arabia would not fit into the carton at the end either, which would have been what led Archimedes or Galileo to do the experiment to begin with.

I have no idea any longer how much water one needs in the bathtub to conduct one's own version of this experiment, on the other hand.

Science generally being a subject one has a tendency to forget as one gets older, unfortunately.

Conversely, what I do only this tardily come to realize is why those eight or nine cartons of books must have been put into the basement after all, which I believe I have said is something else that has more than once perplexed me.

Almost certainly what must have happened was that nobody living in the house at the time was able to make any more sense out of most foreign languages than I myself am able to do now.

Now heavens, how weary I have gotten of looking at that word *Dasein* and having no idea what it means, one can surely imagine one of these people finally deciding.

Or, now heavens, how weary I have gotten of noticing that silly volume which appears to be called *The Way of All Meat*.

Downstairs they go, every last one of the troublesome things.

Granting that this would in no way explain why the translation of *The Trojan Women* happened to be included, although surely this can be dismissed as an oversight.

When one comes down to it there are easier things to do than filling eight or nine cartons with books.

Filling eleven cartons with books not being one of them, in fact.

But what this same assumption would meanwhile also appear to solve, as it happens, is that question as to whether the shelves in this house are to be thought of as being half empty or half filled, which one certainly finds it agreeable to be able to stop fretting over.

Even if what this next reminds me of, which I have not yet come to grips with at all, is the matter of the atlas.

Doubtless I have not even mentioned the atlas lately, to tell the truth.

Which is not to imply that I have not been thinking about the atlas, however.

The reason I have been thinking about it, basically, is because of the way in which the atlas has always had to lie on its side, which I suspect I did once point out was because of its being too tall for the shelves.

Now naturally, there would have always been people in this world who would have failed to make allowances for such taller books when they were building bookshelves.

But what I am actually getting at, here, is that this very same failure might also explain why there does not happen to be one solitary book about art in this house, which is still one further item I have mentioned being perplexed by.

Obviously, your ordinary book about art is quite tall.

So in fact who is to argue, now, that quite possibly there might not have once been just as many books about art on these shelves as there were books in foreign languages, until such time as somebody grew exactly as weary of having a house full of books that were forced to lie flat as he did of having a house full of books he was not able to read?

Downstairs they go, every last one of the troublesome things.

Which is to say that quite possibly there are just as many books about art in those cartons as there are books in German, and all I did was open the wrong one by which to be made aware of this.

As a matter of fact it is not even impossible that every solitary remaining book in that basement is a book about art.

Nor does the simple happenstance of my having found no such books in the one carton I did open in any way eliminate this possibility, surely.

As a matter of fact I could go back down there at this very instant and check.

Nor would I even be required to move the lawnmower again, come to think about it, what with not having put back the lawnmower once I did move it.

I have no intention whatsoever of going back down there to check.

At this very instant or at most likely any other.

And especially since I have still not even come close to resolving the question as to why I went down there yesterday to begin with.

Even if I did not go downstairs to the basement yesterday.

To tell the truth it has actually already gotten to be the day after tomorrow.

Or even more probably the day after that.

Moreover it is raining.

In fact it has been raining since the morning on which I threw out my red roses, which I did not put in either.

By either, of course, I mean also not having put in the days. Either.

Well, I believe it was some time ago that I indicated that I sometimes indicate them and I sometimes do not.

Possibly it began to rain on the day after the day after I went to the basement.

On the day before the day after the day after I went to the basement I was still typing.

I think.

In any case what I have also not put in is that the first day's rain broke a window.

Or rather it was the wind that did that, that night.

Such things can happen.

Oh, dear, the wind has just broken one of the windows in one of the rooms downstairs, having doubtless been all I thought.

This would have been right after I had heard the glass, naturally.

And while I was upstairs.

Actually, a certain amount of the rain is still coming in. Not much, any longer, but some.

Well, most of the wind actually died down again quite quickly, as it turned out.

So that now the whole notion of a warm steady rain is quite agreeable, even.

Even if I am finally convinced that the pain in my shoulder is arthritic after all.

The same thing would hold true for the pain in my ankle, presumably.

Possibly I have not mentioned my ankle in some time.

This would be the ankle I broke when I unexpectedly got my period in the middle of carrying a nine-foot canvas up the main central staircase in the Hermitage and fell, that I am talking about.

Then again the ankle may not have been broken but merely sprained.

The next morning it was swollen to twice its normal size nonetheless.

One moment I had been halfway up the stairs, and a moment after that I was making believe I was Icarus.

In fact very probably it would have been a wind which caused that too, since there were similarly all sorts of broken windows in the museum on its own part, by then.

Although what I had actually just done was shift the way in which I was standing, naturally, so as to close my thighs.

Forgetting for the same instant that I was carrying forty-five square feet of canvas, on stretchers, up a stone stairway.

And naturally all of this had occurred with what seemed no warning whatsoever, either.

Although doubtless I had been feeling out of sorts for some days, which I would have invariably laid to other causes.

At any rate it is that ankle that I mean.

And outside of which I would most likely not mind the rain in the least, as I started to say.

With the exception of missing my sunsets, perhaps.

Although what I have basically been doing about the rain is ignoring it, to tell the truth.

How I do that is by walking in it.

I did not fail to notice that those last two sentences must certainly look like a contradiction, by the way.

Even if they are no such thing.

One can very agreeably ignore a rain by walking in it.

In fact it is when one allows a rain to prevent one from walking in it that one is failing to ignore it.

Surely by saying, dear me, I will get soaked through and through if I walk in this rain, for instance, one is in no way ignoring that rain.

Then again, doubtless it is rather easier to ignore it in my own particular manner of doing so if one happens to have no clothes on at the time.

Well, or no more than underpants.

Although as a matter of fact I stepped out of those on the front deck each time I decided to walk, also.

Well, doubtless I had already gotten soaked while I was out there deciding about the walk in either case.

So that by then it would have scarcely made any difference whether I kept on my underpants or not.

Although what I am more likely admitting by all this is that I may very well have been coincidentally aware of needing a bath, as well. Or at least on the first of those occasions.

Normally I bathe at the spring, of course. Well, or summers as now, in any case.

Oh. And I have finally stopped staining, incidentally, which had begun to look like forever.

And in either event it was actually an amusing diversion, soaping myself and then walking that way until I was rinsed.

Even if for a minute I believed I had lost my stick while I was at it.

When I looked back there it was, however, standing upright.

Which is to say that the stick was already not lost even before I had begun to worry that it might be.

So to speak.

Not that there would have been any point in trying to write anything with it in the rain to begin with, on the other hand.

Well, not that anything I ever write is still there when I go back in any case.

Then again, perhaps it might have been interesting to see one's messages beginning to deteriorate even before they were finished being written after all.

Like Leonardo da Vinci doing *The Last Supper*, one might have felt.

Well, one rather doubts that one would have felt quite like Leonardo.

Even by writing left-handed.

Or backwards, so that one would have needed a mirror to read it.

Meaning that the image of what one was writing would have been more real than the writing itself.

So to speak.

Have I ever mentioned that Michelangelo practically never took a bath in his life, by the way?

And even wore his boots to bed?

On my honor, it is a well known item in the history of art that Michelangelo was not somebody one would particularly wish to sit too close to.

Which on second thought could very well change one's view as to why all of those Medici kept telling him don't bother to get up, as a matter of fact.

Although come to think about it even William Shakespeare himself was terribly tiny, which is something I did once mention.

I mean so long as one would appear to be getting into this sort of thing.

Well, and for that matter Galileo would never even ever

shake another person's hand, once he had discovered germs.

Not that a solitary other soul would believe that there were such things, of course. Even though Galileo kept insisting he had seen them.

In some water, I believe this was.

And they move, too, Galileo kept telling people.

Which became just as significant a moment in the history of science as Michelangelo not going near water at all became in the history of art, in fact.

I do not remember any longer if the water in which Galileo found the germs was the same water in which he had proved that the life of Lawrence of Arabia had to be put in first, on the other hand.

And on later thought it may have been Louis Pasteur who would never shake anybody's hand.

Or Leeuwenhoek.

What I find interesting about the possibility that it might have been Leeuwenhoek, actually, is that Leeuwenhoek was from Delft.

So that one of the people he would have refused to shake hands with would have almost assuredly been Jan Vermeer.

Unfortunately the same footnote that brought up Leeuwenhoek in connection with Delft gave no indication as to whether Vermeer might have taken this as a slight, however.

Well, or as to how Carel Fabritius may have felt about it, either.

Emily Brontë once painted a quite effective watercolor of Keeper which I have actually seen a reproduction of, incidentally, even if I have no idea what I have been saying that has now made me remember this.

Any more than I have any idea what has also now made me remember that Pascal invented the first adding machine.

Or how I even know that he did.

There goes my head again in that way that it sometimes does, doubtless being the only explanation here as usual.

Although one of my sunsets just before the rain was finally another Joseph Mallord William Turner, actually.

Even if what this next reminds me of is that one more thing that John Ruskin became famous for, besides the other thing I have already told about that he became famous for, was watching sunsets himself.

Although the real reason I remember this about John Ruskin is because he actually gave his butler instructions to remind him when it was time to look.

On my honor, John Ruskin once told his butler to announce the sunsets.

The sunset, Mr. Ruskin, being what the butler would say.

Even if something different that has just struck me is that I myself would appear to be saying on my honor extraordinarily frequently, of late.

Every single time I have said it it was only because what I had been talking about was the gospel truth, however.

Such as about Mrs. Ruskin not turning out to have had certain superfluous material taken away by somebody like Phidias, for instance.

Even if for the life of me I still cannot remember what I had been trying to get that monstrosity of a canvas up that stairway for, on the other hand.

Or whatever became of my pistol either, to tell the truth.

The pistol being the one with which I had shot holes into one of the skylights in the museum so that the smoke from my chimney would go out, obviously.

Well, I have just mentioned this. Or perhaps it was only certain additional broken windows that I mentioned.

Nonetheless the last place I would seem to remember still carrying the pistol in was Rome, for some reason.

Well, on the afternoon when I ran into that alley, in fact, which was actually a cul-de-sac. On a street full of taverns below the Borghese Gallery, at the intersection of Calpurnia Avenue and Herodotus Road.

After seeing my own reflection, highlighted against a small stretched canvas coated with gesso in the window of a shop selling artists' supplies, as I had passed.

Still, how I nearly felt, in the midst of all that looking.

Looking in desperation, as I have said.

But too, never knowing just whom one might find, as well.

Although as a matter of fact it may very well have been Cassandra I had intended to paint, on those forty-five square feet.

Or should I have spelled that Kassandra, perhaps?

Even if a part I have always liked is when Orestes finally comes back, after so many years, and Electra does not recognize her own brother.

What do you want, strange man? I believe this is what Electra says to him.

Although it is the back of the jacket on a recording of the opera that I am thinking about now, I suspect.

Well, or because of imagining that somebody may have actually called one's own name, do I possibly mean?

You? Can that be you? And here, of all places?

It was only the Piazza Navona, I am quite certain, so beautiful in the afternoon sun, that had touched a chord.

Still, not until dusk did I emerge from the cul-de-sac.

In Italy, no less, from where all painting came.

So why would I now suddenly be thinking about certain murals by David Alfaro Siquieros, of all people?

And to tell the truth I also have no idea whatever became of my thirty silent radios either, actually, that I once listened to and listened to.

Poor Electra. To wish to murder one's own mother.

Yet everybody, in those stories. Wrist deep in it, the lot of them.

Doubtless the radios are still in my old loft in SoHo, as a matter of fact.

Still. So where are my seventeen wristwatches, then?

It did run on, that madness.

Walking in the rain I have not gone much farther than to where one can see the toilet fastened to pipes on the second floor in the house where I knocked over the kerosene lamp, incidentally.

Even if there is no second floor.

Although what I am really remembering about that ankle now is how astonishingly adept I became at maneuvering my wheelchair, once I had located one.

Skittering from one end of the main floor to the other, in fact, when the mood took me.

From the Buddhist and Hindu antiquities to the Byzantine, or whoosh! and here we go round the icons of Andrei Roublev.

But which in turn now makes me wonder that if I am presently hurting in two places at once, as I undeniably am, would this then mean that I am actually hurting in four?

Except that I have now completely forgotten what the other two places are that I might have meant, unfortunately.

Andrei Roublev was a pupil of Theophanes the Greek, by the way. In fact he was also a sort of Russian Giotto.

Well, perhaps he was not a Giotto. Being the first great Russian painter nonetheless, having perhaps been all one meant.

And Herodotus was almost always spoken about as having been the first person ever to write down any real history, incidentally.

Even if I am not especially overjoyed at being the last.

As a matter of fact I am quite sorry I said that.

Such thoughts again being exactly the sort one would have wished to believe one had gotten rid of with the rest of one's baggage, naturally.

Oh, well. One can be thankful that they have been coming up only rarely these days, at least.

Have I ever said that Turner once actually had himself lashed to the mast of a ship, to be able to later do a painting of a storm?

Which has never failed to remind me of the scene in which
Odysseus does the identical thing, of course, so that he can
listen to the Sirens singing but will stay put.

But now good heavens.

Here I sit, and it is only after all this time that I have remembered the most significant thing I had meant to say about the
basement once I had started to say anything at all about the
basement.

The person who wrote that book about baseball did not make
any sort of ridiculous error in its title after all, as it turns out.

On my honor, there is a separate carton in the basement
which contains absolutely nothing except grass that is not real.

Artificial grass being something I had never even heard of
before, I would swear. So that doubtless I would have scarcely
been able to imagine what it was down there at all, if the carton
had not had a label.

Then again, if the carton had not had a label, unquestionably
I still would have been struck by the manner in which what was
inside of it certainly did look like grass.

The things one tardily becomes aware of.

Even if the whole notion actually saddens me now that I do
know about it, to tell the truth.

Grass being simply supposed to be grass, is all.

Well, or quite possibly the book itself is a sad book, and for
this identical reason, which would have been a point that I
missed until now completely, of course.

In fact quite possibly even those people Campy or Stan
Usual may have been sad too, if somebody once told them they
would have to stop playing their game on real grass.

Although surely even people who played baseball must have
had more important things than that to worry about, or one
would certainly wish to imagine that they did.

Certainly the one they named the disease after must have had
more important things to worry about.

The instrument that Ludwig Wittgenstein used to play was a

clarinet, by the way.

Which for some curious reason he carried in an old sock, rather than in a case.

So that anybody seeing him walk down the street with it might have thought, there goes that person carrying an old sock.

Having no idea whatsoever that Mozart could come out of it.

Doubtless A. E. Housman thought he was just somebody carrying an old sock, in fact, on the afternoon when Wittgenstein found himself with diarrhea and asked if he could use the toilet, and A. E. Housman said no.

On my honor, Wittgenstein once needed a toilet in a considerable hurry, near some rooms at Cambridge that were Housman's, and Housman would not let him in.

Actually the composer who most often came out of the sock would have probably been Franz Schubert, having been Wittgenstein's favorite.

Even if I have no idea why this reminds me that Brahms's friends were frequently embarrassed because prostitutes would call hello to him when they passed.

Or, for heaven's sake, that Gauguin was once arrested for urinating in public.

Or that Abraham Lincoln and Walt Whitman often used to nod to each other while walking the streets in Washington, D.C., during the Civil War.

Presumably this last will at least make it seem less improbable that people like El Greco and Spinoza did exactly the same thing, at any rate.

If hardly in Washington, D.C.

Clara Schumann actually visited the Wittgenstein home in Vienna with Brahms on occasion also, incidentally, if I have not made that clear.

And which was perhaps an additional reason for Brahms wishing that children would go away.

Whereas Schubert was one more person who had syphilis, unfortunately. This being an explanation for why he never finished the *Unfinished Symphony,* as a matter of fact, having died at thirty-one.

And Handel can be put on the list of people who went blind, I think.

But who was somebody named Karen Silkwood, whom I suddenly also feel I would like to tell that you can now kneel and drink at the Danube, or the Potomac, or the Allegheny?

And why do I only at this instant realize that Leningrad was still called St. Petersburg when Shostakovitch was born there?

I have just wrapped my head into a towel.

Having gone out for some greens, for a wet salad, this would be because of.

And in the meantime the more I have thought about it, the more sorry I have gotten about what I said.

I mean about Michelangelo, not about Herodotus.

Certainly I would have found it more than agreeable to shake Michelangelo's hand, no matter how the pope or Louis Pasteur might have felt about this.

In fact I would have been excited just to *see* the hand that had taken away superfluous material in the way that Michelangelo had taken it away.

Actually, I would have been pleased to tell Michelangelo how fond I am of his sentence that I once underlined, too.

Perhaps I have not mentioned having once underlined a sentence by Michelangelo.

I once underlined a sentence by Michelangelo.

This was a sentence that Michelangelo once wrote in a letter, when he had lived almost seventy-five years.

You will say that I am old and mad, was what Michelangelo wrote, but I answer that there is no better way of being sane and free from anxiety than by being mad.

On my honor, Michelangelo once wrote that.

As a matter of fact I am next to positive I would have liked Michelangelo.

I am still feeling the typewriter, naturally. And hearing the keys.

Hm. I would seem to have left something out, just then.

Oh. All I had meant to write was that I had just closed my eyes, obviously.

There is an explanation for my having decided to do that.

The explanation being that I would appear to be more upset about that carton of grass that is not real than I had realized.

By which I imagine what I mean is that if the grass that is not real is real, as it undoubtedly is, what would be the difference between the way grass that is not real is real and the way real grass is real, then?

For that matter what city was Dmitri Shostakovitch born in?

A certain amount of this sort of thing can actually sometimes almost begin to worry me, to tell the truth.

Even if there would appear to be no record as to what name Wittgenstein ever did pick out for that seagull, on the other hand.

Well, my reason for bringing this up again being because it was a seagull that brought me to this very beach, as it happens.

High, high, against the clouds, little more than a speck, but then swooping in the direction of the sea.

Except that the seagull was in no way a real seagull either, of course, being only ash.

Have I mentioned looking in Savona, New York, ever? Or in Cambridge, Massachusetts?

And that in Florence I did not let myself into the Uffizi immediately, but lived for a period in a hotel they had named after Fra Filippo Lippi, instead?

What I write with my stick are not necessarily always messages, by the way.

Once I wrote Helen of Troy, in Greek.

Well, or in what looked like Greek, although I was actually only inventing that.

Even if Helen of Troy would have been only an invented name in real Greek too, come to think about it, since it is assuredly doubtful that anybody would have been calling her that at the time.

I have decided to hide among some women so that I do not have to go and fight over Helen of Troy. That hardly being the manner in which one imagines that Achilles would have thought about such things, for instance.

Or, I have decided to make believe I am mad and sow salt into my fields so that I do not have to go and fight over Helen of Troy. That hardly being the manner in which one imagines that Odysseus would have thought about them, either.

Moreover everybody would have doubtless been too accustomed to calling her of Sparta to have troubled with changing in any event.

Even after they had sailed to Troy in the one thousand, one hundred and eighty-six ships.

Which is how many ships it says in Homer that the Greeks sailed to Troy in, incidentally.

Even if one is personally next to positive that there would have been no way in the world that the Greeks could have sailed in one thousand, one hundred and eighty-six ships.

Doubtless the Greeks had twenty or thirty ships.

Well, as I believe I have mentioned, the whole of Troy being like little more than your ordinary city block and a few stories in height, practically.

No matter how extraordinary one may find it that young men died there in a war that long ago and then died in the same place three thousand years after that.

Although what one doubts even more sincerely is that Helen would have been the cause of that war to begin with, of course.

After all, a single Spartan girl, as Walt Whitman once called her.

Even if in *The Trojan Women* Euripides does let everybody be furious at Helen.

In the *Odyssey,* where she has a splendid radiant dignity, nothing of that sort is hinted at at all.

And even in the *Iliad,* when the war is still going on, she is generally treated with respect.

So unquestionably it was only later that people decided it had been Helen's fault.

Well, Euripides of course coming much later than Homer on his own part, for instance.

I do not remember how much later, but much later.

As a matter of fact it was as much later as twice the time between now and when Bertrand Russell's grandfather met George Washington, approximately.

And certainly any number of things can be lost track of, in that many years.

So that once he had gotten the idea to write a play about the war, certainly it would have been necessary for Euripides to think up an interesting reason for the war.

Not knowing that the real reason must surely have been to see who would pay tariff to whom, so as to be able to make use of a channel of water, as I have indicated.

Although on the other hand it is also quite possible that Euripides just lied.

Quite possibly Euripides knew perfectly well about the real reason for the war, but decided that in a play Helen would be a more interesting reason.

Certainly writers must have now and again done this sort of thing, one would imagine.

So that when one comes right down to it, it is equally possible that Homer just lied, too.

Quite possibly Homer knew perfectly well himself about the real number of ships, but decided that in a poem one thousand, one hundred and eighty-six would be a more interesting number, as well.

Well, as it undeniably is, as is verified by the very fact that I remember it.

Doubtless if I had underlined only twenty or thirty ships when I was tearing pages out of the *Iliad* and dropping them into a fire I would not have remembered that at all.

In fact if Homer had said there were only twenty or thirty

ships doubtless I would not have underlined any numbers to begin with.

Which is to say that perhaps certain writers are sometimes smarter than one thinks.

Then again, Rainer Maria Rilke once wrote a novel called *The Recognitions,* about a man who wears an alarm clock around his neck, which seems less like a lie than just a foolish subject for a book altogether.

Except that in this instance I remember it without even having ever read *The Recognitions.*

And which furthermore now makes me realize that if Euripides had not blamed Helen for the war very possibly I would not remember Helen, either.

So that doubtless it was quite hasty of me, to criticize Rainer Maria Rilke or Euripides.

Even if on third thought what one is only now forced to suspect is that there could have been still a different reason entirely, for the wrong number of ships in the *Iliad.*

Which is to say that since Homer did not know how to write, very possibly he did not know how to add, either.

Especially since Pascal had not even been born, yet.

But be all that as it may, what it also occurs to me to mention here is that I am frequently just as annoyed at how Clytemnestra is blamed for certain things as I am about Helen, to tell the truth.

This would be in regard to when Clytemnestra stabs Agamemnon in his bath once he comes home from the same war, of course.

Needing some assistance. But nonetheless.

Although what I am really saying is why in heaven's name wouldn't she have?

Well, after the way Agamemnon had sacrificed their own daughter to raise wind for those identical ships, I naturally mean.

God, the things men used to do.

Kings and generals especially, even if that is hardly any excuse.

But what also just so happens is that I have sailed from Greece to Troy myself, actually.

Well, or vice versa. But the point being that even with a page torn out of an atlas, instead of maritime charts, the entire trip took me only two unhurried days.

In spite of having been frightened half to death by that ketch, near Lesbos, with its spinnaker taking noisy wind, even.

But which in either case still scarcely comes close to making it a distance that calls for the sacrifice of anybody over, obviously.

Let alone one's own child.

And which is additionally not even to bring up the question as to what possible difference a day or two's extra sailing might make in any event, if your silly war is about to last for ten full years.

But then to top it off there stands the man with a concubine in tow when he finally gets back too, no less.

And yet the way the plays are written, even Electra and Orestes somehow manage to get furious at Clytemnestra for finding the sum of this a bit much.

Again one may be foolhardy for criticizing famous writers, but certainly it does seem that somebody ought to draw the line someplace.

Daddy murdered our sister to raise wind for his silly ships, being what any person in her right mind must surely imagine that Electra and Orestes would have thought.

Mommy murdered our daddy, being all that they think in the plays instead.

Moreover in this case there are plays by Aeschylus and Sophocles as well, even before Euripides.

Nonetheless one is still categorically forced to believe that Electra and Orestes would have never felt that way in the least.

In fact what I have more than once suspected is that the

whole story about the two of them taking their own revenge on Clytemnestra was another lie altogether. More than likely all three of them together would have felt nothing except good riddance.

Or certainly once the bathroom had been cleaned up.

And then lived happily together ever after, even.

So that as a matter of fact what I have furthermore even suspected is that Clytemnestra would have hardly been that much upset about the notion of the concubine after all, or at least once she had gotten the more basic matters off her chest.

Well, or after she had also found out that the concubine happened to be only poor Cassandra, assuredly.

In one of the plays, Clytemnestra kills Cassandra at the same time that she kills Agamemnon.

Surely in real life she would have immediately understood that Cassandra was mad, however, and so would have doubtless had second thoughts on this basis alone.

How she would have immediately understood that would have been the minute Cassandra went into the house and started lurking at windows, naturally.

Although when I say house, I should really be saying palace, of course.

Oh, dear, the way in which that poor child keeps lurking at our palace windows, surely being what Clytemnestra would have had to think.

So that very possibly her next decision would have even been to allow Cassandra to stay on, as a sort of boarder, after the funeral.

Certainly the poor child has no more palace windows back home in what is left of Troy to go lurk at, being another thing she would have obviously had to realize.

For that matter Clytemnestra would have almost certainly learned that Cassandra had been raped, as well, which would unquestionably strengthen this entire probability.

As a matter of fact what I would now be perfectly willing to wager is not only that Clytemnestra and Electra and Orestes lived happily together ever after, but that Cassandra eventually even came to be thought of as one of the family herself.

Moreover I can even further imagine all four of them happily traipsing off now and again to visit Helen, once all of this had been settled.

Surely Clytemnestra would have wished to see her own sister after that same ten years in any event. But what I am only now also remembering is that here is Cassandra being an old friend of Helen's on her own part.

Well, Cassandra having been Paris's sister, of course.

Which is to say that once Helen had gotten to Troy the two of them would have become sisters-in-law, practically.

One says practically because of Helen still having been rather more officially married to Menelaus, naturally.

But still, ten years being ten years in this case, too. So that undeniably Cassandra would have been delighted to renew the relationship.

Good morning, children and Cassandra. Guess what I have been thinking about. How would everybody like to take a little trip to Sparta, to visit Aunt Helen?

Oh let's, indeed! What an agreeable idea, Clytemnestra!

Will Uncle Menelaus be there too, Mommy?

Oops.

One had been forgetting that part, obviously.

Which is to say that after having fought an entire war to get his wife back, doubtless Menelaus would have been less than overjoyed at a sister of the man she had run off with turning up as a house guest.

When I say house, I should again be saying palace, of course.

Then again, what one next imagines is that doubtless Helen would have nagged a little, if necessary.

Oh, now darling, what possible harm can there be in letting her have a window or two, to lurk at?

Well, and most probably Cassandra would have brought

gifts also, to smooth things over.

Trojans having been known for bearing gifts whenever they went anyplace in either case.

Actually, a cat would have been thoughtful. Even if a cat would have perhaps been more appropriate as a gift for Helen, rather than for Menelaus.

I cannot remember if there is anything in the *Odyssey* about Helen having a cat, however.

I say the *Odyssey* rather than the *Iliad* because of the *Iliad* having been over before Cassandra would have brought the animal, naturally.

But which again incidentally verifies that Gustave Flaubert was wrong about a woman having written that book, since surely a woman writing it would have thought to put Helen's cat in.

In fact what does happen to be put in is a dog, belonging to Odysseus.

Actually, the part about the dog is sad, it being the dog who is the first to recognize Odysseus when he returns to Ithaca after having been gone for ten extra years after Troy but then dies.

Ah, me. At least it would appear to have been some pages since the last time I did that.

Or at least noticed that I did.

What I meant was hardly that it is Odysseus who dies after returning to Ithaca, obviously. Obviously it is the dog who dies after recognizing him.

On the other hand Penelope does not recognize Odysseus at all, incidentally.

And which is surely additional proof about a woman not having written that part, either.

Well, surely if a wife had been dutifully avoiding any number of suitors for twenty full years while waiting for her husband to come home she ought to have recognized the husband when he got there.

Although it is the reverse of that statement which is more likely true, actually.

Which is to say that if a woman had written that part one sincerely doubts that the wife would have been avoiding the suitors for all of the twenty years to begin with.

I believe I have voiced such doubts about Penelope before, as a matter of fact.

After all.

Although come to think about it Penelope may very well have not spent the entire twenty years at Ithaca in either case.

Or surely would have at least gone so far as to visit Helen in Sparta herself, being a cousin.

This again being once that everybody had gotten home, naturally.

So that her own visit would have been basically to pick up some news, really.

Yes, yes, it is agreeable to see you again, too, Cousin Helen. But what I am more truthfully curious about is if anybody has heard anything of that husband of mine?

In fact it is this identical visit that her son Telemachus makes in the *Odyssey* itself, come to think about it, asking about his father.

And which is moreover the very scene in which Helen is shown to have that splendid radiant dignity.

But be that as it may, and even if she had no news whatsoever about Odysseus, Helen would have nonetheless had all sorts of other interesting items to report, unquestionably.

Well, and with Ithaca being an island, especially, so that anybody coming from there would have frequently been out of touch altogether.

Heavens above, Penelope. Do you honestly mean to tell me you have not even heard about my brother-in-law and the bathtub, yet?

Then again, for all one knows Penelope's visit might very well have coincided with Clytemnestra's own. Or certainly if Helen had ever invited the whole family at once, say, for some holiday or other, this could have easily been the case.

And in which instance most likely it would have been Clytemnestra who told Penelope about all that herself, then.

Even if she would have doubtless been discreet enough to leave out certain parts until Electra and Orestes had left the table, one imagines.

You don't *mean* it? And with a *net,* first? Now three cheers for you, Cousin Cly.

Oops.

One had been forgetting something here too, obviously.

Which is to say that doubtless Clytemnestra would not have uttered one solitary word until Menelaus had left the table, likewise.

If for that matter Menelaus would have ever let her sit down to begin with.

Menelaus having been Agamemnon's brother, of course.

Certain of these connections do get complicated enough to slip one's mind like this, unfortunately.

But it does remain a fact that the two brothers had married the two sisters.

And which would now appear to indicate that poor Electra and Orestes would not have gotten to visit their aunt that often after all.

Now see here, Helen. Winter solstice or not, certainly it is pushing things a bit far to expect me to allow that woman to set foot into this palace.

Oh, but Menelaus, darling.

Don't oh darling me. Not about this, you won't.

Even if none of this would have precluded Penelope's own visit in any way whatsoever, on the other hand.

So that what one is now naturally forced to suspect is that very likely it was the latter who gave Helen the cat, rather than Cassandra who did.

Well, and doubtless it would have been exactly like Penelope to think of an animal in any event, what with being so accustomed to a dog at home.

Although in fact she had a cat, too. Even if what I had almost been about to forget next is that there is actually a painting showing this, by somebody named Pintoricchio.

I am fairly certain I have mentioned the painting by Pintoricchio showing Penelope's cat.

I am even fairly certain I have mentioned that the cat in the painting is russet.

Even if as I have long since indicated russet is not a name one gives to a color.

I believe it may have been Rembrandt who first established this rule, actually, although in more recent years it was Willem de Kooning who most strongly insisted upon it.

Then again I may have also spoken about a cat of my own as having been russet in spite of this, now that I think back.

That would have only been carelessness, however.

And at any rate none of these cats is by any means to be confused with Rembrandt's own cat, which I bring up only because one might understandably think of Rembrandt's cat as having been russet as well, if for no other reason than russet being a color one automatically associates with Rembrandt.

Rembrandt's cat was actually gray. And had only one eye.

Which may very well be an explanation for why it always strolled right past those gold coins on the floor of his studio without so much as a glance, as a matter of fact, even though I had never stopped to think about that before.

Which is to say that doubtless it had generally passed the coins on the wrong side and so had not noticed them at all.

A good number of people also happened to disapprove of that same cat's name, by the way, which was Argus.

There was an explanation for this, too, of course.

The explanation being that the original Argus had been a dog.

In fact the original Argus was the very dog I have just been talking about, and which is therefore even something of a small coincidence, when one comes down to it.

After all, how often does one happen to be talking about the dog who recognizes Odysseus when he finally returns to Ithaca after having been gone for so many years but then dies?

Or which Penelope becomes so accustomed to that it reminds her to bring other animals as gifts, whenever she visits anybody?

Still, people did voice disapproval over Rembrandt having named his cat the way he did.

Now how could anybody be so foolish as to name a cat after a dog? This basically having been the manner in which such disapproval was voiced.

And which brings up Carel Fabritius once again, also, if only insofar as there would appear to be no record as to whether Carel Fabritius was one of the people involved in this or not.

One guesses that in having still been a pupil at the time he would have very likely kept his opinion to himself, however.

Although doubtless many local merchants would have handled the situation in much this same manner, as well.

Well, tradesmen generally being less apt than most people to express disapproval in any event, so as not to lose patronage.

Have you heard? Rembrandt has gotten a cat that he has named after a dog. Most probably this is approximately the manner in which the local pharmacist would have put it, say, insofar as such a simple statement does not necessarily have to be interpreted as showing disapproval at all, really.

Most probably the pharmacist would have put it in just this manner to Spinoza, in fact, on the next occasion when Spinoza had a prescription to be filled.

Or needed cigarettes.

Then again it is equally possible that Spinoza may have heard about the name from Rembrandt himself.

Well, as when waiting on line in the same shop, for instance, which the two of them were frequently known to do. Certainly as no more than casual acquaintances they would have found this a perfectly harmless subject with which to pass the time.

So. And have you thought up a name for your new cat yet, Rembrandt?

As a matter of fact I am naming him Argus, Spinoza.

Ah, so you are naming your cat after the dog in the *Odyssey,* are you?

One assumes that Spinoza would have answered in something like this fashion, all of this again being merely polite. Assuredly he would have looked at the matter in a different light later on, however.

Now how could anybody be so foolish as to name a cat after a dog? Assuredly it would have been more in this sort of a light that he looked at it then.

But in the meantime what is also highly probable here is that Rembrandt himself would not have been aware of one bit of this.

Well, certainly a man facing bankruptcy would have had little time to waste in thinking about a cat in either case.

So that doubtless as soon as the animal had been named he would have again been preoccupied with other matters entirely.

Such as finishing *The Night Watch,* for instance.

Interestingly, by the way, I had never understood what it was supposed to be about *The Night Watch* at all, when I had only seen reproductions of it.

When I finally walked into the Tate Gallery in London and saw the canvas itself it sent shivers up and down my spine, however.

As if there were a glow from inside of the pigments themselves, practically.

So that I was even more careful with it than with any other painting I had ever removed to make use of the frame from, I suspect.

And especially when I was nailing it back into place.

Even though my fire had almost gone out before I was finished, too, as I remember.

To this day I have never quite been able to solve how Rembrandt managed to bring that off, either.

Well, which is why he was Rembrandt, presumably.

Have I ever said that my pickup truck has English license plates and a right-hand drive, incidentally?

Heaven only knows what it was doing parked at one of the marinas here. But I have been driving it locally ever since.

Although there is one more thing I had wished to point out about that question of Rembrandt's cat before I leave it, actually.

Which is the way in which so many more people happened to be familiar with the writings of Homer in those days than would have been the case later on.

Here we have Carel Fabritius and the pharmacist and Spinoza, all immediately recognizing the name of the dog. Well, and not to mention Rembrandt himself, who chose it.

But for that matter doubtless Jan Vermeer would have recognized it just as quickly, once he in turn became a pupil of Carel Fabritius and Carel Fabritius was explaining about russet and bedspreads.

Well, and as would Leeuwenhoek and Galileo, doubtless, having been in Delft, too.

Conversely if I had named my own russet cat Argus I am next to positive that not one solitary person I knew would have made the connection with Odysseus's dog at all.

As a matter of fact the only individual I can recall personally who ever did make this connection was Martin Heidegger.

I have perhaps said that badly.

In saying that I can personally recall Martin Heidegger having made this connection very likely what I have implied is that I once spoke with Martin Heidegger.

Martin Heidegger is not somebody I once spoke with.

As a matter of fact another implication in that same sentence would presumably be that I might have understood such a conversation if it had occurred.

Which I would not have, obviously, not speaking one word of German.

Not that it is of course impossible that Martin Heidegger spoke English on his own part, although I did not ask him that, either.

Ah, me.

Possibly I had better start over.

I am starting over.

What happened was that I once wrote Martin Heidegger a letter.

It was in answer to my letter that Martin Heidegger indicated his familiarity with the *Odyssey.*

Even though my own letter had had nothing to do with that topic.

Although in fact what I now believe is that I wish to start this whole thing still one more time.

I am starting this whole thing still one more time.

What really happened, once, was that I wrote letters to a considerable number of famous people.

So that to tell the truth Martin Heidegger was not even the most famous person I wrote to.

Certainly Winston Churchill would have been considered more famous than Martin Heidegger.

In fact I am positive that Picasso would have also been considered more famous than Martin Heidegger.

And that the same thing could have assuredly been said about the Queen of England.

Well, and what with fame generally being a matter of one's orientation anyway, surely in the eyes of people who admired music Igor Stravinsky and Maria Callas would have been said to have been more famous themselves.

As no doubt in the eyes of people who admired movies this would have held true for Katherine Hepburn or Marlon Brando or Peter O'Toole.

Or as for people who admired baseball it might even have appeared to be the case with Stan Usual.

But be all that as it may I wrote letters to every single one of these people.

And as a matter of fact I wrote letters to more people than this.

Some of the other people I suspect I may also have written to were Bertrand Russell, and Dmitri Shostakovitch, and Ralph Hodgson, and Anna Akhmatova, and Maurice Utrillo, and Irene Papas.

Moreover I suspect I may have even written to Gilbert Murray and to T. E. Shaw.

Although when I say I suspect in regard to these latter cases it is because with a good number of them I can no longer be certain.

The chief reason I can no longer be certain being simply that I wrote all of these letters a good many years ago.

But too, another reason is that a certain number of the people I have mentioned may in fact have already been dead by the time I wrote the letters.

And in which case I would have scarcely written to them, naturally.

Well, this having been the very situation with such people as Jackson Pollock, and Gertrude Stein, and Dylan Thomas, to whom I naturally did not write, either.

So that all I actually mean is that after so long I have forgotten a lot of these other people's dates.

Which is to say that even though I happen to be thinking about them now as having been people I might have thought about writing to then, they may have obviously not been people I would have been thinking about writing to then after all.

This is not really that complicated, although it may seem to be.

And to tell the truth I had no special messages for anybody individually in any case.

Every single one of the letters having been identical.

In fact they were all Xerox copies of one letter.

All of them stating that I had just gotten a cat.

Well, naturally the letters stated more than that.

One would hardly sit down and Xerox a letter to Picasso, or

to the Queen of England, simply to state that one had just gotten a cat.

It being that I was having an extraordinary amount of difficulty in naming the cat, and did they have any suggestions, that was what else the letter said.

All of this having been contrived in a spirit of fun, of course.

Even if it remains a fact that the letters were quite truthful.

Except perhaps for the fact that the cat was not really a cat but only still a kitten.

After one has had a cat for a certain time one tends to refer to it as a cat even when speaking of the period in which it had not yet become a cat, however.

Even if that is doubtless neither here nor there.

The point remaining that there was the poor thing still poking about my studio with nothing for anybody to call it by.

Until it had almost stopped being a kitten and begun to become a cat for real, in fact.

Almost cat, being what I had even begun to think of it as.

Although doubtless I had better get some help with this difficulty, being what I was also finally forced to think.

What would Joan Baez name an almost cat? Or Germaine Greer? Doubtless I even began to have thoughts along those lines, as well.

Well, unquestionably I began to have thoughts along those lines as well, or it would have otherwise scarcely occurred to me to write those letters.

Even if I have perhaps forgotten to mention that Joan Baez and Germaine Greer were two more of the people I wrote them to.

And even if it was not actually my idea to write those letters in any way at all.

Actually, what happened was that there happened to be certain people at my studio, one evening, and one of these people happened to ask me what my almost cat's name happened to be.

Well, visiting at somebody's studio and having an almost cat climb into one's lap one is quite naturally apt to ask a question of that sort.

In fact whose lap the almost cat had climbed into was Marco Antonio Montes de Oca's lap.

Even if I no longer have any idea whatsoever what Marco Antonio Montes de Oca may have been doing at my studio. Unless perhaps it may have been William Gaddis who brought him.

Although doubtless I have also failed to mention that William Gaddis ever visited at my studio himself.

William Gaddis now and again visited at my studio himself.

And on certain of those occasions brought along other writers.

One would tend to do that sort of thing, basically.

Well, by which I mean that if William Gaddis had been a pharmacist doubtless the other people he brought along would have been other pharmacists.

Assuming he brought along anybody to begin with, I am obviously also saying.

So that this time he had perhaps brought along Marco Antonio Montes de Oca, who in either case did ask me what my almost cat's name was.

And so that what happened right after that was that all sorts of interesting suggestions were offered in regard to a name.

Writing to famous people for suggestions being one of those very suggestions, as it turned out.

And which immediately appeared to ring a little bell for everybody in the room.

So that in no time at all I had a sheet of paper filled with more names of famous people than you could count.

All of this as I say having been contrived in a spirit of fun.

Even if it saddened me.

Well, for never having heard of half of the people who were mentioned, to tell the truth.

Although not that this was by any means an entirely new

experience in my life either, when one comes down to that.

In fact it had sometimes seemed to happen every other time I turned around.

So that as quickly as one had gotten accustomed to a name like Jacques Lévi-Strauss, say, there was everybody talking about Jacques Barthes.

And three days after that about Jacques somebody else.

And in the meantime all one had honestly ever been trying to do was catch up to Susan Sontag.

And of course it was around this same time that one discovered that people who wrote ordinary art reviews in the daily newspapers had stopped calling themselves art reviewers and become art critics, as well.

Which naturally led one to wonder just what one was supposed to call E. H. Gombrich or Meyer Schapiro, then.

Well, or Erwin Panofsky or Millard Meiss or Heinrich Wölfflin or Rudolf Arnheim or Harold Rosenberg or Arnold Hauser or André Malraux or René Huyghe or William Gaunt or Walter Friedlaender or Max J. Friedländer or Élie Faure or Émile Mâle or Kenneth Clark or Wylie Sypher or Clement Greenberg or Herbert Read.

Or for that matter Wilhelm Worringer or Roger Fry or Bernard Berenson or Clive Bell or Walter Pater or Jacob Burckhardt or Eugène Fromentin or Baudelaire or the Goncourts or Winckelmann or Schlegel or Lessing or Cennini or Aretino or Alberti or Vasari or John Ruskin, even.

Although doubtless I am showing off again.

Just for the minute I felt like I needed it this time, however.

And be that as it may everybody did insist that I write to all of those other people who were named.

Even if I did leave out certain of the additional artists who were brought up, finally.

Well, such as Georgia O'Keeffe and Louise Nevelson and Helen Frankenthaler.

Simply feeling silly about sending such a letter to people I had been in group shows with, was all.

Although obviously I was not the one who put Campy Stengel in, either.

Oh, good lord.

Magritte.

Whom I did remember to tack onto the list myself, in fact.

Well, but Magritte now turning out to be exactly like Artemisia Gentileschi, I suddenly realize.

Which is to say that it seems practically impossible that I could have written this many pages without ever having mentioned Magritte before, similarly.

Certainly I have thought about Magritte now and again whether I have mentioned him or not, on the other hand, which was truthfully perhaps not the case with Artemisia.

In fact I have thought about Magritte practically as often as I have asked myself certain kinds of questions.

And which do not happen to be questions I have asked myself only rarely, either.

Well, such as what floor is that toilet on, say, that is on the second floor of the house that does not have a second floor?

Or, where was my own house when all I was seeing was the smoke from my potbellied stove but was thinking, there is my house?

Certainly both of those questions are questions that could make one think about Magritte.

And as a matter of fact I now even remember that when I finally found the road to the house in the woods behind this house after not having been able to find the road to the house in the woods behind this house, just about the first thing I said to myself was, well, here I am at the intersection of Fallen Tree Avenue and Magritte Road.

Even if on second thought I perhaps did not put Magritte on that list after all.

Which is to say that even though I happen to be thinking about Magritte now as somebody I might have thought about writing to then, he may have actually not been somebody I would have happened to think about writing to then.

In all instances lately when I have spoken about my studio, by the way, I have also been speaking about my loft.

Having worked where I lived, if I have not made that clear. Well, or vice versa.

Although in the meantime I have only at this instant been struck by something quite curious.

In fact it is extraordinarily curious.

Not sixty seconds ago I walked into the kitchen for a drink of water, from my pitcher.

While I was walking back I heard part of one of the *Bachianas Brasileiras,* by Villa-Lobos, in my head.

I mean the one that everybody was generally familiar with, with the soprano voice.

Still, the *Bachianas Brasileiras* by Villa-Lobos being something else I am next to positive I have never mentioned before, either.

Even though what I realized simultaneously is that I have heard that identical piece of music now and again whether I have mentioned it or not.

In fact I have heard it as many times as I have thought about Magritte, practically.

Except that every single time I have heard it what I have always said to myself I was hearing was *The Alto Rhapsody.*

And which obviously now implies that every single time I have mentioned *The Alto Rhapsody* what I ought to have mentioned was one of the *Bachianas Brasileiras.*

And moreover that every single time I have mentioned Kathleen Ferrier singing the Brahms what I ought to have mentioned was Bidú Sayão singing the Villa-Lobos.

Even if it may have been Kirsten Flagstad singing.

And in a manner of speaking I was not really hearing any one of the three to begin with.

Hm.

[214]

Once, somebody asked Robert Schumann to explain the meaning of a certain piece of music he had just played on the piano.

What Robert Schumann did was sit back down at the piano and play the piece of music again.

I would find it very agreeable to be able to feel that this has solved anything I have just been talking about.

Whatever I have precisely just been talking about.

In fact I would even happily settle to have not completely lost track of where I was.

I have not at all lost track of where I was.

Where I am is at the point where somebody next borrowed another sheet of paper and actually started to dictate the letter for me.

In fact it may have been William Gaddis himself who did this.

Or one of the pharmacists.

Although what was also suggested around this time was that I should include postcards along with the letters, addressed to myself, so as to give the people who received the letters less excuse for not answering.

Well, your ordinary letter of this type being easily left unanswered, of course.

Whereas surely one would feel more guilty about doing so when the letter had included a postcard addressed to the sender.

Even if what this in turn brought up was the question of proper postage, United States stamps being obviously of little use in any of the other countries the postcards were supposed to be mailed back from.

I believe it was Susan Sontag who thought to point this out, actually.

Or another of the pharmacists.

Still, I did follow the suggestion about the postcards.

Just allowing the stamps to appear to have been forgotten about, as it were.

And which in the end turned out to have been just as well, or certainly at least in terms of having saved the expense.

What with only one of the people to whom I had sent the letters ever taking the trouble to return the postcard in either case.

This having been Martin Heidegger.

And who in fact spoke quite impressive English after all.

Even making use of the subjunctive, as it happened.

Although when I say spoke, I should really be saying wrote, of course.

What I should wish to suggest as a name for your dog is the splendid classical name of Argos from the *Odyssey* by Homer, ✓ having been what was written in English on the postcard from Martin Heidegger.

For some period I was fairly annoyed with Martin Heidegger. Well.

Even if I did finally come to realize that doubtless philosophers had more important items on their minds than names for other people's pets.

Ach, here I sit with such important items as *Dasein* on my mind, surely being what Martin Heidegger must have said to himself, and there is that person in America requesting a name for her foolish animal.

So that in the final analysis it was actually quite kind of Martin Heidegger to have taken the time to write at all, in spite ✓ of having made a mistake when he did so.

And even though it had taken almost seven months before the postcard came back, additionally.

But which may have also very well been the reason for Martin Heidegger's mistake, now that one stops to think about it.

Which is to say that very possibly Martin Heidegger was busily writing one of his books through all of that time.

Very possibly the book he was so busily writing was one of the very books in the carton in the basement of this house, in fact, and which only goes to show how astonishingly small the world can be.

But in either case not until Martin Heidegger had finished writing his book would he have found my letter again.

Or rather what he more likely would have found was only the postcard, having doubtless discarded the letter as soon as he had read it.

Certainly having had no doubts at all that he would remember what he was supposed to write on the card.

Well, and being a famous philosopher having had even fewer doubts that he would remember the difference between a cat and a dog, surely.

Unless on second thought there is a subtle possibility here that Martin Heidegger did not make a mistake after all?

Granting that this has only this tardily come into my head. But still, why couldn't Martin Heidegger have perhaps known that whole story about Rembrandt and his own cat?

And why couldn't Susan Sontag have indicated while she was dictating my letter that I was a painter myself?

Surely in writing to total strangers one would have shown the courtesy to identify one's self in either event.

So that what would have really gone through Martin Heidegger's mind, then, would have been something like, ach, so what I will tell this painter person in this SoHo place to name her animal is what Rembrandt named his.

And which would thus call for a rather different explanation as to why Martin Heidegger still happened to write dog instead of cat, obviously.

The rather different explanation being obviously that Martin Heidegger's English was hardly so impressive as one had thought.

Still, what I am finally almost sorry about is that I never did write to Martin Heidegger a second time, to thank him.

Well, and I certainly would have found it agreeable to tell the man how fond I am of his sentence, too, about inconsequential perplexities now and again becoming the fundamental mood of existence.

Unless as I have said it may have been Friedrich Nietzsche who wrote that sentence.

Or Søren Kierkegaard.

And even if I had long since given the cat itself another name altogether, of course.

Hm.

Except that after all of this talk I suddenly cannot seem to remember what name I did give it.

Doubtless this is only because I have been speaking about so many other cats, however.

Not even counting Rembrandt's, for instance, there is the cat that Medea gave to Helen, and there is the cat I saw in the Colosseum, and there is the cat which scratches at the outside of my window, here.

Well, and then there are all of those cats which would have been leery about going to the garbage disposal area because of so many seagulls doing their scavenging, and there is the cat which Taddeo Gaddi once did a painting of and was speaking about as being russet until Giotto informed him it was burnt sienna.

Which Theophanes the Greek had informed Giotto before that.

I believe that cats may have been mentioned in connection with such people as Sor Juana Inés de la Cruz and Ludwig Wittgenstein and Anna Karenina in some way or other, as well.

Then again I may be in error about Sor Juana Inés de la Cruz, not knowing whether anybody who lived in a convent was permitted to have a cat.

I am assuming that Sister Joan Inez of the Cross lived in a convent.

But which is to say that St. Teresa would not have had a cat in Toledo either, then.

Well, and I now realize I am in error about Ludwig Wittgenstein, too, since any cat of Wittgenstein's would have been just as leery about his own pet seagull as were all of those other cats

[218]

about the seagulls at the garbage disposal area.

Or at least during Wittgenstein's period at Galway Bay, this would have been.

Galway Bay.

Andrea senza errori.

Which is not to say that Wittgenstein might not have had a cat years earlier while he was mowing the lawns at a monastery, on the other hand.

Unless monasteries had the same rule as convents.

So that St. John of the Cross would have been still somebody else who could not have had one.

Jan Steen owned a brewery in which there might have been a cat, however.

Heaven only knows why writing about a monastery should have reminded me of that, although I am pleased to have thought of it nonetheless, having believed for the longest time that I knew nothing at all about Jan Steen.

Although what I am also now remembering is that Fra Filippo Lippi once eloped with a nun, if that is in any way connected with anything?

Well, possibly what it is connected with is that if the nun had not been permitted to have a cat before, she might have gotten one then.

Anna Karenina's cat was run over by a train, if I remember.

I am still somewhat upset about that question of having repeatedly believed I was hearing the *Four Last Songs* by Strauss when what I was really hearing was the *Bachianas Brasileiras* number five, incidentally.

Even if I have forgotten whether there was a cat near Robert and Clara Schumann's piano in *Song of Love,* likewise.

Although what I do only this instant realize is that there happen to be books in this very house by Jacques Lévi-Strauss and Jacques Barthes, actually.

Except now what troubles me is why so many people would have been excited about instructions as to how to behave at table or a guide to the Eiffel Tower.

Unless perhaps it is the guide to the birds of Southern Connecticut and Long Island Sound that I am mixing up, here.

In any instances lately when I have spoken about my pitcher, by the way, I should have more truthfully spoken about a jar.

Pitcher merely having more of the sound of something one would carry to a spring, being all.

Even if for the life of me I have no idea what I have been saying that has now made me think about Marina Tsvetayeva again, either.

Especially since that is one of the saddest stories I know.

What happened having been that the Russians let such a wonderful poet practically starve to death, all alone and in exile.

After having killed her family.

So that she finally hanged herself.

And so that I might have actually driven right past her grave on my way across Russia, too, without ever having known where it was.

Even if nobody ever really knew, for that matter.

God, the things men used to do.

Not that they could ever again find the pauper's grave that Mozart had been buried in either, after the rain had stopped the next morning.

That being a different sort of story altogether, perhaps, but still also sad.

Have I ever said, just to deliberately change the subject, that it was at a garbage disposal area that Van Gogh actually painted his famous canvas called *The Broken Bottles?*

Which is at the Rijksmuseum, I think.

Van Gogh having had that gift for making his pigments sometimes seem to glow, too, by the way.

Except that in Van Gogh's case what one generally catches one's self doing is starting to glance across one's shoulder, as if to figure out where all the sunlight is coming from.

There would appear to be no record as to which particular

paintings Van Gogh painted while wearing the old socks that Alfred North Whitehead later used to put on when he went for walks in the woods near Cambridge, on the other hand.

Although another thing I have perhaps never mentioned is that Ludwig Wittgenstein actually used to carry sugar in his pockets, when he went for walks near Cambridge himself.

The reason he carried the sugar being to give it to horses he might see in fields while he was walking.

On my honor, Wittgenstein used to do that.

For some reason this story is another that reminds me of something, even if I have no idea what, at the moment.

Doubtless I will think of my cat's name in a day or two also, however.

And in the meantime what I have just decided to do is to change the name of the cat which scratches at the outside of my window.

What I am now calling that cat is Magritte.

Well, Magritte having more of a connection with a cat that is not really a cat than Van Gogh does, being all.

Even if the very painting by Van Gogh I have just mentioned is a painting of a fire which is not really a fire but is only a reflection of a fire, actually.

And which perhaps I have never even seen except in a reproduction either, since on second thought I do not remember it at the Uffizi after all.

Wittgenstein was never married, by the way. Well, or never had a mistress either, having been a homosexual.

Although in the meantime when I just said in the meantime I truly did mean in the meantime.

It now being almost an entire week since I additionally said I would doubtless think of my cat's name in a day or two.

And this in turn being by far the longest period I have allowed to go by without sitting at the typewriter.

My shoulder and my ankle no longer hurting as badly as they did, however.

Which is not to say that the pains in my shoulder or my ankle had anything to do with my not sitting at the typewriter.

Or that the pains no longer being as bad as they were has anything to do with my being back.

For some reason all I felt like doing was lying in the sun, for a time.

Which is also to say that it has stopped raining, obviously.

Well, one hardly having been able to lie in the sun if it hadn't. Obviously.

In fact I have been having some rosy-fingered dawns again after all, too.

Even if how I happened to feel through most of the week was depressed, to tell the truth.

I believe I have said that I felt depressed at least once before, actually, while writing these pages.

Although perhaps what I more exactly said I felt once before was a certain undefined anxiety.

Which in that instance would have only been because of my period coming on, however.

Or because of hormones.

And so which would have not really been anxiety at all, but only an illusion.

Even if one would certainly be hard put to explain the difference between an illusion of anxiety and anxiety itself.

And in either case how I still felt this time was depressed.

Even if I had no idea why.

And moreover even if feeling depressed and having no idea why can generally leave one feeling even more depressed than that.

I was fairly certain that none of it had anything to do with not being able to remember the name of my cat.

Well, and too, once the rain had stopped but the woods were still wet everything was extraordinarily beautiful, and all of the wet leaves glistened and glistened.

So that it scarcely could have had anything to do with the rain, either.

Which I had been finding agreeable to ignore by walking in it in any event.

Finally on Tuesday I understood why I was feeling depressed.

Which was the same day on which I noticed that my rowboat would have to be bailed out, incidentally, should I wish to make use of my rowboat.

Although when I say this was Tuesday I am saying so only in a manner of speaking, naturally.

Having had no idea what day of the week it has ever been through any of these years, of course, and which is surely another thing I must have mentioned.

Still, certain days *feeling* like Tuesday, for all that.

And even if I could also not remember having ever bailed out my other rowboat at all, although certainly I must have done so, now and again.

Unless it had never once rained while I still had my other rowboat.

Or I had never had another rowboat.

Certainly I once had another rowboat.

Just as I once had another cat, in fact, besides the cat I once wrote letters to all of those famous people about, and which was why I was feeling depressed.

This having been a cat before that cat, and which I had completely forgotten about when I was doing that list of so many other cats, last week.

In fact I suspect there is something ironical in my having been able to remember Helen of Sparta's cat, or even Carel Fabritius's burnt sienna cat, and not remembering this particular cat.

Especially since this particular cat was not really mine but was Lucien's.

And even though I had a husband at the same time, named Adam, whom I do not remember very frequently, either.

What happened with this cat having been that Adam and I suggested to Lucien that he should be the one to give it its name.

And which Lucien then commenced to look upon as an extraordinary responsibility.

Well, being only four, doubtless he had never had a responsibility before whether extraordinary or not.

So that for a certain period all that Lucien ever appeared to be doing was fretting over a name for the cat.

And which in the meantime we called simply Cat.

Good morning, Cat, being what I would say when I found the cat waiting for breakfast.

Good night, Cat, being what either Adam or I would say when we put the cat out for the night.

All of this having taken place in Mexico, incidentally, in a village not far from Oaxaca.

And naturally in a village in Mexico one puts one's cat out for the night.

Well, the village scarcely needing to be in Mexico for one to do that in either, of course.

Later, in fact, I remember having done the identical thing with my Martin Heidegger cat, once when I was painting in Rome, New York, for a summer.

Although in that instance with the cat having been a city cat I did worry to some degree, perhaps.

Even if a cat which had been locked up in a loft in SoHo for all of its life ought to have found it agreeable to be outside at night, surely.

But be that as it may, Lucien never did seem to decide upon a name for that earlier cat.

Or for so long that very likely it would have been impossible to stop calling it simply Cat by then in either case.

Although as a matter of fact we had taken to calling the cat Cat in Spanish too, sometimes.

Buenos días, Gato, being what I would sometimes say when I found the cat waiting for breakfast.

Buenas noches, Gato, being what Adam or I would sometimes say when we put the cat out for the night.

For three years we called the cat that, either *Gato* or Cat, and then I went away from the village not far from Oaxaca.

Even though I did go back, once, years and years afterwards, as I have possibly said.

And in a Jeep was able to maneuver directly up the hillside to where the grave was, instead of being forced to follow the road.

Having still been making use of all sorts of vehicles, in those days.

Well, having still been looking, in those days.

If having been quite mad for a good deal of the time, too, of course.

Mexico having appeared as reasonable a place in which to begin to look as any, however, whether I was mad or not.

Even if I am convinced that I remained in New York for at least two winters before I did look elsewhere, actually.

And even if one surely does not have to be mad in the least, in being drawn to the grave of one's only child.

So that when one truly comes down to it perhaps I was only partly mad.

Or mad only part of the time.

And able to understand that Lucien would have been almost twenty by then at any rate, and so well on his way to becoming a stranger.

Well, or perhaps not yet quite twenty.

And perhaps not at all on his way to becoming a stranger.

There being certain things that one will never ever know, and can never ever even guess at.

Such as why I spilled gasoline all over his old room on that very next morning, for that matter.

After turning my shoes upside down, naturally, in case of scorpions, even though there could no longer have been any scorpions.

And then watched the image of the smoke rising and rising in my rearview mirror as I drove and drove again.

Across the wide Mississippi.

And yet never once having given a solitary thought to the cat we had called simply Cat at that time either, I do not believe.

Even alone in that empty house where so many memories died hard.

Although come to think about it I do not believe I ever once gave that cat a thought when I had the other cat that I could not decide upon a name for as well, actually.

Which is assuredly a curious thing to have done.

Or rather not to have done.

Which is to say to have not remembered that one's little boy had once not been able to decide upon a name for a cat while finding one's self in the very process of not being able to decide upon a name for a cat of one's own.

Well, perhaps it was not so curious.

There being surely as many things one would prefer never to remember as there are those one would wish to, of course.

Such as how drunk Adam had gotten on that weekend, for instance, and so did not even think to call for a doctor until far too late.

Well, or why one was not there at the house one's self, those same few days.

Being young one sometimes does terrible things.

Even if life does go on, of course.

Although when I say does go on, I should really be saying did go, naturally.

Having doubtless let any number of similar mistakes in tenses slip by before this, it now strikes me.

So that on any occasion at all when I have made such generalizations as if in the present they ought to have been in the past.

Obviously.

And even if it was nobody's fault that Lucien died after all.

Although probably I did leave out this part before, about having taken lovers when I was still Adam's wife.

Even if one forgets whether one's husband had become drunk because one had done that, or if one had done that because one's husband had become drunk.

Doubtless it may have been a good deal of both, on the other hand.

Most things generally being, a good deal of both.

And none of what I have just written having been what really happened in either event.

Since both of us were there, that weekend.

And could do nothing about anything, was all.

Because they move, too, Pasteur kept telling people.

Except later to make even more out of such guilts as one already possessed, of course.

And life did go on.

Even if one sometimes appeared to spend much of it looking in and out of windows.

Or with nobody paying attention to a word one ever said.

Although one continued to take still other lovers, naturally.

And then to separate from other lovers.

Leaves having blown in, or fluffy cottonwood seeds.

Or then again one sometimes merely fucked, too, with whomever.

Time out of mind.

While next it was one's mother who died, and then one's father.

And one even took away the tiny, pocket sort of mirror from beside one's beautiful mother's bed, in which she and her image had both been equidistant from what lay ahead.

Although perhaps it was one's father, who had no longer wished her to perceive that distance.

Even if I have seen my mother's image in my own, in the one mirror in this house as well, incidentally.

On each of those occasions having always made the assumption that such illusions are quite ordinary, however, and come with age.

Which is to say that they are not even illusions, heredity being heredity.

Then again having never painted any sort of portrait of poor Lucien at all, on the other hand.

Though there is the framed snapshot of him in the drawer beside my own bed upstairs, of course.

Kneeling to pet *Gato*.

And he is obviously in my head.

But then what is there that is not in my head?

So that it is like a bloody museum, sometimes.

Or as if I have been appointed the curator of all the world.

Well, as I was, as in a manner of speaking I undeniably am.

Even if every artifact in it ought to have made me even more surprised than I turned out to be at not having thought about Magritte until I did, actually.

And so that even the very marker that Adam had promised to place beside the grave when I did not stay on for that had been in my head for all of those years before I went back, as well.

Without there ever having been a marker.

God, the things men used to do.

What do any of us ever truly know, however?

And at least as I started to say I certainly did finally understand what it was that had made me feel depressed.

Last Tuesday.

When all I had been doing was lying in the sun after the rain had stopped and thinking about cats, or so I believed.

Although to tell the truth I do not very frequently allow such things to happen.

By which I hardly mean thinking about cats.

What I am talking about is thinking about things from as long ago as before I was alone, obviously.

Even if one can hardly control one's thinking in such a way as not to allow anything that happened more than ten years ago to come into it.

Certainly I have thought about Lucien before, for instance.

Or about certain of my lovers, like Simon or Vincent or Ludwig or Terry.

Or even about as early as the seventh grade when I almost wanted to cry because I knew, knew, that Odysseus's dog could certainly catch that tortoise.

Well, and doubtless I have thought about the time when my mother was asleep and I did not wish to wake her and so wrote I love you with my lipstick on that same tiny mirror, as well.

Having intended to sign it Artemisia, except that I ran out of room.

You will never know how much it has meant to me that you are an artist, Helen, my mother having said, the very afternoon before.

But the truth of the matter being that I did not intend to repeat one bit of that just now, actually.

In fact when I finally did solve why I had been feeling depressed what I told myself was that if necessary I would simply never again allow myself to put down any of such things at all.

As if in a manner of speaking one were no longer able to speak one solitary word of Long Ago.

So that even if it were not until right at this instant that I were to first remember having written to Jacques Lévi-Strauss, say, I would no longer put something like that down, likewise.

One scarcely having been able to write to Jacques Lévi-Strauss or to any single other person unless it had been before one was alone, obviously.

Any more than Willem de Kooning could have been at one's studio to dictate such letters to begin with.

Or Robert Rauschenberg could have been there to correct their mistakes.

Or its, since there was really only the one letter.

With Xerox copies.

To all of those additional people.

Who were obviously still someplace, too.

Except that what I also realized in making such a decision was that it would certainly leave me with very little else to write about.

Especially if even in writing about such harmless items as pets I could still wind up thinking about meningitis, for instance. Or cancer.

Or at any rate feeling the way I did.

So that what I realized almost simultaneously, in fact, was that quite possibly I might have to start right from the beginning and write something different altogether.

√ ⎡Such as a novel, say.⎤

Although there is perhaps an implication in those few sentences that I did not intend.

Well, which is to say that people who write novels only write them when they have very little else to write.

Any number of people who write novels no doubt taking their work quite seriously, in fact.

Although when I say write or taking, I should really be saying wrote or having taken, naturally.

Well, as I have only just explained.

But in either case doubtless when Dostoievski was writing about Rainer Maria Raskolnikov he took Rainer Maria Raskolnikov quite seriously.

Well, or as Lawrence of Arabia undeniably did when he was writing about Don Quixote.

Or just look at how many people might have gone through life believing that castles in Damascus was just a phrase, for instance.

Still, what happened next was that I realized just as quickly that writing a novel would not be the answer anyhow.

Or certainly not when your ordinary novel is basically expected to be about people too, obviously.

And which is to say about certainly a good number more people than just one, also.

In fact without ever having read one word of that same novel by Dostoievski I would readily be willing to wager that Rainer Maria Raskolnikov is hardly the only person in it.

Or that Anna Akhmatova is the only person in *Anna Karenina,* as well.

So that as I say, there went my novel practically even before I had a chance to start thinking about a novel.

(*) Unless on third thought it just might change matters if I were to make it an absolutely autobiographical novel?

Hm.

Because what I am also suddenly now thinking about is that it could be an absolutely autobiographical novel that would not start until after I was alone, obviously.

And so that obviously there could be no way whatsoever that it could be expected to have more than one person in it after all.

Even though I would still have to remember to keep out of my head while I was writing any of that also, of course.

But still.

As a matter of fact it might even be an interesting novel, in its way.

Which is to say a novel about somebody who woke up one Wednesday or Thursday to discover that there was apparently not one other person left in the world.

Well, or not even one seagull, either.

Except for various vegetables and flowers, conversely.

Certainly that would be an interesting beginning, at any rate. Or at least for a certain type of novel.

Just imagine how the heroine would feel, however, and how full of anxiety she would be.

And with every bit of that being real anxiety in this instance, too, as opposed to various illusions.

Such as from hormones. Or from age.

Even though her entire situation might certainly often seem like an illusion on its own part, paradoxically.

So that soon enough she would be quite mad, naturally.

Still, the next part of the novel would be about how she would insist upon going to look for other people in all sorts of places whether she was quite mad or not.

Well, and while also doing such things as rolling hundreds and hundreds of tennis balls one after the other down the

Spanish Steps, or waiting during seventeen hours for each of her seventeen wristwatches to buzz before dropping each one of them into the Arno, or opening a vast number of cans of cat food in the Colosseum, or placing loose coins into various pay telephones that do not function while intending to ask for Modigliani.

Or for that matter even poking into mummies in various museums to see if there might be any stuffing made out of lost poems by Sappho inside.

Except that what one senses even this readily is that there would very likely be almost no way for such a novel to end.

Especially once the heroine had finally become convinced that she may as well stop looking after all, and so could also stop being mad again.

Leaving her very little to do after that except perhaps to burn an occasional house to the ground.

Or to write make-believe Greek writing in the sand with her stick.

Which would hardly make very exciting reading.

Although one curious thing that might sooner or later cross the woman's mind would be that she had paradoxically been practically as alone before all of this had happened as she was now, incidentally.

Well, this being an autobiographical novel I can categorically verify that such a thing would sooner or later cross her mind, in fact.

One manner of being alone simply being different from another manner of being alone, being all that she would finally decide that this came down to, as well.

Which is to say that even when one's telephone still does function one can be as alone as when it does not.

Or that even when one still does hear one's name being called at certain intersections one can be as alone as when one is only able to imagine that this has happened.

So that quite possibly the whole point of the novel might be that one can just as easily ask for Modigliani on a telephone that does not function as on one that does.

Or even that one can just as easily be almost hit by a taxi that has come rolling down a hill with nobody driving it as by one that somebody is, perhaps.

Even if something else that has obviously become evident here is that I would not be able to keep out of my heroine's head after all.

So that I am already beginning to feel half depressed all over again, as a matter of fact.

Doubtless making it just as well that writing novels is not my trade in either case.

Well, as Leonardo similarly said.

Although what Leonardo actually said was that there is no better way of keeping sane and free from anxiety than by being mad.

And which has now given me the curious sensation that most of the things I do write often seem to become equidistant from *themselves,* somehow.

Whatever in heaven's name I might mean by that, however.

Once, when Friedrich Nietzsche was mad, he started to cry because somebody was hitting a horse.

But then went home and played the piano.

On my honor, Friedrich Nietzsche used to play the piano for hours and hours, when he was mad.

Making up every single piece of music that he played, too.

Whereas Spinoza often used to go looking for spiders, and then make them fight with each other.

Not being mad in the least.

Although when I say fight with, I mean fight against, naturally.

Even if for some curious reason one's meaning would generally appear to be understood, in such cases.

Would it have made any sense whatsoever if I had said that the woman in my novel would have one day actually gotten more accustomed to a world without any people in it than she ever could have gotten to a world without such a thing as *The Descent from the Cross,* by Rogier van der Weyden, by the way?

Or without the *Iliad?* Or Antonio Vivaldi?

I was just asking, really.

As a matter of fact it was at least seven or eight weeks ago, when I asked that.

It now being early November, at a guess.

Let me think.

Yes.

Or in any event the first snow has been and gone, at least.

Even if it was not a remarkably heavy snow, actually.

Still, on the morning after it fell, the trees were writing a strange calligraphy against the whiteness.

For that matter the sky was white, too, and the dunes were hidden, and the beach was white all the way down to the water's edge.

So that almost everything I was able to see, then, was like that old lost nine-foot canvas of mine, with its opaque four white coats of gesso.

Making it almost as if one could have newly painted the entire world one's self, and in any manner one wished.

Assuming one had also wished to paint outdoors in such chilly weather, that is.

Although the cold had been coming on for quite some time before that too, naturally.

So that I had already been to the town any number of times in the pickup truck, in fact.

Well, scarcely wishing to be caught short for supplies once I am basically locked in here, obviously.

And which is to say that I have now dismantled a good deal more of the house next door, as well.

Making two toilets fastened to pipes on the second floors of houses which no longer possess second floors that I now see when I go for my walks along the beach.

Now and again when I was calculating which of the boards I

could get at next with my crowbar up there, by the way, I was reminded of Brunelleschi and Donatello.

Early in the Renaissance when Brunelleschi and Donatello had gone about measuring ancient ruins in Rome, this would be, and with such industry that people believed they could only be searching for buried treasure.

But after which Brunelleschi returned home to Florence and put up the largest dome since antiquity.

While Giotto built the beautiful campanile next door.

Even if there would appear to be no record in art history as to whether Giotto did that before or after he had painted the perfect circle freehand, on the other hand.

And as a matter of fact Giotto's campanile is square.

Although there is practically no place in Florence from which one cannot see either of those structures, incidentally.

Well, as there is practically no place in Paris from which one cannot see the Eiffel Tower, either.

And which might certainly disturb one's lunch, should one not wish to look at the Eiffel Tower while eating one's lunch.

Unless like Guy de Maupassant one had taken to crawling about on a floor and eating one's own excrement, say.

God, poor Maupassant.

Well, but poor Friedrich Nietzsche, too, actually.

If not to mention poor Vivaldi while I am at it also, since I now remember that he died in an almshouse.

And for that matter poor Bach's widow Anna Magdalena, who was allowed to do the same thing.

Bach's widow. And with all of those children. Some of whom were actually even more successful in music at the time than Bach himself had been.

Well, but then poor Robert Schumann as well, in a lunatic asylum and fleeing from demons. One of whom was even Franz Schubert's ghost.

For that matter poor Franz Schubert's ghost.

Poor Tchaikovsky, who once visited America and spent his

first night in a hotel room weeping, because he was homesick.

Even if his head at least did not come off.

Poor James Joyce, who was somebody else who crawled under furniture when it thundered.

Poor Beethoven, who never learned to do simple child's multiplication.

Poor Sappho, who leaped from a high cliff, into the Aegean.

Poor John Ruskin, who had all those other silly troubles to begin with, of course, but who finally also saw snakes.

The snakes, Mr. Ruskin.

Poor A. E. Housman, who would not let philosophers use his bathroom.

Poor Giovanni Keats, who was only five feet, one inch tall.

Poor Aristotle, who talked with a lisp, and had exceptionally thin legs.

Poor Sor Juana Inés de la Cruz, who I also now remember was one more person who died in a plague. But in her case while taking care of other nuns who were more ill than she.

Poor Karen Silkwood.

Well, and poor all the young men who died in places like the Hellespont, by which I mean the Dardanelles, and then died again three thousand years after that, likewise.

Even if I hardly mean the same young men.

But meaning poor Hector and poor Patroclus, say, and after that poor Rupert Brooke.

Ah, me. If not to add poor Andrea del Sarto and poor Cassandra and poor Marina Tsvetayeva and poor Vincent Van Gogh and poor Jeanne Hébuterne and poor Piero di Cosimo and poor Iphigenia and poor Stan Gehrig and poor singing birds sweet and poor Medea's little boys and poor Spinoza's spiders and poor Astyanax and poor my aunt Esther as well.

Well, and poor all the youngsters throwing snowballs in Bruegel, who grew up, and did whatever they did, but never threw snowballs again.

So for that matter poor practically the whole world then,

more often than not.

And of course without even thinking about that Wednesday or Thursday morning, this is.

Even if for the life of me I have no idea why I am talking about one bit of that now, either. Any of it.

When all I had actually been about to say was that I have no real explanation for not having written anything in these past seven or eight weeks.

Even if I have already listed several, such as going for supplies, or devoting more time than usual to my dismantling.

Although another reason may very well be that I have appeared to be frequently tired lately, to tell the truth.

As a matter of fact what I ought to have perhaps just said was not that I have no explanation for not having written anything in the past seven or eight weeks, but for having been so frequently tired during that period.

In fact I am feeling tired right at this moment.

Perhaps I was feeling tired when I spent that week lying in the sun before I last did do any writing, too, now that I stop to think about it.

So that I am less than positive that I have brought in as many items for winter as I will need after all, actually.

Or that I have done nearly as much dismantling as is necessary, either.

Especially since any number of the boards are still waiting to be sawed, as it happens.

Although I have never considered sawing the boards to be part of the process of dismantling, incidentally.

Being rather a question of turning dismantled lumber into firewood.

After it has been dismantled.

Even if such a distinction is doubtless no more than one of semantics.

And in either case perhaps I will do some more of that, later today.

Perhaps I will find the painting I have lost later today, also.

Although doubtless I have not mentioned that I have lost a painting.

Well, assuredly I have not mentioned having lost it, what with not having written one solitary word since some time before that happened.

It being the painting of this very house, that I am talking about, and which until at least last August had been hanging directly above and to the side of where this typewriter is.

I believe the painting is a painting of this very house.

In fact I believe there is a representation of a person lurking at the window of my very bedroom in it, even, although one had never been able to be positive about that.

Well, because of the brushwork being fairly abstract at that point, basically.

Still, through all of this time I had been certain that I had put the painting into one of the rooms here that I do not often make use of, and to which the door is generally closed.

As a matter of fact it is a room I surely must have mentioned, since I had been equally certain it was the identical room in which I had more than once noticed a life of Brahms and an atlas.

The former having become permanently misshapen because of dampness, in fact, whereas the latter was lying on its side.

Because of being too tall for the shelf.

And with the shelf being the identical shelf that the painting was leaning against, additionally.

Nonetheless the painting is not in that room.

And for the life of me I have not been able to locate the life of Brahms or the atlas either, even though I have also looked into every other room in this house, including the several additional rooms to which the doors are likewise generally closed.

As a matter of fact I have also walked to the house in the woods behind this house, suspecting that I might have been mistaken as to the whereabouts of all three items, but the painting and the life of Brahms and the atlas do not appear to be in that house, either.

In fact the only item in that house which I remembered having ever given even a second glance, in addition to a reproduction of a painting by Suzanne Valadon that is taped to the living room wall, was a soccer shirt with the name Savona printed across its front.

Which I have now washed at the spring and am wearing as I type.

As a matter of fact I have been wearing the soccer shirt for some days.

Even if I have no idea what it is, really, about wearing the soccer shirt.

And even if I am still at a total loss in regard to that painting.

Which I may or may not have painted myself, incidentally, if I have not said.

Actually I have no recollection whatsoever of having painted that painting.

Still, ever since it turned up missing I have had the curious impression that I just could have.

Or at least that I certainly once imagined it as a painting that I might possibly paint but then did not.

Which is the sort of thing that a painter will now and again do, of course.

Or not do, rather.

But in which instance there could have scarcely been a painting for me to have lost after all, obviously.

Or would that have to mean that there might have been no life of Brahms and no atlas either, then?

Except that if there had not been any atlas how could I have once looked up Lititz, Pennsylvania, in it, on an occasion when I happened to be curious about Lititz, Pennsylvania?

And if there had not been any life of Brahms how could I have once lighted some torn-out pages from it on the beach and then tossed them into the air to see if the breeze might make them fly?

When I was trying to simulate seagulls?

Even if most of the pages happened to fall right next to me, as a matter of fact.

Because of having been printed on extraordinarily cheap paper, doubtless.

But so that there must have unquestionably once been a life of Brahms in this house.

And in which a part I always liked was when Clara Hepburn gave Ludwig Wittgenstein some sugar.

Although what I would really like to find even more than I would like to find the painting is my missing cat, to tell the truth.

Even if it is not really a cat and is not really missing, actually.

Well, being only Magritte, who used to be Vincent.

Which is to say that the tape would appear to have blown away from the outside of that broken window, being all.

Still, one had gotten to be quite fond of that frisky scratching.

Although even just to see some floating ash again would be agreeable, too.

Even if one would hardly go to the trouble to name some floating ash, on the other hand.

There is a numeral on the back of the soccer shirt, by the way.

Possibly it is a nine. Or a nineteen.

In fact it is two zeros.

Have I mentioned that I have taken to building fires down near the water, after my sunsets, incidentally?

I have taken to building fires down near the water, after my sunsets.

Now and again, too, looking at them from a distance, what I have done is to make believe for a little while that I am back at Hisarlik.

By which I really mean when Hisarlik was Troy, of course, and all of those years and years ago.

So that what I am more truthfully making believe is that the fires are Greek watchfires, where they have been lighted along the shore.

Well, that certainly being a harmless enough thing to make believe.

Oh. And I have been hearing *The Alto Rhapsody* again also, these days.

Which is to say the real *Alto Rhapsody* this time, what with all of that having finally been sorted out.

Even if it is still hardly the real one either, naturally, being still only in my head.

But still.

And at any rate it is far too chilly this morning to be fretting about inconsequential perplexities of that sort.

In fact it is far too chilly to be typing here to begin with, actually.

Unless I might wish to move the typewriter closer to my pot-bellied stove, some way.

Although what I really ought to do before doing that is to go out to the spring again, to tell the truth.

Having completely forgotten about the rest of my laundry, which is spread across various bushes.

So that by now there could very well be some new skirt sculptures out there, even.

Even if Michelangelo would not think them that, but I think them that.

And even if I will more probably leave the rest of the laundry where it is until I am feeling less tired, on the other hand.

Doubtless I will not trouble to move the typewriter, either, when one comes down to that.

Once, I had a dream of fame.

Generally, even then, I was lonely.

To the castle, a sign must have said.

Somebody is living on this beach.